THE
BURNING
LAND

Also by George Alagiah

A Home from Home: From Immigrant Boy to English Man

A Passage to Africa

GEORGE ALAGIAH

THE BURNING LAND

CANONGATE

First published in Great Britain in 2019 by Canongate Books Ltd,
14 High Street, Edinburgh EH1 1TE

canongate.co.uk

1

British Library Cataloguing-in-Publication-Data
A catalogue record for the book is
available on request from the British Library

ISBN 978 1 78689 792 3
Export ISBN 978 1 78689 793 0

Typeset in Garamond by Palimpsest Book Production Ltd,
Falkirk, Stirlingshire

Printed and bound by Clays, Elcograf S.p.A.

For Frances

PROLOGUE

The old woman, her face etched with the lines of experience and hardship, retied the cloth around her head. She'd just used it to wipe the sweat from her neck and arms. It was a blisteringly hot day in South Africa's Mpumalanga Province on the distant eastern fringe of the country. There was no shade, not on this side of the fence.

She looked back at the compound and could see the shape of the marula tree about five hundred metres away. It had been there long before they'd put up the fence, a landmark to aim for at the end of the day. The way her eyes were troubling her, these days, she could no longer see the huts beyond the tree, but she knew they were there – just as they had been in her father's time and his father's before that.

So it had come to this. Her family had survived the *amabhunu*, the Afrikaners, who had claimed the land for themselves. It was the 'law', they'd said. The *umlungu*, the white man, had told her father he could stay on the land, and his children as well, but he must work for his keep. Tch! How they worked!

Then Mandela and his people had come and said the land would be given back to its rightful owners.

'Ah! But this is a good day,' her father had said.

Next, a government man from Nelspruit came, and he told all the workers they must get together, form a co-op-something and the government would help them buy some land. So the men did this thing, and signed a paper.

'Ah! But this is a good day,' her father had said.

They worked hard but the money was little. They went to see the bank man, but he said the signed piece of paper was no good; he would not borrow her father and the other men any money. And then another government man came from Nelspruit. He told the men the land was

1

not productive or what-what, and now a new owner was coming. He was from another country.

Then a machine came with some men from outside who built the fence. They said everyone must move to a new village.

That was why she was standing in front of her family's furniture. She wiped the dust from a chair, her father's chair, the one he'd sat on when he drank his traditional beer, and eased herself down. She was waiting for her son to come back. He had taken the children and their mother to the new location.

She had just shut her eyes when there was a huge noise, a percussive wave that seemed to get inside her head. She had never heard anything like that before. Then she saw the smoke. It was coming from the other side of the compound, from the place where the *baas* used to live. She heard some of the men there shouting. There was a big commotion. Was this really the place she was born? she wondered. What happened to that world?

That day, in a room in Hillbrow, central Johannesburg, four people – three men and one woman – crowd round a laptop. They are streaming the evening news on SABC, the state-run broadcaster, once the mouthpiece of apartheid and now performing much the same function for the country's new rulers.

The item they are waiting for is not in the headlines. Halfway through the bulletin the newscaster says there's been an accident on a farm in Mpumalanga. The pictures show the charred ruins of various farm buildings and vehicles. The reporter says investigators have been sent to the farm but early reports suggest an electrical fault caused a fire.

'Bullshit!' says the woman. But one of the others, a man in his thirties, wearing glasses, says, 'This is good. They're running scared. They are doing what the old regime used to do.' They look at each other, the four of them, and smile. Their work has begun.

Just a couple of hours later anyone searching for more details of the incident would discover a link to an unadorned website carrying this anonymous entry:

Today a new struggle has begun. Just over a hundred years ago, in 1913, the Boers passed a law to ROB US OF OUR LAND. Now we must fight for it again. In Mpumalanga Province a MESSAGE HAS BEEN DELIVERED. We did not win our freedom to see the LAND TAKEN AWAY FROM US AGAIN. We, the people of South Africa, will not sit and watch our precious inheritance SOLD TO THE HIGHEST BIDDER. Today in Mpumalanga we fired the first shot in our fight against the NEW COLONIALISM. Let them be warned, those who will SELL OUR LAND TO FOREIGNERS, the people of South Africa are ready to RISE UP AGAIN.

It was signed off, at the bottom of the page, simply as 'The Land Collective'.

In rooms elsewhere in the country, others saw the statement and recognised it for the call to arms they had been waiting for. A fuse had been lit, setting in motion a chain reaction that none of them, least of all the group in Hillbrow, could predict or control.

1

Lesedi Motlantshe's murder was one of those pivotal moments that seemed destined to change the course of a country's trajectory. There are some events – a law passed, a speech delivered, a transgression exposed – which are deemed significant only in retrospect, like looking back on a life and realising the point at which things had taken a turn for the better, or worse. This was different. As news of the murder spread across South Africa, its people knew there could be no going back to business as usual. Lesedi Motlantshe was more than a man: he was an idea, a symbol, and with his death that idea had been tarnished.

Lesedi had been one of freedom's children. Born in the eighties, his life mirrored the changes in South Africa as apartheid's pernicious laws were expunged from the statutes. A quick and confident boy, he'd once been interviewed by a TV crew doing a piece on the role schools were playing in changing attitudes to race. The reporter had asked the class of teenagers to define racism. In a flash, Lesedi had stuck up his hand. He'd pointed to one of only three white children in the class and said: 'Racism is like, you know, if I'm unkind to Darren and call him names – "Whitey" and so on.'

The clip had made it onto the evening news. This reversal of the conventional definition of racism – that white people could be the victims – from the lips of a black child seemed to speak volumes for the miraculous journey South Africa was making.

From that day on, Lesedi had become something of a celebrity, not so much teacher's pet as the nation's pet. His words were spliced into countless promotional videos produced by the government. He would be dragged out of the classroom to meet visiting dignitaries from China or Europe. A local TV station had adopted him for its 'Children of the Future' series, which meant he featured in an annual film tracing his every success (of which there were many) and failure (of which there were none). His progress in school, his three years at the University of Cape Town – all of it was chronicled. In short, Lesedi had become a national mascot – the embodiment of South Africa's new beginning.

Now he was dead.

Even in a country inured to violent crime, and a murder rate that saw it perpetually leading the wrong kind of international league table, the notion that Lesedi Motlantshe would one day become a victim – another notch on the grim statistics board – was unthinkable. There wasn't a person in the country, whether they spent their time in a township shebeen or in a gated mansion, who did not know who Lesedi Motlantshe was and what he represented.

So who in their right mind would want him dead?

2

On the day Lesedi Motlantshe was murdered, his father had flown into Dubai, arriving early after an overnight flight.

Despite his immense bulk and thigh-chafing gait, there was an unmistakable swagger to the way Josiah Motlantshe approached the entrance to the hotel. He looked as if he owned the place, the proprietorial confidence enhanced by the familiarity with which the uniformed doorman greeted him. Motlantshe burst out of a pale, lightweight suit, like one of his country's famous meaty *boerewors* oozing out of its skin. The crotch, the knees, the elbows, even the armpits – at every junction of his stupendous body the fabric signalled its stress with a collection of starburst creases.

Josiah was a veteran of the anti-apartheid struggle who'd turned his hand – and influence – to business. He was one of the so-called Black Diamonds, that exclusive club of black millionaires, no, billionaires, thrown up by empowerment schemes established by post-apartheid governments.

He'd been met off the private charter from Johannesburg by one of a fleet of Bentleys the hotel owned. It was just one of the many perks offered by a place that attracted a clientele rich enough to afford such luxury and spoiled enough to feel they deserved it. Its marketing brochure boasted that every wish would be granted and every desire fulfilled. The South African politician-turned-billionaire could certainly attest to that, having had his every desire – including one or two that were not on the official list of services – met with alacrity and, where appropriate, the necessary discretion.

Josiah Motlantshe's personal 'butler', a service assigned to those who stayed in the penthouse suites (and Motlantshe never stayed in anything else), started unpacking the obligatory Louis Vuitton cases, breaking off every now and then to pick up the various items of clothing that were being thrown onto the floor as Motlantshe undressed.

In a vest and a pair of briefs that were barely visible under an overflowing belly, Motlantshe eased himself onto the armchair, its leather upholstery sticking to his moist, hairless skin as he shifted this way and that till he was comfortable. With his pudgy hand he made one final adjustment of his balls, which nestled in the stretched cotton of his briefs, like a pair of oranges in a sling, and he was, at last, ready to make his first call – only to realise he'd left his mobile phone in the sitting room.

'Hello! Whassname! Bring me the phone,' he shouted.

The butler, a slight and professionally obsequious servant of South Asian origin, who had been busy laying out a fresh set of clothes in the dressing room, scurried in and picked up a handset from the bedside table.

'No, no, not that one. I want my own phone. It's there.' Motlantshe pointed to the lounge. 'And put this TV on – I want BBC.' He sat there, every obese inch of him exuding an air of entitlement. He'd come a long way from the time when he was so thin, so bony, that sitting on the wooden benches on Robben Island for more than a few minutes at a time was agony.

So, who to call first? The wife or the mistress? On this occasion duty prevailed. One of his three children answered.

'And how's my Thandi today? . . . It's who? Oh! My little princess. It's a bad line. Daddy is far away in Dubai. You sounded like your sister. So you have not gone to school yet? You are going to be late.'

'I'm not going today.'

'Is my little princess not well?'

'I'm fine, but Mummy talked to the teacher and she said some bad men were outside our school.'

'Bad men? What kind of men? Where is your mother? Bring her to the phone.'

'She's in the garden.'

'Go and fetch her. Hurry up.'

Motlantshe was irritated. He wished he'd phoned the other woman now. He imagined her at the flat he'd bought for her in Sandton. What time was it in Jo'burg? Still early. She was probably in bed. Motlantshe realised he was ever so slightly aroused. He heard the phone being picked up.

'What's going on?' he barked. 'Why is this girl talking about bad men at the school?'

'Is that what she said?' Priscilla Motlantshe sounded amused, which only added to her husband's irritation. 'No, today was meant to be a visit to Newtown. They were going to Museum Africa, but it's been cancelled because of the protest.'

'What protest?'

'You know! These land people. You were talking to Mkobi about it yesterday! Have you forgotten already?'

He knew why he had a mistress. His wife could make everything sound like an accusation. He had, indeed, called the president's office the day before in a last-ditch attempt to have the march stopped or postponed on some legal technicality – at least until after this meeting in Dubai. That reminded him: he needed to get that little shit Mkobi sacked. How the prissy bastard had made it into the president's office he didn't know. Mkobi hadn't put his call through. 'The president is a bit tied up just now,' he'd said, as if he were addressing some junior minister. Motlantshe could have called the president on his direct line, or on his private mobile phone, but that wasn't the point. Who the hell was Mkobi to decide whether or not he could speak to the president?

His temper had not been improved by the fact that Mkobi, the presidential chief of staff, had been right: it *was* too late to do anything about the march, but Motlantshe liked to reach these conclusions for himself and not have some jumped-up bureaucrat treat him like he was a novice. After all, he'd done time in jail for ungrateful bastards like Mkobi. Besides, judging by that voice of his, he was probably one of those homos or something.

'No, I remember, I'm just tired after the flight.'

'Didn't you sleep on the plane?'

There it was again: the accusatory tone. The needling suggestion that the reason he was tired was because he had failed to sleep, that it was his fault. Had it been the other woman, she would have whispered sweet nothings into his ear and told him she would wipe away all his tiredness just as soon as he was back in her arms.

'Okay, I have to go,' he said. 'I'll call after I meet these fellows from London.'

'And don't forget it's Lesedi's birthday this week,' she threw in, for good measure. Lesedi was their only son, born in the days of struggle.

'Of course I remember,' he snapped back.

'By the way, Jo, that minister, the Coloured fellow . . .' Priscilla continued to use the old apartheid lexicon for 'mixed race'.

'You mean Jake, Jake Willemse?'

'That's him, yes. He called here.'

'What's he doing calling you?'

'He said he couldn't get hold of you. He was angry. He wants to know what Lesedi is doing in Mpumalanga. He says Lesedi is interfering. He says if you can't stop him, he'll deal with Lesedi himself.'

'Who told Lesedi to go to Mpumalanga? What's the boy doing over there?'

'He says he wants to see things for himself, talk to local people to find out why they are so upset by this land thing. And, Jo, you have to stop calling him a boy. He's a man now.'

'Why should he be talking to these stupid people? They are being led by extremists. If he wants to be treated like a man, he needs to start thinking like one instead of all this foolishness he talks about.'

'I can remember when you used to talk like that.'

There was wistfulness in her voice, which Motlantshe both recognised and loathed. He knew that everything else that was wrong in their marriage had grown out of this one central accusation – that he had forgotten where they had both started out.

They had met in the seventies. Josiah Motlantshe was the most prominent in a new generation of activists that was emerging inside South Africa, carrying the mantle of leadership while the likes of Nelson Mandela, Oliver Tambo and Joe Slovo were either jailed or in exile. He was an extrovert, a fiery orator. Priscilla was the opposite, but what she lacked in public presence she more than made up for with a quiet determination. When Motlantshe and some others were jailed it was said that, of all the women who were left behind, Priscilla would cope best.

And so she did, raising the son who barely knew his father. Lesedi Motlantshe was brought up on heroic tales of what his father was like and what he would do, come freedom day. But when he had emerged from Robben Island, it had turned out that Motlantshe was a far better businessman than politician, and he believed Priscilla had never forgiven him for that. Instead, she had brainwashed the boy, tried to turn him into a version of the man she wanted her husband to be. At least, that was how he'd put it in the days when he could be bothered to argue with her.

'I haven't got time for that nonsense,' he shot back. 'If he wants to be treated like a man he should be here, by my side, talking to these London people.'

'But you know he doesn't like what you are doing. He thinks the land should be going to our people.'

'It is you who has put this rubbish in his head. The land is not going anywhere. It is staying in South Africa. It is going to make money for the people of South Africa.'

'You mean make money for you.'

'Just call him and tell him to get back to Jo'burg.' Motlantshe flung the phone onto the bed. He could still hear his wife's disembodied voice. He stared at the phone, waiting for her to shut up.

Motlantshe looked up at the TV screen and realised he was seeing downtown Johannesburg. He put the sound up. It was the last thing he needed. There they were, hundreds of men and women doing the *toyi-toyi*, the rolling protest dance so reminiscent of the heyday of the anti-apartheid era. Except this was today, and Motlantshe was about to sit down with the latest land-hungry investors to tell them South Africa was a safe and stable place to park their millions. He thought about calling the executive director of the SABC but decided it was too early. Since their days as activists he'd known the man didn't get going till mid-morning.

He'd have to send an email, which Motlantshe loathed, not least because it required a modicum of digital dexterity that was beyond his pudgy fingers. He preferred issuing his instructions over the phone, and when he had to send an email he usually got his personal assistant to key in the message. Facing the prospect of doing it himself only added to his ill-temper.

He navigated his way to the email screen on his phone, something

11

of an achievement in itself, and started to assemble the words. He found it impossible unless he mouthed the letters aloud. He pushed down on the letter *a* only to see *s* appear on the screen. He did it again, this time producing @. The more frustrated he got the harder he pressed, making it even more likely that his thumb tip would hit the wrong letter. Eventually, he had what he wanted:

Am in Dubai to see these buyers from London. Worried protest going to upset them. This one is a big deal. The one in Mpumalanga. Keep protest coverage down. Call me. JM.

Motlantshe understood the TV business inside out – after all, he owned a channel – and knew how much other broadcasters depended on footage from SABC. Most – with the exception of BBC World and Al Jazeera – had long since shut down their bureaux in South Africa.

He had a few hours before the meeting with the London delegation. Motlantshe looked at his personalised Richard Mille watch and decided he still had time to make the other call before he was due to meet George Kariakis, the middleman who was organising the meeting. It was going to be a long day and he needed the kind of fillip that only his mistress could provide.

That same morning, some four thousand miles to the south, Kagiso Rapabane had glanced around a single open-plan room, the head office of Soil of Africa in Malelane, an unremarkable town in South Africa's Mpumalanga Province. Tourists passed through it on their way to the great Kruger National Park, but it was an experience they rarely, if ever, remembered.

It was going to be a big day for Soil of Africa and Kagiso was there a good hour earlier than was usual. It was the charity's only office. No two desks were alike, and the chairs were an assorted collection that included plastic garden furniture and a 'sofa' that had started life as the back bench on a bus, now bolted onto a couple of wooden pallets.

He rubbed his hands together, trying to generate some life in fingers that had been chilled to the bone on his ride into work. It was midwinter in the southern hemisphere and the early-morning air had an edge like a butcher's knife. He rummaged in his satchel and found a box of matches. Kagiso was not a habitual smoker, but in his line of work, out here in South Africa's forgotten rural fringe, it was the kind of thing that always came in handy. He carried the stump of a candle for the same reason. There were still plenty of farm labourers' huts where the electricity that powered escalators and supermarket freezers in the city had yet to reach a single light bulb. He struck a match and squeezed it through the fireguard on the paraffin heater; it sucked up the flame with a satisfying gulp.

Kagiso went over to the sink in the corner of the room and filled the kettle to the brim; the others would be here soon enough. He switched on the electric stove and watched the spiral filament as it glowed into red-hot life. The water dripping off the outside of the kettle fizzed and spat as he put it down.

He was waiting for Lesedi – scion of the Motlantshe family. The approach from Lesedi had been quite a surprise. When his office had called to arrange a meeting, the initial reaction among the staff at Soil of Africa had been one of suspicion. What were the Motlantshes up to now? Why would the son of a man like Josiah Motlantshe want to have a meeting with Soil of Africa, an organisation dedicated to ensuring that farm workers were given the opportunity to buy and work their own slice of land? Soil of Africa championed the notion, embedded in centuries of folklore and cemented by the humiliation of apartheid's evictions and pass laws, that those who are most secure are those who walk on land they can call their own. He could see why so many of his colleagues thought he was being either duped or naive. Not for the first time that morning Kagiso checked his phone. He was expecting a call. Nothing. No missed calls.

He went outside and stood on the stoep. The white light of a wintry sun shone through the delicate filigree of a spider's web stretched between the thatched roof and one of the timbers on which it was supported. A single dewdrop clung to the bottom of the web, like a pearl hanging from an intricate necklace. A few metres in front of him, a young boy, wearing a T-shirt that reached halfway down his shins, was herding half a dozen rangy cattle down the main street. Kagiso checked to see if the extra chairs he'd borrowed from the church up the road had been delivered. Word had got round that Lesedi Motlantshe – heir to a billionaire – would be visiting Soil of Africa and he knew there would be quite a crowd. Motlantshe himself had proposed meeting some of the farm workers from around the town.

Kagiso Rapabane's transition from favoured civil servant to charity worker was as surprising as it was exceptional. A poorly paid job helping South Africa's rural poor was a far cry from his days at the Ministry of Rural Development and Land Reform in Pretoria, where he was a policy adviser to one Jake Willemse, at the time an up-and-coming minister. Kagiso had been something of a high flyer himself, one of the brightest prospects in the policy department, someone destined to go to the very top. There had been shock and not a little incredulity when it had been announced that he'd accepted a transfer to the rural outpost of Malelane. His industriousness, his renowned discipline, even his lean physique, all of these seemed ill suited to the altogether more laid-back attitude to work in the languid province of Mpumalanga in the eastern reaches of the country.

At the ministry, he'd been something of an enigma: everybody's friend but no one's confidant. You'd have been hard pushed to find anyone who had a bad word to say about him, but in the world of office camaraderie people wanted more of a colleague, someone who was clubbable in a way that Kagiso was unable and unwilling to be. While the others had aspired to owning BMWs, he was satisfied with his Yamaha scooter; while they signed up with a personal trainer – a status symbol in the new South Africa – he would disappear on long, lonely runs. No one knew about his love life, whether he even had one. He seemed inured to the charms of even the most attractive women at the ministry. The men couldn't understand it and the women were intrigued. They wondered what went on behind those bespectacled eyes. His aloofness, his unavailability, was much more alluring than the crude lasciviousness of the other men, brought up in a society hooked on the conventional rituals of men chasing women.

Kagiso's phone rang. He didn't recognise the number.

'Lesedi Motlantshe here. How's it going?'

Kagiso was taken aback for a moment to hear Lesedi himself, not the assistant he had been dealing with up till then, at the end of the line. And he was surprised by how 'white' the accent was. It was reminiscent of the still-white suburbs of Cape Town, certainly not Mitchell's Plain.

'Hey! I'm fine. Are you on your way?'

'Yeah. I think I'm about an hour away, two at the most. I've just stopped to get something to eat. It was an early start.'

'How many of you are coming?'

'Just me.'

'Really? I thought you would be . . .'

'You sound shocked. I know we Motlantshes are meant to travel with an entourage, just to show how important we are.' Lesedi was laughing.

'Well, we'll be ready and waiting.'

'You make it sound like I'm about to walk into an ambush!' Another chuckle.

'No one's going to ambush you here. Listen, you're the biggest thing that's happened here since some American rapper passed through on his way to the Sabi Sabi game lodge. Most of them probably just want to shake your hand.'

'I'd better brush up on my rap, man.' That chuckle again. It was infectious.

'So how do you want to play things today?' Kagiso asked.

'I don't plan on making any big speeches or anything. I just want to listen. I know there's a lot of loose talk about what the Motlantshes are up to and I'd like to reassure people.'

Ever since the meeting had been arranged, Kagiso had rehearsed the various ways in which he might broach their disagreements. He was acutely conscious that he was about to change the tone of the conversation. 'Well, I wouldn't say it's all just loose talk. At Soil of Africa we think there are other ways of taking care of the land *and* the people who live on it.'

'I know. I've been looking at your website. Your achievements are pretty impressive. Maybe there are things we can talk about . . . You know, reach a compromise.'

This was unexpected, but Kagiso remained wary. 'I certainly hope so. People here just see all these land deals and feel betrayed. And the new black owners are as bad as the old white ones. And now we've got all these foreigners coming in . . .'

'Look, I know, there's a lot to discuss. Maybe it would be good if we – you and I – could get a few minutes to chat on our own, away from the others. I don't agree with everything that's going on and I want to find a way to help.'

'Well, just tell your father and his friends.'

'You don't know my father! Anyway, see you just now.'

Their lives couldn't have been more different: Kagiso, the son of a house worker and the beneficiary of a white family's generosity; Lesedi, a child born into the aristocracy of struggle, for whom wanting something was merely a question of asking for it. Their paths had crossed once before when they were both students, not that Lesedi would remember the encounter. It was at a varsity rugby match between Stellenbosch, where Kagiso had studied, and the University of Cape Town, where Lesedi had entertained himself, with the occasional foray into the library. It was a home game for Stellenbosch, and Kagiso now remembered how he'd cycled to the sports ground to watch. He'd been padlocking his bike when Lesedi had rolled up in a soft-top BMW with a couple of friends, who tumbled out of the vehicle with bottles of the Cape's finest fizzy in their hands.

He hadn't felt any jealousy at the time, at least not over Lesedi's wealth. If anything, it was the other man's confidence he'd envied. As a child growing up, he'd never been the one who'd stick his hand up and say, 'Yes, sir, I know the answer.' He feared the humiliation of being wrong much more than he craved the praise that went with being right.

By the time Lesedi Motlantshe had arrived at Soil of Africa's office, a little later than he'd predicted, the sun had worked its magic. It would be a warm day. The two men shook hands and, despite their contrasting backgrounds, Kagiso felt it would be a meeting of equals.

Much later that day, in Dubai, Josiah Motlantshe's phone rang. He opened his eyes, and still he could see nothing. There was a moment of terror before he pulled at the sleep mask. All the pieces began to fall into place: he was in Dubai; he'd come back from the casino (those private-equity chaps loved their gambling) a couple of hours before dawn. He stared at the screen on his phone, waiting for his eyes to focus. It was a number in South Africa but not one he recognised.

'Who is this?' he barked, in his default disposition.

'Hello, is this Mr Motlantshe I am speaking to?' He recognised the Afrikaner accent. 'Mr Josiah Motlantshe?'

'Yes, what do you want? It's the middle of the night.'

'Just a moment, *meneer* – I mean sir. Let me put you through.'

'Hello, hello, put me through to whom?' It was useless: she'd already transferred the call.

'Is this Mr Motlantshe, Mr Josiah Motlantshe?'

'How many times do I have to tell you people? Yes, this is he. And who are you?'

'It's Lieutenant General Jackson Sibande, sir, from the South African Police Service in Mpumalanga.'

'From where? Mpumalanga?'

'Yes, sir. We have some news for you, sir, and I'm just going to pass you on to the premier, Mr Jeremiah Bekelu.'

'For Chrissake, what the hell is going on? . . . Jerry? Jerry, is that you? What the hell is happening?'

'Josiah, something bad has happened here. It's Lesedi . . .'

3

It was barely seven in the morning when Lindi Seaton's phone rang. She fumbled around the bedside table as her eyes adjusted to the neon glare of a London streetlamp streaming through the ineffectual lace curtain. It was too early for Anton Chetty, her boss at South Trust, a high-profile and well-respected organisation dedicated to conflict resolution around the world. She checked the screen – she didn't recognise the number.

'Lindi Seaton here.'

'I suppose it was your idea, was it?'

'Who's this?'

'It's Clive, Clive Missenden.'

'And how lovely to hear from you too. Silly of me not to have recognised your voice instantly.'

'Let's get straight to the point.'

'You've already done that. What exactly is supposed to have been my idea?'

'Come off it,' Missenden huffed. 'All that guff on the radio just now from your man about South Trust having warned that something like this would happen. You couldn't resist it, could you? The poor bastard's hardly been dead a day and you've got it all sorted.'

'You've got a bloody nerve! Just in case it's slipped your mind, I no longer have to listen to your shit.'

'You're at it again, aren't you? Most people put two and two together and get four. Not you! You've gone straight to the conclusion you want, never mind the facts.'

Lindi moved the phone an inch from her ear and sighed. 'If you want to talk to me about Lesedi Motlantshe's murder, call me at my office.'

'I'm just warning you.'

'A warning. That's official, is it?'

'I've left the Foreign Office.'

'Oh? So who's warning me now?'

'I'm just trying to prevent you from making another . . . How shall I put it? Another error of judgement. I'm trying to be helpful, that's all.'

The needling reference to their shared past was not lost on Lindi. 'Helpful. Is that what you call it? As in when you *helped* me out of my job. Piss off, Clive.'

Lindi ended the call. She wasn't sure whom she was angrier with: Clive Missenden and whoever he was working for now, or her colleague, Anton Chetty, for not talking to her before mouthing off in front of a microphone.

Lesedi Motlantshe's murder had made the BBC's *News at Ten* the previous night, breaking news. It was only a brief mention about a member of one of South Africa's most prominent families being found dead shortly after visiting a group campaigning for land reform. The report said South African police had launched an investigation and were questioning a number of Mozambican migrant workers. Lindi had phoned Anton straight away. They'd argued about how, even whether, South Trust should respond. He said he was sure the murder was mixed up with the land thing; she argued back, said they should wait till they had some proof. They'd agreed to talk it over in the office in the morning. Anton hadn't said anything about having had a request for an interview. It was still too early to call him, not if she wanted any sense out of him.

And Missenden, what was he up to? His call had unsettled her, not only because of what he'd said, his 'warning', but because of the memories it had brought back. Lindi Seaton thought she'd left all that behind.

Missenden had been her line manager in what she now regarded as a previous life. That was in the days when she was a junior diplomat at the Foreign and Commonwealth Office, a position she owed to her fast-track appointment straight out of university. Because of her family's links to South Africa, Lindi had been asked to prepare a draft paper on what South Africa might look like post-Nelson Mandela. Among other things, her report contained the memorable, if dramatic, assessment that if land ownership became an issue, the ensuing agitation would 'make what happened in Zimbabwe look like a picnic'.

She'd argued that apartheid's legacy of white ownership might be eclipsed by the more recent land purchases: everyone from Gulf sheikhs, Chinese government agencies and private-equity magnates, many of them based in London, had been at it. Whether justified or not, she'd said the British government would be dragged into the affair, held responsible for the actions of 'land-grabbers' based in its own jurisdiction.

It had taken Missenden all of a couple of minutes to give his verdict on Lindi's report. 'Shrill' – that was how he'd described it. In the following weeks, what was supposed to be a draft for Missenden's eyes became a water-cooler topic in the Africa department. The general assessment among her colleagues, doubtless egged on by Missenden, was that, despite her impeccable credentials – starting with a degree from an ancient university – she had, somehow, missed the point. In an era when the prime purpose of British missions abroad was to boost trade and investment, her report was deemed wrongheaded and unhelpful. A transfer to an unspecified role in HR followed. Some months later she walked out of the Foreign and Commonwealth Office, carrying few reminders of her brief career in diplomacy and her self-confidence in tatters.

So now, despite her perennial irritation over Anton's impetuosity, she rather hoped he was right. It had been a long time coming but she savoured the thought of an I-told-you-so moment. It would be in stark contrast to her prevailing mood since leaving the British diplomatic service – a dead weight of regret at having failed to stand her ground and fight. Her failure to do so had played into a private and punishing evaluation of her own worth.

It was a self-deprecating assessment at odds with how others perceived her. Lindi Seaton stood out from the crowd. If you met her once, you were unlikely to forget her: it was the intensity with which she seemed to relate to other people. Never wholly comfortable in front of a crowd, she came into her own one on one. She had the right question at the right moment. It was a reflex, a way of coping with the awkwardness she always felt when she met someone for the first time. There was an apparent intimacy, which Lindi did not intend and from which she would all too often have to extricate herself. It was a characteristic many loved her for. Clive Missenden, however, was not among them.

Lindi gathered her work things, looked out of the window, decided she would not need her waterproofs, and manoeuvred her bike through the front door of her ground-floor flat.

4

Lindi arrived at South Trust's King's Cross offices, a converted Victorian warehouse now hosting architects, tech start-ups and a firm of human-rights lawyers. No sign of Anton Chetty. On this day, of all days, you'd have thought he'd manage to get into the office on time. She knew where to find him, but she also knew that to search him out would be more trouble than it was worth, a cue for one of his now familiar rants about not needing a nanny.

True to form, Anton was in his usual spot at the café down the road. He always claimed his best work was done there, in the coffee house, at the table in the front corner by the full-length window.

Now living in London, Anton still took more than a passing interest in South Africa. He'd been born there, grown up there, and had even been jailed there. For him, the personal had always overlapped with the professional. He was the charismatic, if shambolic, director of South Trust, which was generally regarded as the most effective outfit involved in conflict resolution outside the United Nations. Most of its work was in poor countries, almost all of which were in the southern hemisphere. 'Local solutions for local problems' – that was its tag line. Independently funded and staffed by men and women whose hands-on, real-time decision-making was the antithesis of the committee-ridden structures of conventional diplomacy, South Trust had negotiated deals in places where others feared to tread. It had no official or statutory powers but plenty of influence.

Anton had been up half the night – at least, that was what it felt like. Once he'd heard the news about Lesedi Motlantshe's murder, he'd been on the phone to old contacts in South Africa. None of them had any answers to his enquiries about Lesedi's murder and, like Lindi, warned him against rushing to conclusions by linking the killing to land sales.

But Anton had eventually slumped into a fitful sleep, convinced he was onto something. When a journalist called first thing in the morning, he found himself giving voice to his suspicions. It was the clip Clive Missenden had heard, prompting his early-morning call to Lindi.

Now nursing a hangover and gulping his second espresso, Anton was determined to find something, anything that might give credence to his overnight hunch. He scrolled through numerous news sites, followed threads on his Facebook and Twitter accounts. A campaigner at heart, he wanted his news unadulterated and he made sure he was plugged into what activists on the ground were saying – in this case in South Africa. He gave short shrift to the speeches given by the appa-ratchiks in the ruling party, the silver-tongued revolutionaries in their Canali suits, with a penchant for the finer things in life. He knew some, and if he didn't know them personally, he knew their type. And he largely ignored the international newspapers and their websites. 'What the hell do those parachute journalists know about anything?' he would say to whoever would listen.

As far as Anton Chetty was concerned, from whichever quarter the editorial judgements came, they had a common refrain: 'Here we go again,' they implied, as if the prospect of yet another African country throwing it all away was as inevitable as the summer rains over Johannesburg. If there was one thing he despised it was the way Western journalists expected so little from Africa, and the self-satisfaction that seeped from their journalism when they thought they had been proved right in their prejudice.

In the years that he'd been in charge, Anton had steered the Trust away from getting involved in South Africa, despite his strong personal interest in his erstwhile homeland. He knew too many of the people who now ran the country and, perhaps more to the point, they knew him. He came with baggage; excess baggage, they would say. When old comrades, now ministers and advisers in government, came to London they would give Anton a wide berth. They had become masters of pragmatism, and found it irritating that he was still talking about ideals. He was rarely, if ever, invited to functions at the Trafalgar Square High Commission. The feeling, it had to be said, was mutual.

But the murder of Lesedi Motlantshe changed everything. No more squeamishness about being accused of interfering in South Africa. To Anton's febrile mind, Lesedi's death was not an isolated and untimely killing but the latest and most chilling act of violence among the many he'd been monitoring in Mpumalanga Province.

For some months now there'd been a number of apparently inexplicable and largely unreported attacks on farms in the province. Until now, no one had been killed and nothing was ever taken. Hardly the stuff of headlines. But time and again farm property or equipment would be damaged. On one farm the tractors' tyres had been slashed. Somewhere else an experimental crop of *mielies* was hacked down. In another place an intruder had disabled the computerised timer on an irrigation system. Elsewhere a dam had been blown up.

All the incidents had been chronicled in a blog, under the name of the Land Collective. Anton couldn't remember when he'd first come across the site, but once he had, it had become compelling reading. Every instalment drew attention to the fact that the farm in question had been sold or was about to be sold. Far from being random acts of vandalism, the incidents were brought together in a single narrative. Yet, as far as Anton could make out, the authorities chose to treat each one separately: to acknowledge a link – even behind closed doors – would be to accept that the post-apartheid consensus was breaking up and the political hegemony of the ruling party was being eroded.

Much to Anton's private satisfaction, the Land Collective had been highlighting something that had long been on his own mind. Anton had always believed that land ownership would become an issue in South Africa, just as it had been in other countries where colonial settlers had carved up the best land and parcelled it up among themselves. Each nation had dealt with it differently. In Kenya white mischief was met with black rebellion; in the Portuguese colonies of Angola and Mozambique, Soviet-backed revolutionary movements had nationalised the land at a single stroke of a Communist pen; and in Zimbabwe a desperate Robert Mugabe had let loose his thugs in a populist move to shore up his faltering hold on power. Anton wasn't sure how it would pan out in South Africa, but he believed there would be a day of reckoning before long.

He went back to the website, picking through previous statements about various incidents on farms, hoping to find a clue as to why Lesedi had been murdered. Nothing. Not even a hint that revolutionary inflation might account for sabotage turning into assassination.

He couldn't help feeling that these incidents in South Africa were symptoms of the unfinished business he'd talked about so often. It was the price that had to be paid for the way in which the 'real' struggle in South Africa – as he put it – had been tamed and repackaged so that race rather than wealth had become the defining characteristic.

That, to Anton, was apartheid's big lie: that the great divide was all about race. The painstaking demarcation of areas between whites and others: *nie-blankes, vir debruik deur blankes.* The classification of people according to skin colour: natives, Indians, Coloureds, whites. Anton was dark-skinned, darker than many so-called blacks, a genetic trace of the Tamil blood that ran strong in his veins but which he barely acknowledged. One of the lasting legacies of the apartheid system was the way in which its brutally simple racial categories superseded more subtle cultural and ethnic differences. So, in the old days, when he was growing up in Durban on South Africa's east coast, he was simply 'Indian'. Whether he was Tamil or not was irrelevant. The point was to distinguish whites from non-whites, nothing more.

For Anton, replacing white leaders with black was merely a stepping stone to the real prize – the communal ownership of wealth-making. There were rare, unguarded moments, usually on a bellyful of whisky, when he would tell his colleagues: 'Whether you are being fucked by a black bastard or a white bastard is irrelevant – you are still being fucked!' In his book, a black capitalist was barely an improvement on a white one.

Of all the adjustments he'd had to make since he was released from jail into European exile, the most difficult had been the need to leave his particular brand of politics behind. He remembered how all those matronly Scandinavian women and their earnest, sandal-wearing partners had been shocked to hear that he didn't just want to change the colour of government but the entire edifice on which it was built. In the early days, when he was still something of a celebrity on the 'struggle' lecture circuit, he'd noticed the collective unease in the audience whenever he started talking about changing the whole system, lock, stock and barrel (one of his favoured rhetorical phrases).

It was the same whether he was talking to the politics department at some university in Sweden or to genteel activists in a cathedral city in middle England. In their polite, ever-so-respectful way his hosts in the anti-apartheid movement would suggest, never demand, that he talk about his experiences in prison or how, as a child, a Catholic priest had instilled a sense of social justice in him. At the time, the thing that annoyed him even more than their liking for these insipid tales of victimhood was the way they were always so terribly reasonable. Why couldn't they just confront him, actually look him in the eye and say: 'Shut the fuck up about the revolution. You're here to make people feel good about themselves, not make them feel guilty for being part of the system you hate so much!'

He dragged his eyes away from the rain-spotted window, wondering how long he'd been lost in reverie. He found a recent and detailed account from the Land Collective about a strike by workers at an orange farm in Mpumalanga Province. It described how the trouble had flared up after a whole crop had had to be discarded because the pesticide had been contaminated with petrol. The farm owner, one Piet Meyer, had immediately blamed the workers and sacked the elderly foreman. The old man's protests – that he had had nothing to do with what had happened – had fallen on deaf ears. Meyer's attitude – as reflexive as swatting one of the ticks that would land on his leathery, sun-freckled skin – was a throwback to the old era. Anton read the first paragraph:

SACK FIRST and ask questions later – NOTHING has changed. So now the union bosses have been called in. What a joke. They are part of the SYSTEM. They will take six months to write a report and then they will negotiate in a FIVE-STAR hotel and the PEOPLE will be FORGOTTEN. The only thing the farmer is interested in is the FAT PROFIT he is going to make when he SELLS THE LAND. Yes, he wants to SELL his farm to whoever will give him most money. FOREIGNERS want the land but Meyer does not care – he just wants MILLIONS of rands. Nobody asks what will happen to the WORKERS. What are YOU going to do about this? Are you going to leave this INJUSTICE to stand?

It was only ten thirty in the morning and Anton already felt tired and exasperated. He peeled off his rimless glasses, massaged the bridge of his nose, and tugged at his goatee. He heard the hiss of the espresso machine and looked over to the counter where Saleh, the Turkish café owner, was taking a breather before preparing for the midday rush.

'Get me another double-shot coffee, man,' he shouted.

'You look like shit,' came the reply. 'Whatever you were up to, I hope it was fun. You should eat something. Let me fix you a couple of eggs.'

Anton felt his stomach churn. 'Listen, I don't need a fucking mother, I need a coffee.'

A couple of minutes later Saleh arrived with the coffee and placed a large tumbler of fresh orange juice next to it. They smiled at each other. Anton looked at the juice the way he used to look at cough medicine when he was a kid and downed it in one long gulp. Then he turned to the screen again.

He found nothing in the international press about the incident at the orange farm. In his experience rural affairs only twitched the interest of foreign correspondents if the fortunes of white farmers were at stake. They rarely, if ever, departed from this central theme. The plight of an ageing black foreman didn't register on the Richter scale of news judgements. So when it came to land and how it was distributed there was always the story of the lone white farmer to fall back on – the one who heroically stands up to thugs but, in the end, abandons the fight and joins the growing numbers heading for the departure gate and a life of bilious exile overseas.

There had been plenty of crime on South Africa's vast commercial farms in the years since democracy. The farmers who owned them, still almost exclusively white, had had the misfortune to be both isolated and relatively rich, certainly in comparison to the poverty all around them. They were sitting ducks. Hundreds had been killed. The murders were the collateral of botched robberies by gangs of increasingly frustrated youths for whom the great promise of freedom had been as beguiling as a strip-tease but, ultimately, just as unsatisfying.

There was a mention on the website of a provincial farming magazine in South Africa. In this version, the incident at Meyer's farm had been reduced to nothing more than an advice column on the need to supervise farm labourers. There was an interview with a representative from De Kok and Sons, suppliers of farming equipment, fertilisers and pesticides. The spokeswoman said the company had decided – in the light of events at the Meyer farm – to have another look at the instructions that went with their products. They were thinking of making them simpler, perhaps using cartoon characters and pictures to illustrate what needed to be done.

'We know some of the employees find it difficult to read,' she was quoted as saying.

He still had the Land Collective website open and clicked back to it. What a contrast! There were the names of the foreman and some of the farm labourers. It even named the brand of pesticide and how the petrol might have been mixed with it. It was like an online training session on how to replicate the sabotage.

News of the event at the Meyer farm would have spread from farmstead to farmstead quicker than a dose of foot and mouth. And yet the magazine had chosen not to report any of the detail. Anton Chetty thought he had the answer. They were frightened of contagion – not of the agrarian kind but the political variety.

It was enough to get his blood up. God! This was like the old days. A cause to get stuck into. He flipped the cover back over his tablet, chucked it into his rucksack and headed for the door.

'Hey! I'm running a business here – what about some money?' shouted Saleh.

Too late. Anton was already out of the door. He darted across York Way, all traces of the hangover now miraculously gone.

He plunged into his office building, which overlooked the Eurostar railway line to Paris.

Wayne, whose job description as the building's janitor was entirely at odds with his preferred occupation of reading the *Sun* newspaper while slumped on his seat, barely looked up when Anton shouted, as he did every day, 'Stop reading that fucking rag,' while bounding up the stairs – the closest he ever got to a daily exercise routine.

'Nice of you to make an appearance, Mr Chetty,' Lindi called, as he rushed past her desk.

'Stop being an old bag and come into my office. And bring me some bloody coffee.'

He peeled off several layers of clothing. More than two decades abroad, first in Stockholm and latterly in London, had failed to make a dent in his sartorial tastes. He still wore a selection of safari suits – the only allowance he made for the inclement weather was to wear a woolly jumper under the jacket. It made him look bulkier than he was – comically so, given his spindly legs. He was short, no more than five foot six or seven but, unlike many men of his stature, he was entirely relaxed about it. 'Sit down, you bugger. My head is going to fall off if I have to look up at you any longer,' was a refrain directed at ministers and minions alike.

He hunted for the TV remote control, looking under last week's newspapers, on the floor beside the sofa until, eventually, he found it perched on the edge of the bookshelf. He pressed the power button and heard the little click before the flat screen on the wall burst into life. For a moment, he imagined it was a detonator setting off a bomb. Yet more fantasies from the glory days. His 'cell' in Durban, a group of college friends, really, had had rudimentary training in bomb-making, taking instruction from a pamphlet smuggled to them by the ANC's military wing. He remembered going through the step-by-step instructions, using rice packed in women's tights as a substitute for explosive. How they'd dreamed of striking a blow for freedom, obliterating some iconic building or statue. Like so much else in his earlier life, it had never quite happened that way.

He looked through the door into the rest of the office. How long can it take to make a couple of mugs of coffee?

Lindi finally walked in, two mugs precariously held in one hand and her notebook in the other. He grabbed one of the mugs, took a sip and nearly gagged. 'Christ! What the hell is this?!'

They swapped mugs, Lindi taking back the peppermint tea that was her habitual work-time tipple.

He knew he was heading for a ticking off and waited for Lindi to speak first.

'You should have told me last night that you were going to do an interview.'

'I didn't know I was. Some journalist caught me off guard first thing this morning.' Anton sounded almost apologetic, unusually for him.

She brushed off his explanation with a wave of her hand. 'Whatever. The fact is we're out there now saying that one of South Africa's most famous families, not to say most respected, is somehow embroiled in the land business. Talk about going out on a limb.'

'Okay, I may have pushed it a bit too far—'

'A bit too far?' Lindi interrupted. 'You've practically gone the whole distance. I've already had a couple of journalists calling me.'

'What did you say to them?'

'That I'd call them back. A bit lame after your performance but it buys us time to get this straight. And they're not the only ones who are curious.'

'What do you mean?'

'I had a call from an old colleague of mine. I was still at home. It must have been minutes after your thoughtful contribution on the airwaves this morning.'

'From the Foreign and Commonwealth Office?'

Lindi shook her head. 'He's no longer a diplomat. Anyway, he said your statement – or whatever it was you said – must be my doing. If only he knew.'

'I don't get it.' Anton frowned.

'It's ancient history. Years ago, when I was at the FCO, I wrote a paper about how explosive the land issue would be in South Africa.'

'You told us that at your interview. Remember? I was impressed – a woman after my own heart. It was partly why you got the job.'

'I also said the British government would be dragged in because of all the London-based investors cashing in on land deals.'

'You were bloody right about that too.'

'That's the bit the FCO didn't like. I say FCO, but the paper only got as far as Missenden. He killed it.'

'You're losing me. Who's Missenden?'

'The guy who called me this morning. Anyway, the call was a sort of warning. That was the word he used.'

'Warning?' Anton's voice was a few decibels higher. 'I hope you told him to fuck off.'

31

'That's not quite how I put it but, yes, I told him to mind his own business.'

'Anyway, who does he work for now?'

'That's my next task of the day.'

Clive Missenden looked out over London. He had the best view in town. He'd made the most of the revolving door between government and business. People paid to see the cityscape he now took for granted. His office was high up in the Shard, which, like so much real estate in the city, was now owned by foreign conglomerates – in this case the Qataris. He swivelled his leather and steel chair to face the sheet-glass desk. Apart from a laptop, a landline, a mobile phone and a mug of coffee, it was entirely bare. Here was a man who saw no need to commit anything to paper. Hanging on the wall that faced the floor-to-ceiling windows were several framed photos: an aerial view of a phalanx of tractors ploughing a vast field, another shot of a plantation of some sort, and a third, taken against a backdrop of verdant foliage, showed two men shaking hands, one of them suited and white, the other black and in traditional garb. His office, sumptuous in a clinical sort of way, and an anteroom with a secretary, were all there was to show for Africa Rising Investments. The company was registered in the British Virgin Islands, and its British CEO was a one-time City trader who now seemed to spend most of his time in hotels and the back of a private jet. This CEO was the man in the photo.

The mobile phone vibrated on the desk. Missenden saw that it was Jake Willemse in South Africa and pressed the green icon to answer.

'Returning your call.' Willemse was curt. 'I haven't got much time. I suppose you've heard about Motlantshe's son?'

'That's why I rang. What the hell was Motlantshe's boy doing there? So much for you reining him in. Now we're going to have every friggin' journalist nosing around.'

'It's okay, we're dealing with it. I've spoken to Josiah and it doesn't change anything. He's still on the case.'

'Well, that's reassuring, but we might have to do better than that.' Superciliousness came naturally to Missenden.

'Who says? Is this coming from the top?'

'You know how it is, Jake. I'm his eyes, ears and voice. He only has to think something and I'm already there. We need to shut this whole thing down, no need for all this publicity. I'm hearing on the grapevine that even the bloody *FT* is getting interested in doing something on land. You'd expect that sort of thing from those pinko-liberals at the *Grauniad* . . .'

'The what?'

'The *Guardian*. Oh, never mind. Anyway, we don't want this thing snowballing.'

'Like I said, we're working on it, we'll make a plan.'

'You need to pin it to someone and quick,' said Missenden, catching his own reflection in the desk. 'This deal is only the beginning. Mark my words, with all this guff about climate change making farming impossible you'll have the whole world and his sister queuing up for your land. The Chinese, the Gulf sheikhs, they're all on the lookout for more.'

'The police have arrested a Mozambican labourer and—'

'Don't give me that bullshit, Jake,' said Missenden. 'Nobody's going to believe some wretched, shirtless Mozambican was responsible for this.' A change of tone. 'And, besides, we'll need those chaps when, if, this project gets off the ground.'

'Don't worry, it will get off the ground.'

'It better had. As I recall, you have quite a lot riding on it. All that talk about foreign investment in the land. Got you quite a few good headlines here. And then there's your little share, only a fraction of what you'll get as you climb the greasy pole I'm sure but, still, something to be getting on with.'

Missenden thought he was playing the conversation rather well, imagining Willemse squirming at the other end.

Jake Willemse was one of a new breed of South African politicians, who evoked 'the struggle' in their speeches but were privately contemptuous of those who still believed it offered a rubric for government. They'd attend the ruling party's conferences for as long as it took to be noticed, then make a quiet exit. They pretended to listen as the grey-haired veterans relived their glory days, singing revolutionary songs. The young Turks would watch it all from the sidelines, as if they were indulging a grandparent who still thought he was the head of the family. One by one, these men and women had either died or been given a seat on the Board of Elders, the political equivalent of a care home. The Elders were allowed to attend big state occasions, like the start of a new parliamentary session, but were otherwise hardly seen or heard.

For Jake Willemse and his generation of fellow ministers – products of business schools around the world – out of sight meant out of mind. With the veterans out of the way, they could pursue 'the project', to drag South Africa into the twenty-first century, at least their version of it.

'I know what I'm doing and I know what has to be done,' Jake said.

'Never doubted it, mate.' Missenden could tell he was getting to Willemse and rather enjoyed it. 'Oh, one other thing. You ever heard of South Trust?'

'Of course I have. They were quite busy in Congo recently. Frankly, their success put our great leader's efforts at mediation in the shade. What about it?'

'Bunch of interfering do-gooders, if you ask me. Run by one of your chaps, an Indian by the name . . .' He paused, dredging his memory.

'You mean Chetty, Anton Chetty. I don't know him personally, but I know all about him. Old school, a has-been, the type who still thinks it was the Kalashnikov that delivered freedom.'

'He might be a has-been but he's quick off the mark. Gave an interview in London this morning. Said he thinks the Motlantshe boy's murder is linked to calls for land reform. Not very helpful, I must say. Don't want any of our people getting nervous about their money in this deal, do we?'

'I'll see what I can do. We're working on a statement. "A wanton, misguided act of criminality, not politically motivated" – something like that.'

'While you're at it you might want to watch out for his sidekick, Lindi Seaton, another of your compatriots. What is it with you South Africans? Grew up in London. Her parents came here as exiles. Technically she's British. She was with me at the FCO. My hunch is that one of them, or both, will be heading your way. They've got credibility. Once they start digging around and talking, people will listen.

Anyhow, I think that's about everything for now, Jake. I know you'll sort out this unholy mess.'

Anton's phone rang.

'Hey! Howzit, *bru*!' From the phrase, from the subtle change in Anton's accent Lindi knew straight away he was talking to someone in South Africa. She listened in to one half of a conversation.

'*Jirre*, man! On what?' He wrote down a web address. 'Hold on, hold on.' He gesticulated to Lindi, pointing to what he'd just written. 'Pull it up,' he said, before continuing with the conversation.

Lindi had the link on the screen.

'Okay, listen, man, I'm going to call you back. Let me watch this thing. All right, *hamba kahle*, man.'

Slowly, deliberately, he placed the phone back on the desk and turned to Lindi. He looked ashen. 'This is much worse than I thought.'

Lindi touched the 'play' icon and clicked.

The footage was dated for the previous day. It appeared to have been taken in fading light. That and the poor resolution of the images – presumably shot on an old mobile phone – gave the scene an eerie quality, like some amateur horror movie. Whoever was holding the phone was following a group of other men, all wearing beanies pulled right down to their eyes, with their jumpers and jackets lifted over their chins. They were hurrying along a dirt track, the camera bobbing up and down until it veered off the path and settled on a vehicle.

It was a BMW, a four-wheel-drive model. The driver's side door was wide open. One of the men jumped in and pretended to drive, sound effects and all. The customised zebra-skin seat covers added a touch of Africa to the cold efficiency of Bavarian engineering. The group moved on, walking away from the car and into the bush. Every now and then one of the men would point ahead, like wildlife rangers following a trail of spoor in one of the nearby game parks. The camera pushed in on the first find. A pair of shiny shoes. The gold buckle glinted into the lens, incongruous in this landscape, like some exotic species. A bit further on, the group gathered around another specimen, this time a light-coloured shirt, probably white, it was difficult to tell. But there was no mistaking the red smear on the otherwise pristine material. The man holding the camera was having difficulty getting the shot he wanted. You could hear his voice. (Anton translated the Zulu.) It prompted one of the others to pick up the shirt and hold it up as if he were trying it for size.

Lindi and Anton now knew what was coming. It was like some macabre treasure hunt, except that the clues were not subtle and the prize would not be a surprise.

'I don't know if I need to see any more of this,' Lindi said.

'You do,' Anton replied. 'This is going to show you just how nasty things have got. I couldn't believe what my friend told me just now. Who are these guys? Why would they be filming all this and then posting it on the web?' Anton turned back to the screen.

It felt as if the men were now a good distance from where they had found the vehicle. Whoever was at the other end of this trail of designer clothes had obviously tried to run away from his attackers. By the time they found the beige chinos, thrown over a bush as if they had been put out to dry, it was clear this was not just about killing someone, it was about humiliation. The proof was just a few metres on. There was a man's body, a black man.

His underwear had been pulled down around his knees. There was a bloody gash where his scrotum should have been. Whoever had held the camera made no allowances for those of a more delicate temperament.

Lindi turned away. 'This is disgusting. It's like watching one of those snuff movies you hear about.'

Anton brought a hand up to his mouth. He retched, tasting a gutful of fear.

Slowly, the camera panned up the torso, passed the beginnings of a rich-man paunch and another fleshy, gaping wound on the chest. Finally, it settled on a grotesquely misshapen head. Skin that must once have been shiny and pampered was now a dull blue-grey. The man's mouth had been pulled open, as if he were about to unleash some primordial scream, but stuffed into it was his own penis and a crocodile-skin wallet.

'I need to get some fresh air,' said Lindi, already heading out of the door.

Anton shut down the computer. He felt utterly washed out.

Lesedi's grotesque murder would unnerve those in power in a way that went way beyond the crime itself. He knew it would stir a visceral foreboding among South Africa's elite. There was a time when he would have relished the thought. Now it just made him want to curl up and hide in a dark place.

He knew what the authorities would be thinking. If only it had been a Du Plessis or a Westhuisen who'd been battered to death on that farm; if only the vehicle had belonged to a Schmidt or a Smith. That would be so easy to explain. Newspaper editors, local councillors, the provincial premier – everybody who had a stake in the way things were – could get on their high horse and bemoan this throwback to an era that South Africa had left behind. But this, this was different. This was not a man who was killed because of his colour but because of what he represented.

Lindi returned. There was some colour in her cheeks again. She'd tied her thick, wavy brown hair into a knot sitting high on her head. The roots just above her forehead glistened with the water she had just splashed on her face.

'I think it's time you headed down there,' Anton said. 'The sooner the better.'

'I'm not sure where I'd start. Where do we fit in?'

'Listen, I think there is something going on that neither the government or the unions—'

'Nor.'

'What?'

'Neither/nor, either/or . . .' Lindi paused mid-correction. 'God! I'm sorry. It's like your swearing, it just pops out. Can't help it.'

'I can't remember what the fuck I was saying now.'

'The government or the unions,' she said, grateful she'd remembered the train of thought.

'I think there is something going on that neither the ministers *nor* the unions want out in the open. They must know about all the attacks on farms. And now this.'

'Hold on. Despite your intervention this morning, we don't actually know that the attacks on farms and Lesedi's murder are the work of the same people.'

'All I know is that people are taking matters into their own hands.'

'What people and what matters?' she asked.

Anton beckoned her over to his desk and pointed to his laptop. He'd already opened up the links he'd been browsing in the coffee shop. He pointed to the website. 'What's this?'

'It's from something called the Land Collective. They monitor land sales. Every time there's been an incident on a farm there's an entry about it. Look at this. It was written the day after a warehouse fire in Graskop, I checked the dates.'

He read the entry:

We want to salute the BRAVERY of our BROTHERS and SISTERS for what they did at WORLD'S END FARM. It takes COURAGE to stand up for what you believe. That farm was going to be SOLD but nobody asked the WORKERS. There was no CONSULTATION. The PRESIDENT says he is on the side of farm workers but he stays QUIET while FOREIGNERS try to STEAL our land. The workers have buried their FATHERS and MOTHERS on this land but nobody talked to them. Now someone has spoken for the workers and they have SPOKEN with FIRE.

'Whoever is writing this stuff is pointing to the real land issue, not the one the journalists obsess about,' Anton continued. 'It's not about whether the land is owned by a black man or a white man. It's whether it's owned by a South African or a foreigner. He's challenging the government and he's taking a huge risk.'

'It could be a woman,' Lindi butted in.

'Whoever it is, he or she is a link to all the incidents. He knows what's happening on the ground. It's as if he's organising the whole damn thing.'

'You think this Collective group is behind all these incidents?'

Anton shrugged, part admission, part exasperation. 'All I know is that they're trying to make damn sure everyone knows about them.'

'So have they written about Lesedi's murder?'

'Yes, it must have been posted late last night.'

'And?'

'They condemn Lesedi's killing, say it's nothing to do with the campaign against land sales.'

'Christ, Anton! And you go on air making it sound as if there was a link.'

'Like I said, they must have posted it very late: it wasn't there when I went to bed, well after midnight. Anyway, my point still stands. There's some sort of a link. Motlantshe junior visits a land-reform outfit in Mpumalanga and the next thing he's dead. Somebody didn't like him mixing with those guys.'

'Yes, but *who* didn't like him mixing with those guys? It could be the government that was upset about his visit. That's the point. It all depends on what Lesedi was doing there.'

'Look, this is my country, I know some of these people, I feel it in my guts. You need to get down there.' He took off his spectacles and placed them with uncharacteristic care on his desk. He looked straight at Lindi. 'In the old days you'd get a bunch of protesters and they'd sing revolutionary songs and raise their imaginary Kalashnikovs in the air, do a bit of *toi-toing* in front of the farmer's house and then it would be lunchtime and they'd wander back home or to the shebeen. Big business, the police, the government know how to deal with that kind of thing. They cut a deal with the union bosses, offer a little bit of extra pay, which is eaten up by inflation, and then everybody goes back to what they were doing before – pissing on the little man. This is different. Lesedi's killing is a game-changer. We may be seeing the start of something much bigger.'

Anton's phone rang again. This time it was the landline.

'Hello. Yes, this is Anton Chetty.'

'It's Mbali Modise here from the South African High Commission.' Anton put his index finger to his lips and pressed the speaker button. 'We haven't met but I feel as if I know you.'

'Oh! How's that?'

'Well, like they say, your reputation goes before you.'

Anton raised an eyebrow at Lindi.

'Now would that be in a good way or a bad way? What can I do for you?'

'We heard your interview on *Today* a few hours ago. I was just . . . we were just wondering if you'd like to come in and talk to the High Commissioner about your concerns.'

39

'No, I wouldn't like to come in.'

'It's just that Lesedi Motlantshe's death has shocked us all and we, the government, we're obviously as keen as anybody to find the culprit and you seemed to suggest there was a link with the government's land-reform programme.'

'Is that what it's called?'

'Excuse me?'

'Selling land to foreigners, that's land reform, is it?'

'Getting back to your interview. We were just wondering whether you had any thoughts on who might be responsible for Lesedi Motlantshe's murder.'

'I have plenty of thoughts, my friend, but I'll keep them to myself. As you know, we're a neutral organisation.'

'You didn't sound very neutral this morning. Anyhow, if you do have second thoughts, maybe you'll come to us first.'

'Oh, you know me. I wouldn't make a move without talking to you all first. Have a good day, Ms . . . ?'

'Modise.'

'Ms Modise, that's right. Thanks for your call.' Anton slapped the phone back into its cradle. 'Patronising bitch! That was the High Commission.'

'They must be getting twitchy in Pretoria. The High Commission wouldn't have made that call off its own bat. And what did she mean come and talk to them first?'

'They're frightened by the publicity,' said Anton. 'I'd say they're more worried about their precious land-sales programme getting a bad name than worrying about Lesedi. Listen, I've got a board meeting, another four hours of listening to the great and good pontificating. Let's thrash out what we should do. Where were we?'

'Whether I should go or not. The thing is, we never get involved unless we're invited and both sides want us to intervene. But who's inviting us in this instance?'

Normally he would find it hard to argue with her logic, but Anton was in full flow by now.

'The most important rule of all is that we are here to *prevent* conflict, not wait till it happens and then start picking up the pieces. Let's leave that shit to the cotton-frocked aid workers.' Anton stopped himself. If he hadn't, Lindi would have done it for him. She knew that particular rant inside out. She thought it was mostly unfair and bordering on misogynist. In Anton's world, the aid workers were never men in jeans.

'Find these people,' Anton said, 'the Land Collective, you know, whoever is writing this stuff for them, and you have one side. As for the other – well, it's the big farmers, it's the government, the greedy bastards right here in this city, it's the Arabs, Chinese, it's the unions – the whole lot of them.'

'I think you've just about covered all bases.'

'So you'll go?'

Lindi's mind drifted back to the call she'd received earlier that morning from Missenden and then even further back to the way he'd treated her at the Foreign Office. Just the thought of it was like being humiliated all over again. She'd lost count of the number of times she'd told herself that she'd moved on. She knew now that she hadn't. It wasn't so much what Missenden had done but her failure to react, to stand her ground, to call him out that left her feeling, well, less than the woman she wanted to be.

'I'll go,' she said at last. 'I'll need a couple of days to get ready.'

'Sure? You don't want to think about it?'

'I have thought about it.'

5

In South Africa, the violence started within minutes of the police statement: a Mozambican labourer in Mpumalanga Province had been
arrested on suspicion of being involved in the murder of Lesedi
Motlantshe. Across the country there were reports of attacks on
foreigners. It didn't matter where they came from: an exotic accent was
enough. In barely forty-eight hours, parts of South Africa began to look
like a war zone.

'Let them cook,' the man shouted, as the fire-fighters tried to muscle
their way through the crowd that had gathered around the western
entrance to Ponte City. Above the screaming heads, a window on the
fifth floor of the building belched thick black smoke. Occasionally the
wind would clear it, revealing the hungry flames probing for new
material to devour. From several other windows, occupants of the
building leaned out, pleading for help. But their fear-filled cries were
drowned in the noise below, the wailing police sirens, the deep-throated
mechanical murmur of the fire-engine pumps and, above it all, the
taunts of the crowd flinging their filthy curses like bloodthirsty spec-
tators waiting for the kill in a gladiatorial contest.

'We don't want foreign rats in South Africa!' a woman shouted.

Immediately, as if on cue, those around her took up the chant: 'The
rats must go! The rats must be killed!'

Much higher, from the crown of Ponte City, there was a curling,
twisting stream of smoke. On the ground, a section of the crowd
suddenly surged in one direction, no one really knowing what they
were looking for but all of them scenting spilled blood. The police had
cleared a space around a twisted body on the pavement.

'Fucking Mozambican was trying to run,' someone said, as if that was
explanation enough as to why the man lay lifeless where he'd fallen.

43

'The place is full of them,' another said, adding, 'You can smell them.'

The fifty-four-storey doughnut-shaped Ponte City, which dominated the Johannesburg skyline, had once been one of the most desirable places to live. Built in the mid-seventies, the tallest residential building on the continent, it stood tall and proud, like a middle-fingered rebuke to those who hoped apartheid's foundations were crumbling. But for all its architectural precociousness, the Ponte was left isolated in the eighties as the Group Areas Act, which strictly assigned different parts of the city to different races, began to lose its force and the complexion of downtown Johannesburg began to change.

The adventurous white city-dwellers, who had revelled in their fast-lane lives, found a new enthusiasm for the mundane charms of the suburbs. As the white tide retreated, it was replaced by a swirling torrent of black people, many of them from outside the country's border. Africa, in all its spectacular colour and chaos, lashed the Ponte building, like a wave crashing into a cliff. It didn't stand a chance.

By the mid-nineties the Ponte echoed to the sound of a dozen languages, a Babel-esque din which foretold the worst fears of white South Africans, who worried that they would be left marooned in their final redoubt, unable to understand the world around them and misunderstood by it. With white flight went the businesses and their taxes; with the taxes went many of the public services that had once made Ponte the gold standard of urban living.

Ponte's new immigrant colony, from Nigerian traders and Congolese pastors to Mozambican labourers and Somali shopkeepers, lived in the Catch-22 of the black economy, where they were in the city but not of it. If they tried to pay their bills, their dubious immigration status would be exposed. If they tried to sort out their residence permits they would be thrown out. So the plaster peeled off the walls, and the plumbing sprang leaks and the rubbish piled up. The building itself, with its great cylindrical cavern, became a dumping ground, the detritus rising in layers, like geological accretions, until it stood several storeys high.

More recent attempts to rehabilitate the building had met with varying degrees of success. Flats in the uppermost floors were renovated and a few adventurous types had moved in, like an expedition force sent into the unknown. But for the most part, Ponte City remained what it had been for twenty-odd years – a home from home for those for whom the African dream was still just that: a work in progress.

Now even that meagre hope was threatened, engulfed in the indiscriminate flames of xenophobia.

6

Outside Nelspruit, in Mpumalanga Province, the few people left in the squatter camp, the 'informal settlement', as the bureaucrats call it, stare at the man. He's an outsider. That much is obvious: his clothes are too clean; they fit him like he actually bought them, not like the rags they are standing in. They only have to look at him to know he's a South African, not like them, migrants. They are the marginal people, the cleaners and labourers, the servants and night-shift workers who creep around the shadowlands of every nation on earth.

What does he want? He greets them, or tries to. They just turn away, suspicious. He wants to ask them how it happened, this devastation. Did they recognise anyone, perhaps those who led the thugs? Did the police come? No answers. Just the silent accusation that whoever he is, whatever he wants, it is too late. He wants to tell them it was not his fault.

Shack after shack, reduced to a pile of smoking embers and buckled corrugated-metal sheeting. Here and there he sees the remnants of the small, meagre lives of these people, so essential to the rural economy but unrecognised by it: a stack of enamel bowls ready for an evening meal that was never eaten; a cracked mirror in which someone, against all the odds, had tried to show a presentable face to a world that couldn't have cared less; a portrait of the late Samora Machel, Mozambique's charismatic revolutionary leader, still pinned to the plywood partition that lies on the ground. He knows about Samora Machel, his struggle against Portuguese colonialism in the sixties and the subsequent, even more vicious, battle with the apartheid regime in South Africa, which had been grafted onto the history syllabus when he was in secondary school.

Staring at the faded poster of the smiling leader in his heyday, he's weighed down by a profound and almost debilitating sense of disappointment. Machel's victory, winning back the right of an African people to call the land their own, seems so empty now. South Africa should have been next. But here he was, still caught in a fight over land. There was a betrayal at the heart of this latest struggle in South Africa that eclipsed anything its Portuguese colonisers had done in Mozambique. When the Portuguese took the land, when they exploited its natural largesse, they had done so as conquerors: they hadn't pretended otherwise. The whole point of the exercise was to enrich people many thousands of miles away, not those whose sweat seeped into the ground as they toiled under an African sun. But in this new battle in South Africa, it was men who had won the land in the name of freedom who were enriching themselves at the expense of those who'd been so naive as to think the great struggle had been about them.

Now he's back in town. He sits at a table, alone and in the dark. A single light bulb hangs uselessly in the centre of the room and the curtains are drawn tight. His mahogany skin is rendered pallid and gaunt by the blue wash of a computer screen. His tired eyes stare through spectacles that mirror the screen. Long, elegant fingers, normally so deft and expressive, lie beside the keyboard, motionless. He wants to write but can't think where to start. The thoughts are there; the words are elusive. He, too, has seen the video that Lindi and Anton witnessed.

It was never meant to be like this. Sabotage, yes. Propaganda, yes. All of that and more – but not this. Not murder. This hideous mob violence was never part of the plan. In Johannesburg, the iconic Ponte City is on fire; here in Mpumalanga Province the homes of Mozambican migrant workers have been ransacked; and even in far away Western Cape a sixteen-year-old Somali girl is gang-raped and left bleeding by a drainage canal on the edge of the Khayelitsha squatter camp. Where did all this anger come from?

In his mind, he turns over every word he's ever written since they – the Land Collective – started their clandestine campaign against land sales. Which phrase, which sentence, which exhortation could anyone have construed as licence to murder? He realises he'd never really thought about who was reading his statements or understood how they might be transmuted in the reading. He deals in ideals; it had never occurred to him that others might trade in vengeance. He imagines how, like a game of digital Chinese whispers, his messages might have been forwarded from reader to reader, each one adding their own meaning to those words he'd thought he'd composed with such care and purpose. He was never in control. He knows that now.

He keys in a series of passwords, following an encrypted path till he reaches his destination. His last entry is there. It was written late on the day of Lesedi Motlantshe's murder. He rereads it.

Lesedi Motlantshe was a SON OF AFRICA, a child raised on the milk of freedom. He did not deserve to die. Our campaign is to PROTECT THE LAND, NOT KILL ITS PEOPLE. It was not Lesedi who wanted to sell the land to FOREIGNERS. It is the SYSTEM. The deals are being signed by big men sitting in Johannesburg, London, Dubai – not here in our BELOVED MPUMALANGA. Lesedi was born rich but that is not a crime. His life was the life many of our people have dreamed of. Whoever has killed him has not advanced our cause. This HEINOUS ACT will alienate us from many people who looked at Lesedi like their own child. WE ARE NOT THUGS, we are not *tsotsis*, we are ACTIVISTS. Those who have done this thing must go to the police. We must not let our cause be derailed. We must not let the blood of this innocent man stain our HISTORIC MISSION.

It's a little after two in the morning. In a few hours' time he would have to set off for work. To his other life.

He isn't sure if he'd fallen asleep. His laptop is in screensaver mode, a logo bouncing off the edges, like some infinite game of snooker. Could he, could they, the Land Collective, change the direction of this violence? He looks around the room. A hint of dawn light is just discernible through the curtains. He taps the keyboard and is back where he was, a blank screen waiting for the words that might reach those who have unleashed this wave of chaos.

His boots, discarded by the doorway to the room, are still covered with ash from the squatter camp. He starts to type.

I have just returned from HILL VIEW. My boots are covered in ash, my clothes are smelling of smoke from the fires that have left thousands of our FELLOW AFRICANS homeless tonight. Our BROTHERS and SISTERS from Mozambique have paid a high price for this FOOLISHNESS. This chaos is just what the LANDOWNERS AND THEIR MINISTER FRIENDS want. They want us to fight among ourselves. They want us to believe that the problem is the Mozambicans. But they are POORER than we are. They are the POOREST OF THE POOR. That is why they come here, working for NOTHING. They are POWERLESS. They are our comrades in this NEW STRUGGLE for our land. The police ARRESTED A MOZAMBICAN BROTHER but they had NO PROOF that he was involved in the murder of Lesedi Motlantshe. They want people to think this is a struggle between South Africans and Mozambicans. But it is not. This is a struggle between those who WORK THE LAND and those who want to sell it to POLITICIANS AND THEIR RICH FRIENDS OVERSEAS. It is OUR LAND, it belongs to ALL South Africans. This violence must STOP NOW.

7

The photograph, in its simple black frame, had hung on the wall outside her parents' study for as long as Lindi Seaton could remember. She must have walked past it a million times. In the mornings, the sun glinted off the glass, obscuring the picture and reflecting a shard of light across the narrow hallway. It was only in the afternoon, as the sun moved over the house, that you could actually see the figures in the photograph – they emerged from the glare one by one, a slow and gentle revelation of their collective history, a curtain parting before a new act in a play.

This wasn't just another of the many family portraits that jostled for attention: it was a picture that said something about the Seatons. It took pride of place among all the other framed photographs that had been bumped and knocked so often that the wall looked like a particularly careless example of crazy paving. This one photograph – taken in South Africa in the mid-eighties – was a kind of visual shorthand. It said, 'This is who we are.'

On the left of the photo was Harry Seaton, his hair thick, curly and dark. He had one arm around a plump black woman – her apron spoke of her status in the household, but Harry's protective arm evoked her special place in the family's affection. On the other side of the woman was Helen Seaton, her head tilted towards the black woman in another, understated, sign of closeness. In front of them stood three children – two white, one black. Lindi was there, slightly to one side and looking across at her older brother, Ralph. He had his arm around a boy who, in turn, held Ralph's waist. Harry, Maude, Helen, Lindi, Ralph and Kagiso, Maude's only son. A portrait of togetherness in a divided nation.

Many years and thousands of miles away, that photograph of the Seatons and their house-worker, Maude, would grow in significance.

51

It would come to occupy an almost totemic position in their recollection of a time when their credentials as opponents of apartheid were understood and taken for granted. After all, hadn't Harry written the leader columns that had so irritated the apartheid government? And there was Helen's voluntary work at the Legal Resource Centre that saw a stream of black petitioners queue up every day, clutching bits of paper that could change their lives. So how natural and effortless it was that Maude should be treated as one of the family.

But that was then; this was now. You couldn't relive all that in a North London terrace.

Slowly, and unwittingly, they were drawn into an allegiance to their new life in London. In this they were led by Lindi and Ralph. Helen and Harry were the parents of the new kids in the local school. As the children made friends so Helen and Harry found they were pulled into a new social circle – a group of people brought together not by choice or conviction but by the arbitrary drawing of a line on a street map: they were all in the same school catchment area.

For the Seatons, who they had once been became less important than who they were now. The other mothers at the school had been quick to notice how confidently Helen wore her collection of bold ethnic jewellery and asked her where she'd got it – but that was the limit of their curiosity. There were no Brownie points for having once tried to chip away at the edifice of apartheid. It was Helen who felt this need for a separation from their former life most keenly. Once or twice, over a hurried cappuccino at Ribbons & Taylor on Stoke Newington Church Street, she'd noticed how a reference to her campaigning days in South Africa had been ignored, like a conversational cul-de-sac. The heartfelt conviction that had propelled her actions in Johannesburg didn't translate well in the tired aftermath of a hectic school run. Here, in the frazzled mess of soggy anoraks and young children, her past accomplishments seemed neither relevant nor interesting.

And that was where the photograph came into its own. Hanging in the hallway that linked the study to the rest of the house, it made its point unceremoniously. For all the apparent nonchalance with which it had been placed on the wall, the photograph had a quiet eloquence. It said: here was a family that was comfortable with race, even if in the country outside the opposite was the case.

Now, as Lindi's eyes scoured the photograph, she mused that it was accurate in every detail, but the image as a whole managed to convey an impression that Lindi no longer felt was honest. It was greater than the sum of its parts. She had come to think of that photo like one of those mirrors in department-store fitting rooms that make even the most generously proportioned customers look good in an unwise choice. The mirror doesn't lie: it just plays around with the truth.

As she grew up and began to make up her own mind about what was happening in South Africa, Lindi couldn't stop herself thinking that her parents had taken the easy option. She knew there were South African-born teenagers like her in London, whose parents really were a part of 'the struggle'. She remembered the memorial service for the father of one of her friends. Afterwards the congregation had taken over the upstairs room in a pub. There had been plenty of talk about what he'd been like, how he'd always been the guy who would go the extra mile. Nobody said how he'd actually died, except that he'd been on a mission in one of the camps run by the African National Congress, in those days spearheading the liberation movement. It was always that way with the real activists. It had seemed to her that the less you knew about them, the more important their role in 'the movement'. Not like her parents and their friends, who were constantly talking about the struggle as if it were a club anyone could join.

And there was the whole business of her name. Lindi was the diminutive of Lindiwe, 'the awaited one'. It wasn't that she didn't like being called Lindi (though she got bored with explaining its meaning) but that she suspected it was a part of her parents' image of themselves. How contrived to give your child a Zulu name, even if the only Zulu person you knew really well was the woman who washed the dishes and ironed the clothes. She was a part of their myth: that's what Lindi thought when her mind took an uncharitable bent.

Lindi did what she always did when these thoughts came to the surface: she gave herself a gentle ticking off and willed them away. Self-control had always seemed a strength to her but it invariably felt like a dowdy little virtue against the expansive mood that was her

53

family's natural state. She'd spent so many years being the practical child, the one who injected a note of realism into a conversation, that she could no longer tell whether that was the way she was wired or whether it was merely a reaction to her family. She preferred the latter explanation, but worried the former was more accurate. What if she was always going to be the serious little girl in the photograph, the one who wanted to be spontaneous and free, like her brother, but so often retreated into studied reliability?

A clinking of bottles down in the cellar ended this train of thought.

Harry was dusting off a couple of bottles of his precious Meerlust Rubicon. This choice was a kind of vinic semaphore – it was his way of saying how special this meal was going to be. Every year an old friend in Johannesburg, Marney van Rensburg, would send a case of Rubicon. It was a private joke. Back in the old days, when Harry worked for Marney on the *Rand Daily Mail*'s special investigations team, a particularly incisive piece of journalism was always celebrated with a bottle of the Meerlust vineyard's finest. Never mind that it cost a hefty portion of their joint pay-packets – though mostly they found a way of hiding it in their expense claims.

As he brought the first glass to his lips the older man would always lean back in his chair and say, 'One day, when the revolution comes, Harry, we'll all be drinking this stuff. But till that day – we mustn't let the bastards have it all to themselves. Drink up, man.'

The memory always brought a smile to Harry's lips.

He emerged from the cellar, saw Lindi, and put his arm around her. They stood in silence together, staring at the collection of memories on the wall. He glanced from a childhood photo of Lindi to the woman beside him now. A flick of the eye but a journey across time. Not for the first time he marvelled at the change. When had it happened? He'd seen it all and yet he'd seen nothing. It occurred to him that the change was less to do with individual features and more to do with the way they had accommodated each other. He could remember how, as a child, her ears, her lips, her eyes had all seemed to compete with each other. The ears stood out too much, the lips were too full and the eyes too big. Each seemed to make a claim to be the defining feature. He thought

54

back to the way Lindi used to fold her lips inwards in a self-conscious attempt to hide them. And how those big, staring eyes made her look as if she were in a constant state of shock. Now her features had settled into happy coexistence in a face that had once been round but now resembled a heart. Those large green eyes – 'At least one of my genes survived,' Helen would say – were no longer out of proportion; instead they lit her face. And her ears, well, you couldn't even see them now, buried under a tumbling wave of thick brown hair.

He could never look at her without being overcome with a powerful protective urge. There was something vulnerable about her. In truth, he'd always known what it was. Lindi needed protecting from herself, her self-imposed need to be conscientious, to be productive.

As his mind focused back into the present, Harry wondered how long he had been standing there with Lindi: he hadn't even noticed that she'd snuggled her head into his shoulder.

'I'm proud of you, my girl,' he said leaning down, kissing the top of her head.

It was a chilly September day, one of those that takes everyone by surprise after the gentleness of a wishy-washy British summer, and there was something rather comforting about an oven stuffed with a joint of beef, potatoes and Yorkshire puddings sitting in sizzling hot trays. Besides, a roast lunch had its special place in the Seaton family story. Years ago, when they were trying to persuade their reluctant children that going to England would be fun, Helen and Harry had drawn up a list of all the wonderful things they could look forward to. As time went by and hardly any of it had come to pass Ralph and Lindi would tease their parents. 'I wonder when we're going to get to England,' they'd say.

The parental list of inducements had included snow on Christmas Day (never); a milkman in a striped apron who brought bottles to your door (not where they lived); double-decker buses with conductors who shouted, 'Hold on tight now' (they'd all been made redundant); and Concorde streaking across the sky (taken out of service). The only thing from the list that had survived intact was the Sunday roast – and even that hadn't turned out to be quite the British staple that Harry and Helen had suggested. The Seatons had adopted the ritual of a Sunday lunch with all the vigour of converts, even if most of the locals had moved on to more varied fare.

'Listen, you must give Marney a call. He's retired now but I bet he's still plugged into what's going on,' he said to Lindi, handing her a piece of paper with Marney's address and phone number on it. She glanced at it and saw that he'd moved down to Knysna, a coastal resort in the south of the country. Even with her second-hand knowledge of South Africa she was aware that Knysna was not exactly the place to be to judge the pulse of a nation. Put your ear to the ground in Knysna and all you'd detect would be the sound of a thousand feet shuffling in and out of fish restaurants and curio shops.

Helen had packed a parcel for Maude. 'It's just a few goodies,' she said, pointing to a package in the corner of the dining room.

'A few goodies! There won't be space for me to carry anything but a toothbrush if I take that lot,' she said.

'You must check out the old house,' Ralph said. 'Hey, Dad, I wonder if our goalposts are still there.'

'Not that you or Kagiso ever managed to hit the ball between them,' retorted Harry.

The two boys, Ralph and Kagiso, had been an unlikely pairing and not just because one was white and the other black, or because one was the son of a servant and the other the son of the employer. Those things didn't matter in the Seaton household. No, it was their temperaments that were so different. Ralph was boisterous while Kagiso was solemn; one was loud, the other quiet; one confident, the other diffident. Harry and Helen had often thought Lindi a better playmate for Kagiso. They were both earnest, so neither would dominate the other.

'Where is Kagiso now?' asked Ralph. 'You must try to hook up with him, Lindi.'

'Maybe he's moved on,' she replied. 'He might not want to be reminded that he was the housemaid's son.'

'That's a bit harsh,' said Harry, clearly affronted at what Lindi was implying. 'We treated him exactly the way we treated you two.'

'The last time Maude talked about him he'd left his government job,' said Helen. 'Apparently he'd gone to work for some cooperative or other in the rural areas. He'd told Maude it was real grassroots work. She wasn't even sure that he was being paid properly. He hadn't sent her any cash for months and he was always so good about that. Maude was so funny talking about it on the phone.' Helen now mimicked Maude at her irritable best. 'I asked him what for he was so worried about grassroots. I told him we are not *inkomo* pulling grass from the ground. I told him what we need is maize-meal and medicines. I tell you! That boy he likes to dream.'

'It's certainly going to take more than dreams to turn things around now,' said Harry. 'I'm not sure how you recover from a thing like Lesedi Motlantshe's murder.'

Harry had known Lesedi's father. His interview with him had angered the apartheid government of the time. The article had ended with Motlantshe saying he looked forward to the day Harry would interview him in a Pretoria office, and BOSS (the notorious Bureau of State Security) would be protecting him rather than monitoring him. In fact, it was shortly after the double-page spread that the first threats against Harry and the family had begun to drop through his letterbox.

Harry recounted the occasion, then added, 'Well, he certainly took to life in Pretoria.'

'And then some,' said Ralph. 'Isn't he one of the richest men in South Africa?'

'He certainly is. I suppose I should say, "Good luck to him," but it still leaves a bitter taste in the mouth.'

After lunch Lindi headed west from Stoke Newington towards Finsbury Park, where she shared a flat with friends. Her journey took her through one of the most cosmopolitan parts of London. She'd become blind to it but friends from her university days who'd settled outside London would occasionally remark at how there were more foreign faces than English ones. What they meant was that there were more black and brown people than white.

Kebab restaurants jostled with pound stores and pavement vendors. The Finsbury Park mosque had long since lost its radical associations but not its huge congregation. On Fridays, after prayers, the men would crush into the numerous cafés, with the Al Jazeera Arabic news channel providing a constant stream of information to argue about.

Lindi cycled past one of many internet cafés in the area, its window plastered with advertisements for phone cards, all of them promising the cheapest rates yet to keep in touch with people back home. She wondered what they told their fathers and mothers, brothers and sisters. Did they admit to being lonely, or did they dare to tell them that they loved this place and they wanted to stay? These Somalis, Algerians, Moroccans and Pakistanis were buffeted by the same competing emotional tides that generations of migrants before them had struggled with. Some longed to call this grimy city their home but worried that it might never fully accept them. Others saw how their children embraced its mayhem and materialism, and knew in their heart of hearts that they would never get away, as they had promised the folk back home. All around Lindi were people whose lives had been transformed – for good or ill – by journeys begun in a fit of hope, but often lived in the limbo of not knowing for sure if they had made the right move.

In only twenty-four hours' time, it would be Lindi's turn to find herself in a foreign country.

8

The uniformed immigration officer at O.R. Tambo International Airport left his station, taking Lindi's passport with him. 'Wait there,' he said, barely looking back at her. Lindi turned around and shrugged her shoulders, acknowledging the evident impatience of the man waiting behind her in the queue. The immigration clerk was back within minutes, a suited official in tow.

'Come with me,' the second man said.

'Why?'

'We are going to talk.'

'Talk? Talk about what?'

'What you are doing in South Africa.'

'I can tell you right here. I'm like everyone else in the queue. I've come to visit South Africa.'

'We are going to my office. You can come with me or I can ask one of those policemen to escort you.'

He started walking and Lindi followed. It dawned on her that they were expecting her. How was that possible? Just the question was unsettling. As for the answer, every option was as chilling as the next. Either they had been told or they had made it their business to find out. It had been Anton's idea for her to come in as a tourist. Perhaps that had been a mistake. He'd called Lesedi's death a 'game-changer', something like that, but even he might have underestimated what was at stake for the authorities here.

They entered an airless room. Lindi took a deep breath. The unadorned walls – save for the obligatory portrait of the president – were painted in that indiscriminate version of cream common to official places everywhere. There was a single desk and a single chair, which the official took, leaving Lindi to stand, like a naughty schoolgirl in front of the head teacher.

'So what is the purpose of your visit?'

'I grew up here, and I've come back to see family and friends,' Lindi replied, her words rehearsed numerous times on the plane.

'Where are they?'

'Who?'

'Your relatives, these people you have come to see.'

'They're all over the country.'

'Is that so, all over the country? Like where?'

Lindi knew she was going to have to feed him something, something bland, someone on the coast, somewhere that evoked a holiday. 'Oh, I haven't got a firm plan yet but I'll probably head down to Knysna at some point.' She knew what was coming next.

'And who is there?'

'My father's oldest friend.' So Marney van Rensburg had come in useful, after all.

'And what about here, in Johannesburg?'

'Look, I really don't have to give you a blow-by-blow account of my plans. What's all this about?'

The man ignored the question. 'So you're not doing any work here?'

The official's mobile phone rang. He looked at the number and moved towards the door. Lindi could just about hear his voice. 'Yes, she's here.'

So they knew who she was. They must have known what flight she was on. Anton's last words to her had been 'Be careful.' She'd assumed the comment was habitual, but now realised it was specific to this trip.

The man was listening to whoever was at the other end of the call. It was not a conversation: he was being told what to do. Finally, he took the mobile away from his ear, came back to where Lindi was standing and picked up the desk phone. 'The passenger is ready now. Come and get her.'

Turning to Lindi, he forced a grim smile: 'So, you are welcome in our country. Just remember you are here to enjoy yourself. We want you to play, no work. You understand.'

It was an order, not a question.

'If we find you behaving badly we will know what to do.'

Anton had arranged for Lindi to rent a spare room at the BBC office in downtown Johannesburg, South Africa's commercial heartland – the kind of city that says to the capital, the seat of government, 'You can have the politics, I'll take the money.' Anton's habitual disdain for journalists, and foreign correspondents in particular, did not extend to the World Service, the BBC's international radio station. It recruited many of its broadcasters locally, and the editors back in London were men and women steeped in the affairs of the region they were reporting on.

'You couldn't have them on the *News at Six*, could you?' Anton would ask rhetorically. 'I mean, they actually know what they're talking about.'

The Africa editor at the World Service's headquarters in London's Portland Place – a legendary figure whose love for Africa seemed to have grown, inexplicably, with every new and brutal war he'd covered – was an old friend of Anton's and the two had come to an informal arrangement. It was the kind of you-scratch-mine-and-I'll-scratch-yours deal that underpinned many a story.

After Lindi had passed Immigration (she was taken to the front of the queue and the formalities took less than a minute), she turned on her phone to find several messages waiting for her. There was one from her father, and another from Ralph. She ignored them for the time being and scrolled down to one that had been sent from a Johannesburg number. It was from the office manager at the BBC. The woman had said she would be at the airport – despite Lindi's insistence that she could get a cab – but now apologised that it was turning into a very busy morning and that she'd been asked to go straight to the BBC bureau.

Lindi was glad. She hadn't been looking forward to having to make small talk on the journey into the city. She looked up from the palm-sized screen and took in her first view of South Africa since she had left the country as a child. She didn't so much look at it, as breathe it in.

There was a lightness to the air, a welcome contrast to the stale, regurgitated variety she had been inhaling all night on the plane. It wasn't like one of those old Graham Greene novels in which the protagonists always seemed to be wading through the thick, treacly, cloying heat of a tropical backwater. This was fresh and rarefied, a product of

Johannesburg's position on the highveld, and it imbued everything Lindi looked at with a clarity so at odds with the leaden state of her mind as she'd walked off the plane an hour earlier. It lifted her spirits. Perhaps her mission was going to be all right after all.

The car park, spread out below her, was crammed with vehicles, their assorted but distinct colours coming together in a vast mosaic. Every now and then, a car inching its way into a bay or gingerly heading for the exit would catch the sun and and reflect it back.

Airport compounds around the world are like a no man's land separating the culturally neutral and uniformly branded malls of the terminal buildings from the diverse and sometimes chaotic cities they serve. O.R. Tambo International was no different. Ahead of her, on the perimeter of the car park, Lindi could see vast advertising hoardings. The mobile phones or the latest fuel-efficient cars they were peddling were exactly the ones that were being foisted on hapless consumers back in Britain, except that these were peopled with bronzed faces (nothing so offensive as a truly black face). Around her the wait-your-turn commercial discipline imposed inside the terminal was beginning to break down, giving way to an altogether more robust form of commerce. The porters' liveried uniforms implied a certain decorum but their insistent appeals to carry Lindi's bag came from desperation sharpened in the harsh training ground of life in one of Johannesburg's townships.

'Taxi, you want a taxi? I know a good-good driver,' said the porter nearest Lindi. 'He's my brother, he going to get you home sharp-sharp,' the man said, before curling his tongue and expelling a shrill whistle aimed towards the car park.

This as-yet-tentative transaction caught the attention of another man in uniform. He was large with a belly straining at a belt that was only barely visible beneath the rest of his bulk. He wore his uniform like a badge of superiority. He ambled towards Lindi. From a few yards away he started shouting in Zulu at the porter, who retreated a little.

'I'm sorry, madam, but those chaps are *tsotsis*. They will take all your money,' he said. 'The airport authorities recommend you take the licensed cabs from the rank over there and I will organise it all for you personally.'

Despite the many warnings she'd been given about being careful at the airport – the most recent delivered in rather stern language by the BBC's office manager – Lindi decided she was not going to reward the officious and bloated attendant with what would be his latest victory over the porter, still hovering in the wings. She noticed now that the porter's trousers were held up by a length of twine and bunched up around the waist. 'Thank you, but I'm quite capable of looking after myself,' she said curtly.

'Don't mind him, madam.' It was the porter. 'He likes to scare tourists. You see how fat he is – that's because all the taxi drivers give him some per cent. He's eating pies all day.' At this all the other porters laughed. The attendant looked back; he knew he was the butt of the joke.

'Yes, well, I'm not a tourist so don't think you can play games with me,' said Lindi. 'Where is this wonderful brother of yours?'

'You have to go to him, madam. The airport is not allowing him to pick up here.' He reached down for Lindi's bag.

'Oh, all right, then. Let's go.'

'So you coming back after holiday, madam?'

'Well, I'm coming back but not from holiday. I've been away for many years. I was born here.'

'You are welcome, madam. You are an African. Now you are home again.'

Back in Britain, Lindi had applied her own rigorous, not to say fastidious, benchmark for achieving the right to be called an African. By that measure most of the white South Africans she knew, including her parents, didn't qualify, despite their habitual use of the sobriquet. It had always struck Lindi as presumptuous and dishonest. It was all very well calling yourself an African when you were safely ensconced in Britain. That was what she had thought. She had always refrained from calling herself either African or an exile. That was for others to judge. As a white person, it seemed to her, you had to earn the right to be called an African. It couldn't simply be an accident of birth. And yet that was all it had taken for this porter to confer the description on her. For him it was not an award, not a title bestowed on you for services rendered. It was what you were. It was simply a fact. It didn't come with any value judgement. He wasn't offering her a compliment. That she would have to earn.

Looking back, Lindi found new sympathy for the mostly white South African community she'd grown up with in London, an uneasy mixture of the disgruntled and disenchanted peppered with a smattering of draft dodgers and genuine activists. Whatever their varied antecedents, being 'African' offered a patina of credibility – even to those whose flight to London had been an act of pragmatism rather than political activism.

She began to understand, too, her own father's resentful exile. What role did he occupy in this melee of migrants? Even as a child, Lindi had sensed his unease, remembered a sort of lassitude. He'd been quite surly in those early years.

She remembered how he had always been too tired to do the things that came naturally to other fathers. They'd go to the park but he would just go through the motions. Lindi – ever attuned to his moods – would try to compensate. She'd contrive to make those prosaic outings far jollier than they could ever or should be. In her early teens she had already accepted this mantle of responsibility, this requirement to be something more than her years warranted. The more listless Harry had been, the more energy Lindi would find. She had tried to keep up with Ralph, trying to match his boundless demands. As she'd grown older, she'd begun to resent her father's lacklustre, enervating presence.

'Dad's so boring,' was how she'd put it to Helen one day, the closest she ever got to protest. 'He never wants to do anything.'

Helen couldn't bear the thought of her children thinking of their father in that way. But her attempts to get Harry to talk about it always ended in a row. It was like a cold undercurrent that ran beneath the surface of what was otherwise a warm relationship of deep affection and occasional passion. Helen would point to the threats and the precariousness of their lives, once Harry's paper had been banned by the South African government. He, in turn, would say that so many others had found a way to stay and that he had cut and run just as the edifice of apartheid was beginning to shake and shudder.

It had been different for Helen. Having decided not to work while they settled into London life, she found new purpose as she immersed herself in running the house. She would creep out of bed early, sometimes only a couple of hours after Harry had returned from another night-shift on the *Daily Telegraph*, get showered, dressed and have breakfast ready by the time she had to wake up the children. In short, she tried to do all the chores Maude had once done for them, including, much to the amusement of the other mothers on the school run, pressing the family's laundry.

'You iron their knickers!' they shrieked in unison.

In the collective challenge of motherhood they offered an intimacy that helped Helen to make the transition from who she had been to the person she had to become.

It took her quite some time, years, really, to understand that in this respect she had something that Harry could not find. He had gone from being something of a minor celebrity in the liberal circles they had moved in – he could walk into a café in the old Hillbrow, Johannesburg's equivalent to Paris's Rive Gauche, and be instantly recognised – to just another hack working on other people's stories. The occasions when Helen had tried to introduce her friends' partners to Harry had been unsuccessful. He could barely suppress his contempt for what he regarded as the peculiarly English fascination with garden sheds and DIY. 'If I hear one more person tell me they're going to be "pottering about" at the weekend I'll go nuts,' he used to rail. He'd wanted sharp arguments and soulful camaraderie – instead he got a pint of warm, still beer.

He longed for those rare visits from other South Africans who'd also found themselves marooned in the no man's land of voluntary exile. Helen, too, looked forward to the sometimes raucous weekends. She'd noticed that even the anticipation of a visit was enough to lift Harry's spirit. It comforted her that somewhere in all that muddled resentment and emotional lethargy was the man of passion she had married. For weeks after one of those weekends their life seemed blessed, sprinkled by stardust and touched by the bonhomie of friendships forged in more invigorating times.

Lindi and the porter got to the car. The boot was open and he dropped her bag into it. He pushed it shut only for it to bounce open again. He shut it once more, this time with a little more vigour. Again, it gaped open. The driver came round to the back of the car. He saw the look on Lindi's face.

'Don't worry, madam. There is a little trick and this foolish boy does not know how to do it.' He brought the boot down slowly and deliberately and just before the point of contact with the chassis he gave it a slight sideways shove. It clicked into place. 'You see,' he said, with a huge smile.

As she was getting into the car Lindi saw the driver give the porter some money. He, too, was getting his 'per cent'.

Lindi rummaged through her rucksack and pulled out the piece of paper with the address of the BBC World Service office. She read out the street name and number.

'Oh, you work for the BBC,' the driver said.

'How do you know it's the BBC?'

'Every taxi driver knows the BBC,' he said. 'And how is Mr Whitaker, these days?'

There was no answer from the back seat. The driver looked in the mirror. 'You don't know the famous Mr Whitaker?' He made it sound like a terrible rebuke.

Then the penny dropped. Lindi realised the driver was talking about Robert Whitaker – Anton's friend and the *éminence grise* at the BBC's Africa section. 'Oh, you mean that Mr Whitaker.' She made it sound as if she might have been thinking of someone else.

'Yes, yes. We like him in Africa because he gives our leaders a tough time. Ah!' He hummed the signature tune of the programme. 'Oh, yes, we like it very much. That man is not scared! If you are cheating, he calls you a cheat. If you are lying, he calls you a liar.'

'Oh, he's fine, I think,' Lindi said limply, regretting she didn't have something more eloquent to match the tribute she'd just heard.

'And what story have you come to write? Are you going to the international trade fair? I picked up some press people from there last night.'

'No, I'm not a journalist. I'm just meeting someone at the BBC office. So how are things here?' she asked. It is a question asked of taxi drivers the world over and many a traveller's assessment of a country – whether it's a journalist in search of a lead, a tourist in search of a good time or, as in Lindi's case, just someone in search of an insight – begins with the answer given by the man behind the wheel.

'Ah! No, everything is fine, madam.'

'What about the murder we heard about? It was news even in London.'

'Oh, you heard about that in London? That is in Mpumalanga Province, madam. It's far away. You are quite safe here in Johannesburg.'

It occurred to Lindi that all these assurances about safety might actually have the opposite effect on tourists. 'I know it's far away but wasn't the man famous?'

'You mean the man who was killed?'

'Yes. His name was Lesedi Motlantshe.'

'Oh! You are very up on the news, madam. You know our country very well. Yes, that boy he comes from a very rich family here in South Africa.'

To the taxi driver Lesedi was a 'boy', a label stuck, like some birth-mark, to all those who are famous in childhood. They are never really allowed to grow up but remain preserved, public perception locking them into a youth they are mostly keen to leave behind.

'Is that why they murdered him – because he was rich?' she asked.

'Yes, I think that is so.' He didn't sound convinced. Lindi saw his face in the rear-view mirror. She realised she had not looked at the driver properly till then. He was an elderly man. A pair of horn-rimmed spectacles sat heavily on his nose. Coiled springs of grey hair lined his temples. The rest of his head was covered with a tweed flat cap. Years of perspiration had soaked through it, leaving a crooked, tell-tale trail of salt.

'But why didn't they take his car?'

'Ah! Madam, I think you are a secret journalist!.' The driver laughed. 'You like to ask questions, too many questions.'

'Well, it's not just journalists who like to know the truth. Anyway, he obviously wasn't killed for his money. I read that nothing was taken.'

'Well, I think some people are just angry. They see that some people are getting fat while the others are still hungry.'

'Is that what you think?'

'Yes, but I am not angry, madam. I am thankful to God almighty for what I have. These young men – the ones who are causing all this trouble in Mpumalanga – they think they should be rich also. They want to drive BMWs and what-what but they don't want to work.'

'That sounds a bit unfair,' said Lindi. 'Maybe there are no jobs,' she added, recalling the statistics on unemployment in one of the many briefing documents she'd read.

'That is true, madam, but you can't be making jobs by killing people. Those Motlantshes – they fought for our freedom. Now they are getting their reward.'

'But freedom wasn't about getting rich,' she blurted out, and instantly wanted to retract the comment. She knew she sounded pompous but the driver's rebuttal, when it came an instant later, still surprised her.

'So you only want the white people to be rich,' he said. Lindi glanced at the mirror long enough to catch the driver staring at her. Gone was the avuncular demeanour. What she saw, instead, were eyes that accused her of being like all the other travellers who'd sat in that very seat, the ones who liked their Africans to be exotic and poor rather than urbane and rich. She'd barely been in South Africa for an hour and she'd already broken the cardinal rule of conflict resolution – stay neutral.

She was also beginning to understand that the old rules about wealth and poverty, honed over centuries of European class war, did not apply so neatly in this country, with its particular history in which the colour of a man's skin was the great dividing line, the social fissure that defined both public politics and private morality. What was it Anton used to say? 'Whether you are being fucked by a white man or black man the result is the same – you are still being fucked.' Perhaps he was wrong. Perhaps there was a hierarchy of wealth in which a black person with money ranked higher than a white one. Lindi told herself she would have to put all that aside, bundle it up and lock it away in her mind.

There was an almost palpable awkwardness in the car, as if someone had uttered an obscenity. Both driver and passenger knew they had wandered into difficult territory, like a pair of ramblers who suddenly find themselves off the beaten track. It was the taxi driver who brought them back to more familiar ground.

'We have made sure the weather is fine for you today, madam,' he said, finding refuge in that hoary old conversational set-piece. 'Ah! But it was raining last night.'

He was the kindly old gentleman again.

'That's good,' said Lindi, looking out of the window and no longer in the mood for talking. They had left the three-lane highway and were cutting through one of Johannesburg's eastern suburbs. What she saw was a study in siege architecture. Mostly you couldn't see any of the houses: they were hidden behind two-metre walls, leaving only the roof tiles visible from the road. The walls were topped with horizontal rows of thin wire stretched taut, between regularly spaced posts, like guitar strings and frets – except the only music you'd hear from these strings was the hum of low-voltage electricity. Virtually every gate had a sign strapped to it showing a fierce-looking dog. South Africa's record-breaking crime rate was the stuff of legend but Lindi found the lengths to which its citizens went to protect themselves rather depressing. That, and the subtext of the earlier conversation with the driver, left her feeling subdued. The effervescent mood in which she had looked at a southern sky when she walked out of the terminal building had all but deserted her. She put it down to the effects of a broken night in a crowded plane.

By now they had reached the city centre. The sterile and fearful suburbs had given way to brash and busy streets. The cab pulled up at a set of traffic lights, the corner of Commissioner and Rissik Streets. Lindi became aware, despite the creeping gloom that had threatened to bury her just a moment or so earlier, of a flicker of warmth, of amusement, tantalisingly close to the surface, ready to wriggle out into the open and into her consciousness. She worked backwards, reversing her thoughts, till her eyes settled on the circular red light in front of the car. Her parents, even after all these years in Britain, still called them 'robots', as they had done growing up in South Africa. As a child it had always conjured up this vision of the traffic lights sprouting arms and legs and striding away from the scene, leaving the drivers to fend for themselves. She was ten years old again, peering out of the back window of 'Old Faithful', their ancient Volvo estate, as Mr Robot turned to her, winked with his red eye, and disappeared down the road.

The pavements were crowded. Lindi noticed a pair of policemen on each corner of the cross roads. Their battle-blue uniforms, the tapered trousers tucked into shin-high boots, the bulletproof vests and, above all, their guns, seemed to belong to a war zone, not the morning rush-hour. She noticed how the policemen cradled their weapons, as you might hold a baby.

'Are the police always here?' she asked.

'Ah, no! They are just here to make sure there are no problems.'

'What sort of problems?'

'Ah, no! It's nothing, madam. It's just that after this business in Mpumalanga they don't want any troublemakers here.'

On the pavement the men and women who side-stepped and shimmied past each other had that same purposeful air you see in commuters the world over, their eyes apparently fixed on some distant finishing post, which lured them on just as surely as a long-distance runner might keep her eyes on the prize.

The taxi pulled over. 'We are here, madam. That is the building you are looking for,' he said, pointing just ahead of them through the windscreen. He got out, lifted Lindi's bag and shut the boot in a deliberately slow and smooth motion while throwing her a knowing smile, like two old friends sharing a private joke. She handed over some notes, suppressing the urge to explain what she had meant to say earlier. The taxi driver held out his hand: no hard feelings.

Lindi stepped back onto the pavement and watched the car ease itself into the heavy flow of traffic, another version of the frenetic movement that was now parting either side of her on the pavement. There was a hum of activity all around her, like a social tinnitus, but it was never distinct enough to identify its source straight away. Very few people were talking. They surged one way or another, heads down and concentrating on the mission. An urban anthropologist in some far distant time might study this daily migration and exclaim at the way nobody actually bumped it into anybody else, guided by an inner sense of space and proximity. It was only when Lindi concentrated her gaze at a particular point in this streetscape that she was able to tune into its sound. From inside the shoe shop, just opening for trade, the forced chirpiness of morning radio, and from the newspaper boy, a punchy verbal précis of the story of the day – the lustful indiscretions of a local celebrity. And further up the road, the metallic clatter of a dustcart as it swallowed the detritus of a downtown night.

Lindi caught the sweet early-morning whiff of freshly baked pastries and bread. It was coming from a mobile stall a few metres away from her. The prices were written in permanent marker on the glass cabinet that shielded the shelves of food. 'Sausage rolls – R10/-, jam rolls – R2/-, bunnichow – R20/-.'

So that's how you spell it, she thought. Bunnichows – soft white loaves with their centres hollowed out and filled with curried meat – had been a treat in the Seaton household, a special reward for a good week at school or comfort food on a particularly gloomy winter's day. As children, half the fun had been derived from pushing their little fists into the loaf and pulling out handfuls of airy white bread, which they would stuff into their mouths. Harry was the bunnichow expert and he'd help them ladle his 'special' curry into the hand-made cavity. Eating bunnichow was always accompanied by a lot of shrieking as the filling inevitably oozed out of the bread and trickled down their faces and hands.

In later years they had switched to vegetarian fillings because Ralph had become convinced that the filling was in fact made of bunny-rabbit meat. Nothing Harry or Helen said could assuage his fear that a fluffy little mammal with a white bobble tail had ended up in the saucepan. The memory brought a smile to Lindi's face. It gave her a connection with this frenzied place, which was all the more welcome because it had been unexpected. It was the first inkling that this city, this country, was, in fact, an integral part of her family's story – her story. She remembered, again, with a twinge of regret, the way she had sometimes berated her parents for being so hung up on their past, on being South African. What had seemed to her an imaginary and exaggerated connection with this nation might have been, after all, exactly what they said it was – a visceral, umbilical link with the place in which they had been born and raised.

Lindi pulled up the handle on her bag and headed towards the building the driver had shown her. Once inside she saw that the BBC office was on the third floor and waited for the lift, along with a dozen or so other people. When the doors slid open she expected the kind of

Darwinian rush that sorted out the men from the boys back in London. One or two did stride into the compartment, like their life depended on it, but many more stood back to allow her into it. The lift was filled with a smell that combined takeaway breakfasts with the over-generous application of aftershave lotion. On the third floor Lindi saw the BBC's logo on one side of the lobby and headed towards the glass doors next to it, mentally reminding herself of the office manager's name. The receptionist, a young woman with perfectly manicured nails, was talking into a phone held awkwardly between her neck and shoulder while signing a receipt note for a delivery.

'I'm looking for Comfort Ramphele,' Lindi said, when the receptionist finally put down the phone.

'Just head down the corridor and she should be at the first desk as you enter the big newsroom,' she said.

Lindi walked into a large, open-plan office. There must have been a dozen desks, each cluttered with PC screens, TV monitors and head-phones. On one wall a line of clocks showed the time locally and in Lagos, Nairobi, London, Washington and Beijing. Underneath them, as if surveying the newsroom, was a life-size cut-out image of a beaming Nelson Mandela, his right arm raised in an iconic closed-fist salute. The great man had signed the picture. Lindi saw that its wooden base was screwed to the floor, presumably because it was the kind of memento for which there was a lucrative market.

On another wall there was a row of screens, each tuned to a different channel – CNN, ENCA, BBC World and Al Jazeera. The six or seven people in the office had congregated under them. Like supplicants at an altar, they were staring at the screens. Lindi recognised one, even in profile. The woman, a British-Asian, had become something of a celeb-rity a few years earlier for her reports on the implosion of Iraq and Syria. They had been robust, partly to do with the economy of language but also because she delivered them in an unforgettable mockney that was at odds with the more conventional tones of other BBC correspond-ents. She was now based in Johannesburg.

Anton had taken an instant dislike to her. 'Frontline bimbo,' he'd called her. 'All talk, no analysis.' On the edge of the group stood a plump, older-looking woman. Lindi guessed she might be Comfort

Ramphele, the office manager who'd been unable to meet her at the airport.

As Lindi began to move towards the huddle, the woman turned around. 'I'm sorry, we were so busy following the news I didn't see you coming in. I'm Comfort.'

'I'm Lindi Seaton from South Trust. I can wait if you're busy.'

'No, no, that's all right. It's time they all got going anyway. This is a terrible business,' she said, as if Lindi must be aware of what was going on.

'What's happened?' Lindi questioned. 'I haven't checked the news since I got on the plane last night.'

'We had this terrible murder about three or four days ago . . . but you know about that, I'm sure. Well, it's just escalated from there. They're sending in the troops now – that's what we were watching, an announcement from the minister of state security. He was saying—'

She was interrupted by the British-Asian correspondent, shouting from the other side of the room, 'Comfort, call Tito and tell him to get his arse over here in half an hour. Tell him we'll probably stay over. And tell Daniel to pack all the gear into the Kombi and follow us. I'll go with Tito and let Daniel know exactly where we're going to end up.'

'Tito is meant to be off from tomorrow,' offered Comfort, clearly knowing full well what the reply was going to be.

'Oh, for Christ's sake, he can have his bloody days off when we get back. It's not like Susie's working or anything. They can go whenever they like. I'm going to make some calls.' Her voice trailed off as she went into a partitioned room.

Comfort looked as if she wanted to apologise. 'It's always a bit tense when we're trying to get people on the road,' she said. 'Look, that office is free – it's the one Robert told us to set aside for you. Why don't you go in there? Grab some of the papers, and you probably want to get online anyway. I've written the password on a piece of paper. There's a coffee machine just off the reception where you came in. I'll be with you as soon as I can. Any friend of Robert's is a friend of mine.'

Lindi went into the room and shut the door behind her. She opened her laptop and booted it up. She stared at the screensaver, a photo of the family taken the previous summer on a walking holiday in the

Pyrenees. Ralph's girlfriend, who had recently become the latest in a long line of ex-girlfriends, was in the shot. She logged into her email inbox. There was a long message from Anton. It had been sent at 4 a.m. London time. Typical! He'd probably not slept since getting home from seeing her off at the airport. She started reading the message, which began in characteristically robust vein: *Fucking hell, it's all kicking off.*

There was a whole line of exclamation marks, just in case the expletive had not been enough to grab her attention. *We might be too late already*, it continued. Lindi scanned the email. He'd forwarded a link to a news item. It was headlined, 'Pangas the Weapon of Choice as South Africans Turn On Foreigners', a reference to the all-purpose wooden-handled blade that many farm labourers used.

Lindi opened the page in Vice News. The report was subtitled, with no voiceover from a reporter. What the raw video material lacked in finesse, it made up for with the sheer shock of what appeared on the screen. A mob gathered round a shack in a squatter camp. One of them, a bandana wrapped around his face, smashed the feeble door to the dwelling and threw a bottle of fuel through it before chucking in a burning rag. Worse than the act itself was the manifest glee on the faces of the mob as the camera turned to them.

'Come out!' shouted one man. 'We are waiting for you.'

Another lifted his panga and ran his tongue over the edge of the blade.

'Today we are going to taste Mozambican blood,' he said.

In the background you could hear screams from the hut. The camera turned to show smoke billowing out from under the tin roof. After what seemed like an implausibly long time, a woman's hand could be seen pushing a young girl, no more than ten years old, into the compound. She stood, blinking into the glare, shivering. She was motionless, paralysed with fear. A youth walked over to her, grabbed her hair and, as he pulled her away, said to the crowd, 'Let her see what will happen when her father and mother come out.'

And they do. The mob surged past the camera, obscuring the view. You could see a flash of a panga blade as it was raised high in the air before it slashed down – again and again. The screaming, both from the victims and perpetrators, was animal, fear and hate unhinged from the conventions of civilised behaviour. A couple of minutes later, the sound of a police siren could be heard, getting louder as it approached the chaotic scene. One by one the mob dispersed. The child approached the corpses of her parents and sat down next to them. No tears. She seemed to be keeping watch. That's what the police find when they arrive.

Lindi flicked back to Anton's email.

All this must have been happening while we were sitting in Terminal Five having a coffee, Anton had written, as if the two things were somehow connected. An eyewitness to one attack, interviewed on the BBC World Service, had said the crowd had been screaming, 'Where are the *amakwerekwere*, the foreigners, those filthy Mozambicans – where are the Mozambicans?'

This is bad [*Anton had written*]. There are tens of thousands of Mozambicans in SA, especially on those farms up there in Mpumalanga, and God knows how many other migrant workers from Zimbabwe and the other neighbouring countries. There are plenty of people who've been waiting for a chance like this to drive them out. You know as well as I do, xenophobia is not just a European thing.

Lindi could feel the suffocating weight of responsibility bear down on her – followed closely by the inevitable question: 'Am I up to this?' She could sense the incipient menace of self-doubt and knew that, if she did not manage to stamp it out, it would overwhelm her. It was like having the walls of a room slowly but surely close in on her, pushing out the air, starving her of oxygen. Over the years she'd learned that the only way to deny its power over her was literally to let the air in. She got up, opened a window, then went to the door and left that ajar to get a draught through the room. It usually worked and it did now. She knew she was dealing only with the symptom and not the deep-seated well of anxiety from which the fear arose but it would have to suffice for the moment.

The correspondent had come to Comfort's desk; Lindi could hear her unmistakable voice but not see her.

'London says the World Service has run an interview with an

eyewitness to last night's attacks. Get someone here to track it down, find out who it was and let me know. Maybe we can take the guy into the squatter camp and do a walkie-talkie with him – that'll keep the News Channel happy for a bit and we can concentrate on *Ten*.'

'It must have been Julius who did the interview. He's been in Nelspruit since Lesedi's murder.'

'Okay. Tell Julius to line him up for me – we should be there just after lunchtime, about two-ish,' the correspondent said. 'By the way, who's the visitor?'

'You remember Robert told us to hire out that room to someone from South Trust? That's her.'

'Oh, so that's Whitaker's Oxford totty. He sent me her CV. Well, she'll need more than her friggin' master's in African development or whatever to sort this lot out. And all those beads and bangles. Very ethnic, right up Whitaker's street. Is Tito here?'

'He's in the car park. He's in a terrible mood.'

'Well, that's hardly breaking news! See you when I see you.'

As she listened to the conversation, a grim determination replaced the anxiety that had enveloped Lindi just a few minutes earlier. How bloody typical, that British proclivity to put people into their little boxes. And this from a woman who might have been expected to remember that a generation earlier her own people were being caricatured as garlic-munching, over-populating foreigners. And to think she had defended the correspondent when Anton had made his own snap judgement about her.

For as long as Lindi could remember she had fought the collective inclination to put people in their place, to give them a label. She had first come across it in secondary school, the way her classmates had instantly put her in a box marked 'Posh'. It hadn't helped that her parents, in a fit of political righteousness, had placed her in the local comprehensive where she was like some alien species. Her academic diligence prompted much curiosity but rarely any admiration. She hated being different but lacked the social guile to mask it. She blamed it on her parents, imploring them to be more like everybody else's fathers and mothers. She used to make up prosaic weekend outings, imaginary trips to the shopping centres her mother loathed to replace the nights out in some crumbling community theatre where a travelling troupe of South African actors were putting on their latest experimental play.

She'd thought it would all end when she got to Oxford. But there it turned out she was not posh enough. One weekend house party at a fellow student's country mansion had convinced her that she had no foothold in that world of privately schooled confidence and monied excess. 'Your friend's a bit serious,' she'd heard someone say sotto voce to the friend with whom Lindi had travelled from Oxford. She knew enough about their type to understand that being accused of seriousness, like being a bore, was about as damning as it could get. And now this woman had decided that Lindi owed her presence in the BBC office to the amorous preferences of an ageing editor back in London. How different from the reaction of the airport porter just a couple of hours previously. He'd taken her at face value. Lindi clung to that thought.

That afternoon, Lindi checked into a guesthouse in Greenside.

She fought the temptation to lie down on the bed and forced herself to look at the list of calls she needed to make: there was an agricultural union representative, a Member of Parliament (an old friend of Anton's), some journalists, a legal-aid charity, the bishop's office in Mpumalanga. Hardly what you'd call the makings of a tourist itinerary.

The phone on the side table rang.

'The taxi you ordered is waiting for you. Do you know how long you will be?' asked the receptionist.

'What taxi? I've only just arrived.'

'We went out to check and he said he's waiting for someone. We assumed it was you. None of the other guests has ordered a taxi.'

'Well, there's been a mistake. I'm not going anywhere.'

Lindi pulled back the blind. The taxi was still there. She decided to get on with her calls and keyed in the first number. She was about to press the green 'call' icon on her smartphone but stopped, a reflex: the less easy she was to track, the better. She put her mobile down and picked up the landline phone. She'd use that instead.

Finally, she got around to the call she'd been wanting to make from the minute she'd set foot in South Africa. She searched her contacts for Maude's number.

'And how's my baby?'

Even after all these years Maude's voice was as familiar as her own mother's, and Lindi, who long ago had taught herself to put away childish things, felt, in an instant, like a little girl again. These were the very words she'd hear every morning as she stumbled, sleepy-eyed and groggy, into the kitchen where Maude would be preparing their breakfast.

'Your mom told me you would be calling and I have been waiting by the phone.'

'I've got a parcel for you from Mom,' Lindi said, unconsciously reverting to the South African idiom. 'I've been dying to call you all day but I've been so busy.'

'I know you have some important work here. Tch, tch. This is a bad thing that's happening here,' she said.

Lindi heard Maude click her tongue and remembered how the disapproval it implied used to weigh down on her more heavily than any scolding meted out by her parents. Maude's admonishments were all the more powerful for their rarity, whereas her parents' daily complaints about homework not done or clothes left on the floor had lost their potency with each repetition.

'Isn't it terrible, this whole business? Maude, I have to go to Mpumalanga tomorrow but I promise I'll come and see you when I'm back in Johannesburg.'

'You're going where? Mpumalanga?'

'I have to start somewhere and that's where the trouble is. And it's where my boss wants me to go,' she said. 'I think I'll be there for just a couple of days.'

'Kagiso is there – that's where he's doing his work. His office, they call it Soil of Africa. He used to work here in town in a good government job but he left. I don't know what for he wants to go and sit in the bush but he's there.'

'What a coincidence, Maude.'

'Yes, he's there,' the old woman said, with a hint of ruefulness.

'Isn't it amazing that he should be in Mpumalanga of all places? How can I get hold of him?'

'You can phone him. He never answers the phone but for you maybe he'll do it.'

'Oh, I'm sure he's just got a lot of work, Maude.'

'Yes, he's working hard for those people in the bush but his own mother is here.'

'Listen, give me his number and I'm going to tell him he's a naughty boy. I'll bring him back to Jo'burg with me.'

'Okay, my baby. I'm going to wait for you.'

Maude read out the number in a deliberate and hesitant way that told Lindi she was an older and less confident woman than the image of her she carried in her mind.

Lindi took a deep breath before she called Kagiso.

9

A couple of hours earlier, Kagiso Rapabane was wedged into the back of a Johannesburg taxi. The needle on the speedometer nudged 80 k.p.h. The minivans that most commuters used, not the metered cabs that ran from the airport or the city's posh hotels, are notorious for their often deadly disregard for the rules of the road. But, for once, Kagiso was glad the driver was in a hurry. He was in Johannesburg for two meetings – one official, the other not.

Kagiso had hitched a lift with a colleague from Malelane in Mpumalanga Province. It had taken them the best part of five hours. Their meeting with an overseas funder, who was getting nervous about the recent violence, had been delayed, and by the time Kagiso had jumped into the taxi to head off for the second appointment, it was past six in the evening and he was running an hour late.

It was the tail end of the rush hour, but the driver had swerved into a stretch of Oxford Road that had just emptied its traffic onto the highway and put his foot down, swerving back into the southbound stream at the last second amid a blare of horns and shouting. Kagiso had been first on the taxi at the rank in Rosebank and he was on the back bench, next to the window. The seat seemed to be only loosely attached to the chassis. It rolled and bucked, like a flat-bottomed barge in a heaving sea. He grabbed the bench in front of him, trying to stop himself sliding on the shiny, transparent seat covering and into a woman of the most generous proportions, who had positioned herself in the middle of the back row. She sat there, her knees apart, a bag of groceries on one side and a cardboard box on the other. Her voluminous breasts rose and fell with each breath, straining at the buttons of her nylon housecoat.

Outside, the huge sign advertising the Nelson Mandela Children's

Fund flashed past, a fleeting reminder of one man's conscience, its promise of a better life now receding as quickly as the hoarding. No one said a word. For many of the dozen or so other passengers this was the last enervating lap in a day that had begun at five that morning. The silence was interrupted only by the ringtone of a phone or a curt instruction to the driver.

'Short left,' somebody shouted, meaning the driver should pull over at the next left turn. Kagiso pulled out twenty rand and handed it to the person in front of him who, in turn, handed it forward, like a game of Pass the Parcel. Other notes and coins were making a similar journey up the cab where the driver, flicking his eyes from the road down to a cashbox next to him and back up again, managed to count the takings and send back the appropriate change. Kagiso took the change and received a surly look from the woman next to him as he stretched his leg towards her so he could squeeze the coins into the tight pocket of his jeans. He looked outside again and they were passing Wits Medical School. Not long now till they got to Hillbrow, where he would be getting off.

'Next robot,' he shouted, hoping the instruction would alert his immovable neighbour that he would shortly have to squeeze past her. When the time came she stuck to her spot, and Kagiso had to try to get over her to the door without touching her – a movement that was as ungainly as it was impossible.

Eventually, he fell out onto Claim Street and made for the Hot Line internet shop on the other side, almost colliding with a youth riding a shopping trolley down the gentle slope towards Klein Street. Ahmadu, who ran the shop, had just put a handful of *egusi* with yam into his mouth. He held out an arm, which Kagiso shook at the wrist. 'Howzit,' he said.

'Can't complain,' said Ahmadu, one of the many Nigerian traders who had colonised the area. The shelves were stacked deep with DVDs, the output of Nollywood, Nigeria's prolific but variable film industry. These days he made almost as much from renting out the films as he did from the phone business, but both were eclipsed by the lucrative room rentals and the express abortions that invariably followed. The clients for his medical services were always too desperate to wait for the state's lumbering alternative. Ahmadu asked no questions, and he wasn't told any lies. As long as the bills were paid he didn't care.

Ahmadu was watching one of the films on a laptop, engrossed in a storyline that had a young bride telling her mother that her marriage was floundering.

'Are you denying him?' the older woman in the film asked.

'Eh-heh! You see now, that's the problem,' shouted Ahmadu, at the screen. 'Our women are behaving like white women. They don't want to take care of their man.'

Kagiso ignored the comment. 'Are the others here?'

Ahmadu nodded. 'They came over an hour ago. You are the last,' he said, with what sounded like reproach. He reached out to a shelf behind him, never taking his eyes away from the laptop, worked his practised fingers behind the last few DVDs and pressed a button. Kagiso waited by a back door until he heard the latch release, then pushed.

He walked down a dark corridor with several doors leading off it. He didn't bother with the light switch. Experience had taught him that the bulb had long since blown. He pushed open another door, which brought him into a hallway, lit by a flickering neon strip. On one side of it there was a stairwell going up to what had once been the rather desirable apartments of Rondebosch Court. Its original purpose had been to act as a service entrance for domestic servants and tradesmen; now it provided a route for those who needed a discreet way in and out of the building – whether it was the suited men who used one of two apartments that Ahmadu rented out by the hour or the women who carried the consequences of these clandestine encounters in their bellies.

Kagiso bounded up the steps two at a time, no longer even seeing the sign that advertised 'same-day abortions' and 'womb cleansing'. The greasy grey hand smears along the wall were proof that the progress of others up and down the stairs was much slower and hesitant. On the first landing, he passed two women. One was bent over, her eyes shut, her face glazed with sweat. She had one arm around the shoulders of the other woman. Kagiso looked down, as if to suggest he hadn't seen them, to spare them the embarrassment of being noticed, and took the next flight of steps.

He walked along the second-floor corridor, its thick, undisturbed air infused with the heavy smell of cheap, fatty meat being fried. Behind each door he heard the muffled ritual of families coming together in that brief interregnum between the end of one day's efforts and the preparation for the next. Eating, drinking, chatting, listening, watching, arguing, loving and lusting – it all had to be squeezed into a couple of hours. Voices competed with the indiscriminate cacophony of a TV soap opera, the intermittent canned laughter and applause a cue to shout even louder. Adults tried to get themselves heard over the incessant squabbling of children; women scolded men who, in turn, took it out on their kids.

Kagiso reached the end of the corridor, looked back towards the stairwell, knocked three times on the last door on the left, then used his key to open it and walked into the room.

'Nice of you to join us,' François said. He was smiling.

'My meeting was delayed. I got here as quick as I could.' Kagiso looked around the room. He couldn't decide which was worse – the second-hand odour of other people's cooking, which he'd just left behind, or the stale smell of cigarette smoke that caught the back of his throat now. 'Sis, man! How many times have I told you guys to open the windows?'

'He arrives late and the first thing he does is give us a tongue-lashing.'

Sharmi Meer had one leg over the end of a threadbare sofa. Her jeans were tucked into black knee-length boots. Her black hair, cut short, framed a face of angular, strong features. There was a muscularity about her, enhanced by her choice of clothes. Sharmi dropped her cigarette stub into a mug in front of her. It hissed as it sank into what was left of the coffee. She pulled her leather jacket tight across her chest as Kagiso opened the window above her.

'You missed your calling. You should have been a headmaster.'

Kagiso saw the bottle of Klipdrift on the packing case that doubled as a table. It was half empty. There were a couple of Coke cans next to the brandy and a column of plastic cups.

'Where's Two-Boy?'

They heard the lavatory chain being pulled and pulled again. Sharmi shouted across the room towards the toilet door. 'Stop being so gentle.

One firm jerk, man!' She looked at the others. 'All these times we've been here and he still can't do it.'

Two-Boy shuffled in.

'You'd be bloody hopeless if a girl wanted a bit of rough,' she said, smiling. 'Pour me a Klippies-and-Coke and let's get on with this.'

Two-Boy, the fourth member of Land Collective, was a software engineer at SABC. A tall man, he nonetheless could not disguise his ample belly, though he carried it with some aplomb. He wasn't embarrassed by his weight. The tail of his shirt hung out from under his knitted jumper, and the laces on his suede ankle boots were untied. His dishevelled look and the fondness for a little *dop*, as he put it, belied a rare gift for navigating his way around the ether unnoticed. He saw Kagiso. *'Heita!* Howzit?' He looked sheepish.

The two men shook hands, touching alternate shoulders as they did so.

'How many of those have you had already?' Kagiso asked.

'For Chrissake, leave him alone. I think we've got more than Two-Boy's drinking habits to worry about,' said Sharmi.

'Yah. Let's do this quickly and get out. It's not looking good,' said François. 'I just drove past Ponte City. There's still a big crowd there – probably a few hundred. They say they're not leaving till every last foreigner is thrown out of the building. And the cops are just lounging about. Every now and again someone tries to get back in to restart the fire. Even the Red Cross people are being shoved around.'

'It makes 2008 look like a picnic,' Sharmi said, a reference to an earlier bout of xenophobia in which immigrants had been killed as competition for scarce jobs had turned to violence. 'It doesn't bloody help that SABC reports it as fact that a Mozambican killed Motlantshe's poor little rich bastard.'

'Stop that, man!' Kagiso glowered at Sharmi. 'He's not even buried and you're badmouthing him. The fact that he was rich has got nothing to do with it.'

'Oh, I must have got this all wrong. I'm so sorry.' Sharmi played the mock-innocent. 'And there I was thinking this was all about rich people fucking over the poor people. I seem to have got the wrong end of the stick. All this secret sabotage we've been organising and it turns out I didn't even know who the bad guys were.'

'You know that's not what I meant. We're not here to pass judgement on Lesedi. We're here to make sure his murder doesn't derail us.'

'We're not here to pass judgement? Christ! Where is this coming from? The guy makes one measly trip to your friggin' cooperative or whatever and suddenly he's the people's hero.'

They had history, the two of them. You had to know someone well enough to have seen their weaknesses and understand how to exploit them. She knew she could keep going, locked in a self-perpetuating cycle of trying to goad him into saying something she could pounce on and use for another line of attack. It had happened so many times before.

He'd rejected her once, walked away when they should have talked. It had made her feel used, tawdry. So now she did the talking. For Sharmi this whole enterprise – and it was Sharmi who had pushed the group from debate to direct action – had been visceral. She was the only one of the four who could claim any direct link to the old anti-apartheid struggle. Her father had been imprisoned on Robben Island for six years and died shortly after release, disillusioned and mad. For her the Land Collective was as much about getting even with a state that had robbed her of a father, never mind that that state was now in black hands. It was about striking a blow. The act itself was cathartic. She'd never understood how you could want change – real change – if you didn't want it in your guts.

Sharmi looked across at Kagiso. She decided to hold fire. For now.

'This thing has got scary. We're not in control,' Kagiso said.

'But we're not meant to be in control,' said François. 'This is exactly what was supposed to happen.'

'No, it wasn't. We never sat here and said, "Let's have execution squads roaming the countryside and, just to make sure they get the message, let's make sure they *donner* some Mozambicans." This is just mayhem now. It isn't political.' Kagiso rolled his head around trying to unwind the tension locked into his muscles. He had a splitting head-ache.

'Of course it isn't all neat and tidy,' said Sharmi, her hostility barely disguised. 'What did you think was going to happen when we did that first job and you started firing off all those anonymous statements?'

'Look, I'm not saying we planned Lesedi's murder or that we predicted all this Mozzie-bashing,' said François, picking up where he'd left off. 'And I'm not saying any of it is good. But I suppose we did want this thing to develop a momentum of its own and that's what's happening.'

'Come on, François! You know as well as I do that this is not what we had in mind.' Kagiso was pacing from one end of the room to the other.

'It is exactly what we had in mind.' Sharmi stood up. Now. This was the time to move in. Sharmi felt the surge of adrenaline. 'Now the bastards are going to sit up and listen. What did you think – another fire here, a power cable cut somewhere, a few more of your terrific words and the land deals would stop? This – what's happening out there – this is what's going to make them scared.'

'Listen, there's no point arguing over whether we're responsible or not. The fact is that it's happening.' Two-Boy could see where this was going. The next thing, Sharmi would accuse Kagiso of being squeamish and then there'd be an almighty row that would take another half an hour to resolve. 'What we have to decide is whether any of this helps us,' he continued. 'If it does, well, we can just sit back and have another drink. If not, we've got some thinking to do and quick. What's happening at Ponte is happening all over the place. I had a look at the wires coming into the newsroom before I left.'

'Well, it doesn't help us. That should be clear enough to anyone,' said Kagiso, shooting a glance at Sharmi. 'Lesedi's murder changes everything. Even the people we're supposed to be representing thought of him and his father as heroes. This is a gift for Pretoria.'

'Okay, so the first thing is to put some distance between us and the murder,' said Two-Boy. 'What you've written so far is not enough. We've got to find a way to make it absolutely clear we had nothing to do with Lesedi's killing.'

'Unless of course we *did* have something to do with Lesedi's death,' Kagiso said, staring at each of the others in turn.

There was silence. It wasn't just the absence of sound but a moment of utter quiet that filled the room, like a poisonous gas leak. Each of the others absorbed what had been said and what had been implied.

'We're not going there.' François broke the silence.

'No, let's go there. Go on, point your fucking finger.' Sharmi was now just a metre away from Kagiso. 'Tell us who you think is behind this. Which one of us do you think is so low and dirty? Come on, say it.'

'*Jissis*, man. Stop this *fokken* nonsense now,' François said, walking over to where Kagiso was standing. 'You of all people should know better. It was your idea, remember? What we do with our own teams is our own business. Ask no questions, get told no lies. Isn't that what you used to say?'

'This is different,' Kagiso stressed. 'We're talking about a murder here.'

'Oh, no! Not a *murder*. Oh, let's just leave that sort of thing to the land-owners, shall we?' Sharmi was finding her stride again. 'Let them drag people off their own land to die in some godforsaken place. We'll just keep our hands clean.'

'This was a brutal killing. No ifs or buts, just a gruesome and sense-less murder. Full stop!'

'Give me a fucking break.' Sharmi was looking straight at Kagiso. 'It may come as a surprise to you but this is what the struggle looks like, and if you're finding it so difficult to swallow why don't you just leave the rest of us to get on with it? Just for the record, I for one think he was fair game.'

'Cut it out, both of you.' Now it was François's turn to shout.

'No, no. Sharmi wants me to spell it out so here it is. Who knew where Lesedi was going to be last Thursday? The folk in Malelane: they hero-worship the Motlantshes so I think it's safe to count them out. Probably his family: they may be corrupt bastards but I don't think even they would stoop to killing their own children. And then there's the four people in this—'

'If you two don't stop this, I'm out of here.' François turned to Kagiso. He put his hands on the other man's shoulders. 'Come on, man,' he said. 'It's too late to be coming up with this *kak*. What's done is done. Now we got to ride this thing.'

Kagiso pulled away from him and stared out of the window. The other three stared at his silhouette, a figure disembodied from the man they thought they knew but one who had, in just the few minutes since his arrival, dismantled the brittle foundations of their clandestine enterprise. Finally he turned around. 'I'm sorry,' he said.

'Okay, okay, let's just crack on,' François said, as if he were calling a residents' association meeting to order. His mundane tone convinced no one in the room but they latched on to it, like drowning men will reach for almost anything that might keep them afloat.

'There is somebody else,' said Two-Boy.

'What you talking about?' asked François.

'Kagiso just listed the people who knew about Lesedi's movements. There's somebody else. Willemse knew.'

'Who? That minister, the rural-affairs guy?'

'Yes, he sent a message to the news editor to make sure SABC wouldn't cover the meeting in Malelane. I saw the email.'

'Yeah, but that doesn't mean he wanted him dead,' said François.

'I wouldn't put anything past him,' said Two-Boy.

'Especially if he'd got wind of what Lesedi was up to,' said Kagiso. He was relieved: Two-Boy had offered another direction in which he could take his suspicions. He'd asked the question, had any of them been implicated? He wasn't really sure he wanted the answer. There was only one person in the room who'd have had the nerve. 'Lesedi told me he'd tried on a number of occasions to talk to his father and Willemse about doing things differently.'

'And think about it. Think what happened to the last person who questioned the land deals,' said Two-Boy.

'You mean the guy who was supposed to be in charge of land affairs or something over there in the provincial government? I wouldn't say he was questioning the deals. He just didn't think enough cash was coming his way. What the hell was his name?' asked François.

'Gwethu, Simon Gwethu. No saint, that's true, but two days after he gives an interview saying not enough money was staying in Mpumalanga he has a car accident.'

'*Jissis!* You're damn right, Two-Boy. Remember?' François looked around the room. 'The investigation lasted a couple of days and they declared it an accident.'

'What do you think?' Kagiso looked at Two-Boy.

'I certainly would not rule Willemse out, or whoever is pulling his strings. If we're right and this thing is being orchestrated by some big players here and abroad, and there's billions of rands at stake, they'd do anything to make sure the money keeps flowing,' Two-Boy said.

'I don't think they're nearly as loth to bump people off as you seem to think they are,' said François, looking at Kagiso.

'I'm with François on this one,' said Two-Boy.

'Which bit exactly?' said Kagiso.

'All of it. I think Willemse and his mob are perfectly capable of silencing Lesedi and I think his death means we know where we stand. Those bastards have drawn a line in the sand.'

'Okay, that settles it for me,' said François. 'From now on we have to assume that anyone in their way will get the same treatment. If they get wind of who we are, we're targets too.'

'Well, they've already sort of got wind of who we are,' said Two-Boy.

Sharmi said, 'You've heard something, haven't you?'

'Look, I was doing my usual trawl through the news editor's inbox and he's having some interesting correspondence with the top floor. It seems Pretoria is leaning on the CEO, so he's leaning on the news editor.'

'What have they got on us?' asked Sharmi.

'They don't have anything on us as individuals but they've obviously read Kagiso's last entry.'

'What was in it? I've lost track,' said François.

'It's the one in which Kagiso talked about being in that squatter camp outside Nelspruit, you know, defending the Mozambicans,' said Two-Boy.

'I'm still not with you. How does that identify us?' François turned to Kagiso. 'You took all the usual precautions?'

'Yes, of course.'

'Look, Pretoria knows they're going to have to stop blaming the Mozambicans and so on sooner or later . . .'

'If they can,' said Sharmi.

'Yeah, that's right. But they know they have to try. If they can't point to any evidence that it *was* a Mozambican, they're going to start looking pretty silly. The Mozambican ambassador has already handed a note of protest to Foreign Affairs and the UN's refugee woman here has put out a statement condemning the violence and saying it's the government's job to put a stop to it. You probably saw it.'

'Yaah. "Impending genocide" was a bit melodramatic but I thought it put the government on the spot all right,' said François.

'Anyway, they know they're running out of time. They need someone or something else to take the place of the Mozambicans as the bad guys. And that's where you come in.' Two-Boy corrected himself. 'That's where WE come in.'

'How can they make it stick?' asked François. 'We're on record condemning the murder.'

'They don't know who we are – do they?' said Sharmi. What had started off as a statement ended as a question.

'No, they don't but the boss wants SABC to play its part in finding out,' said Two-Boy. 'How did he put it in the email? "We are an independent broadcaster but when national security is at stake, we have to play our part." I think that's what he said, anyhow.'

'If SABC is an independent broadcaster then I'm a black man,' said François. 'I think he meant job security, not national security. Your *fokken* boss is so far up the ANC's arse he wouldn't remember the way out even if he wanted to get out.'

'Anyway, tonight's late news will have an item raising suspicions about a shadowy group that's trying to derail land reform. They've even found some academic at the University of Johannesburg to say he's been monitoring our statements and that it all adds up to a conspiracy. That's harmless stuff. But this is the bit that matters – he'll say this underground group is probably responsible for Lesedi's murder and that it could be the first of many.'

'It's nice to know someone is actually reading the stuff,' said Sharmi. It raised a chuckle around the room. 'How does that feel? Some greasy-haired academic poring over every word you write.'

Two-Boy reached for the bottle of Klipdrift – conspicuously avoiding Kagiso's eyes – and poured himself a generous glass, which he topped up with what was left of the Coke. He lowered himself halfway down to the floor, then let his bulk drop the rest of the way. His head resting against a wall, he shut his eyes and took a long swig of the drink. It seemed to give him a second wind.

'The bottom line is this – they're looking for you,' he said, pointing at Kagiso. 'Well, not you by name, but whoever is responsible for the statements. The case is being handed over to the anti-terror unit, the Cheetah Squad, or whatever they're calling it these days. I've seen some of the stuff they're sending the news guys. They think you – I mean the writer – are either a meddling journalist, because they're written statements, or some sort of extremist. They think you're being helped, and they're hoping the help is coming from abroad. That way they get to call it a foreign plot. The report will say a member of an underground extremist group has been in the area and will ask people who've seen strangers to come forward.'

'Did they describe the person they're looking for?' asked Sharmi. 'You know – did they say whether it was a man or woman? Any racial description?'

'No. But they did say they're getting evidence that someone from outside the province was in the area and probably organised the murder . . . I think they called it "a planned assassination".'

'What kind of evidence?' Sharmi again.

'Didn't say. My guess is they're bluffing and all they have to go on is Kagiso's last entry. I think that's the only reason they know we've been in the area,' said Two-Boy. 'But I can't be sure. It's possible someone might have noticed you when you went to the camp that was attacked.'

'But so what if they noticed Kagiso? It doesn't prove anything – doesn't mean you're linked to the Land Collective. It's your job at Soil of Africa to visit farms and so on,' said François, looking at Kagiso for reassurance.

'Yeah, visit farms, but squatter camps is another thing. I'd never been into that one till the other day. So I probably stood out as an outsider.'

'You're seen in the camp and the next thing the Land Collective mentions the camp. It all adds up. It's not exactly rocket science,' Two-Boy added, stating what now seemed blindingly obvious.

Nobody else spoke for a minute or so. They had known there would come a moment when they would have to account for what they had embarked on all that time ago. They hadn't recognised it at first, but this was it. Up till now their secret campaign had been precisely that: secret. It wasn't attached to them. Now it was turning personal, the authorities were going to make it that way.

Kagiso looked at each of them in turn, as if he were seeing them for the first time. Each had had a different motive for being involved. Their commitment to the cause was as varied as their characters. For François, this was a mission of atonement, making up for a privileged past. As for Two-Boy, there were times when Kagiso wondered what he was doing in the same room as the rest of them. He sometimes thought it was no more than the sheer mischievous joy of cheating the system, breaking through virtual walls that kept Two-Boy onside. And Sharmi?

She was the genuine article, the real deal – he knew that. Sharmi was in it head and heart. She, more than any of them, had the sheer audacity and courage to take on the establishment, however explosive the outcome might be. In truth, he admired her conviction, even if the consequences for all of them could be disastrous, not to say fatal. The thing that made Sharmi so dangerous was that she was so alluring.

'It's going to get messy,' he said. 'Are we ready for this?'

One of his phones rang. It was the number he gave to friends and family. He looked at the others. 'Shit! I'm sorry. Today was hectic, man, and I just forgot to turn the thing off. Let me answer it quickly.'

Kagiso slid his finger across the screen, put the phone to his ear and heard a voice that seemed familiar, but one he couldn't place. He walked over to the window, turning his back on the others.

'Guess who?' said a female voice.

'Who's this?'

'It's me, Lindi.'

'*What?* Where are you?'

'Didn't Maude tell you I was coming?'

'We've not talked for a while. I'm sorry, I'm in the middle of something. I'll call you back. About half an hour.' And then Kagiso added, 'It's great to hear from you.'

He turned the phone off and was about to speak. Sharmi interrupted. 'Who was that?'

'Just an old friend.'

'All very furtive,' she said. 'Your fault for keeping your phone on, but for your penalty you have to tell us who it is.'

'It's no one you know.'

'Ooh! We getting a bit irritable, are we?' She looked at the others. 'I think our little bush-boy from Mpumalanga has got a dirty little secret here in the big city. Planning a bit of a fumble tonight, are we, Kagiso?'

'Look, it's late. We need to move. I'm going to Lesedi's funeral tomorrow, then back to Malelane. Let's catch up in a few days' time.'

'Hang on a minute. What have we decided? Ponte City is on fire, foreigners are being hacked to death and we're just going to carry on as normal? This is surreal,' said François.

'There's nothing to decide,' said Kagiso. 'At least, the decision has been made for us. We have to assume we're wanted, or I am, anyway. We need to lie low and work out what our next step is. My advice is that you suspend any hits you've got in the pipeline. If you've got into a routine, stick to it. Don't do anything you wouldn't normally do. If you've left tracks, get rid of them. If you've got any bridges to burn, now is the time to do it.'

'Should we switch to the back-up phones?' asked Two-Boy. He was looking at Kagiso.

'Yes, but remember, we use them only to contact each other and only in an emergency, to warn someone of an imminent threat. If we don't hear from each other, that's good. I'll call when we need to meet next.'

'Amen,' said François. 'All right, let's go. Two-Boy, you first – through the front. I'll go next through the shop. Kagiso, you staying or going?'

'I'll tidy up and leave last,' said Kagiso.

'Okay, that means you're out the front, Sharmi.'

They had parted like this on many occasions before but this was the first time the precaution actually seemed necessary. They were like soldiers who – faced with the reality of conflict – suddenly realise what all that training was for. When her turn came Sharmi half opened the apartment door and looked back into the front room.

Kagiso was still sitting on the sofa. Apart from the packing case there was hardly any other furniture in the room. He looked marooned.

'Are you going to be okay?' she asked.

'Yes, I'm fine. And thanks.'

'For what?'

'For asking.'

Sharmi lingered, perhaps thinking there was more to say or hoping there was.

Kagiso put an end to that possibility. 'Just turn the light off as you go. I'll hang around for a few minutes,' he said, then added, 'Sharmi, we're on our own now. It's each to his or her own for the next few days, maybe weeks. You can't afford to make any mistakes.'

'I know.' Sharmi waited by the door. 'I know what I'm doing, Kagiso. You all think I'm over the top but I'm serious about this.'

'I've never doubted that . . . or your guts,' he said. 'But you've got to think with your head, not your heart.'

'Is that what you do?'

Kagiso ignored the question. 'Okay, I'll see you.'

'Yeah, see you.'

Kagiso heard the front door latch click into place. He found himself staring at the space where Sharmi had been standing. It was as if there was a gap, like looking at a stencil of her shape. She'd taken something with her, her high-voltage presence. The room, the air, was thinner, poorer without her in it. That was how it seemed. It wasn't the first time he'd felt that way after he'd been with her, even on those frequent occasions, such as this one, when they had fought. Especially when they had fought. The fighting always brought to mind its opposite. What was that? Tenderness? Not really. Intimacy? Of a kind. Attraction? Yes, he knew where that came from. It went way back, but not so far that he couldn't remember its intensity, the sheer intoxicating thrill of meeting her, arguing with her – yes, even then. That first time, the only time, their mutual desire had emerged in the physicality of the encounter: there hadn't been time for affection, just energy. Now only the energy remained, finding expression in the words they used, ugly ones, hurtful ones. It was a relationship of sorts, a substitute for what they might achieve if only they could break the habit, make room for something else.

Kagiso was not a man given to impulse but he wondered if he might catch Sharmi before she left the building. Not now, he told himself. Another time, maybe when all this was over.

He got up, walked over to the window and opened it wider. The pungent air caught the back of his throat. He could see the Ponte building as he looked east, the windows of its lower façade intermittently reflecting the blue and red flashes from the emergency vehicles. From this distance it resembled a light show. Normally, you might hear the brassy beat of West African Hi-Life blaring out of one of the other apartments. Now there was nothing, except the shrill sound of sirens, the mechanical scream of a city in trouble. Across the street, each window framed a silhouette. Directly opposite him, he could make out a huddle of people. They, too, were looking east. What they saw was not a building but an uncertain future.

Kagiso imagined looking down on all this. He pictured one of those satellite images you could download. There he was, a tiny speck. Some distance away in Ponte City, its summit still advertising the good life on a huge screen, a family crouched in one room, faceless and dumb. Could there really be a connection between their predicament and the actions of the Collective? He remembered the game they used to play at Stellenbosch, trying to prove there were only six degrees of separation between any two people on the planet. The idea, then, was to make the link. Today he wanted to prove the theory wrong. He didn't want any responsibility for what was happening outside and what had once been set in motion in this very room. Kagiso shut the window, as if that would absolve him of any blame for what was unfolding outside.

He glanced around the room, picked up the mugs, the plastic cups and the nearly empty bottle of Klipdrift and took them into the kitchen. He found the Pick 'n' Pay bag that Two-Boy must have used to carry the liquor and emptied the soggy cigarette butts into it. He pulled the kettle plug from its socket. Across the narrow hallway he checked the single bedroom. As usual, the mattresses, discoloured and stained, were leaning against a wall. There were several holdalls on the floor. Ahmadu had always said they belonged to his tenants, though Kagiso had never seen any. There was one last thing to do before he left.

Kagiso found the 'received calls' list on his phone and selected the most recent one. Lindi answered almost immediately. 'It's Kagiso. I'm sorry about earlier,' he said.

'That's all right. Typical of me to think you'd remember all these years later.'

'No, no, you actually sound the same.'

'I'm not sure how I should take that. Can we meet?'

'I'm only in Jo'burg for a night. I live in Malelane these days – that's in—'

'I know where it is. Maude's told me all about how you live in the bush now.'

'Yeah, she's a bit sore about my move. Look, I'm going to a funeral tomorrow. It's for—'

'Lesedi Motlantshe. I know. It's partly why I'm here.'

'For the funeral?'

'Not exactly. It's a long story. Shall we try to meet there and then arrange something?'

'Okay, that sounds good.'

'I bet I spot you before you spot me.'

'You're on. Have you changed a lot?'

'I certainly hope so. Oh! By the way, I think you should call Maude. None of my business but I promised her I'd ask.'

'I'm going there now. Do you know where it's happening and so on?'

'I've sort of hooked up with the BBC and they're covering it.'

'I didn't know you were into journalism now.' Kagiso sounded surprised.

'I'm not. Look, all will be revealed tomorrow. See you. Can't wait.'

Once outside, it took Sharmi less than ten minutes to walk to her car. That was careless, using her Beetle to get to the meeting. She got in, slammed the door and closed her eyes. It was like bringing down the shutters, trying to block the pathways to the place her mind wanted to go. Those few seconds, back there in the room just before she left . . . she knew she'd missed a chance. There'd been a moment of . . . of what? A connection, like a couple of synapses brushing up against each other, then drifting apart. A fleeting, yet perceptible, sense that they might have been thinking in the same way, together, at the same time. They hadn't just been left in the room on their own for a minute or two, they had shared it, occupied it, not as two separate individuals who find themselves near each other, but as two people open to each other. She should have grabbed the opportunity. That was what she was feeling now. But the moment had gone, and as she thought about the next few days, Sharmi knew she might have lost the chance for good.

'Burn bridges . . . no mistakes . . . It's each to his or her own,' Kagiso had said. Is this how it would end, being hunted down one by one?

She opened her eyes, took a deep breath and turned on the ignition. It was dark. Sharmi knew she had to get rid of the car. She pulled away from the pavement and headed for Yeoville, an inner-city suburb of Johannesburg that sat on a ridge overlooking the city. Yeoville was almost as old as the city itself, established in the 1890s as a lofty refuge from the dirty, chaotic and sometimes violent gold-mining town that was growing out of the veld below. Like much of the area around it, Yeoville had been through a familiar cycle of nineteenth-century gentility, fifties edgy chic and late-twentieth-century urban decay. Now it was a melting pot of African sounds and customs, a home for traders and traffickers alike. There was always talk of a renaissance and a few brave souls, like the trekkers of old, were taking a bet on its gentrification and moving in, not least because they couldn't afford to live anywhere else in the city. But for the most part it was what it was – a place where no one asked any questions because the answers were never that simple. Sharmi knew it was the kind of place she needed now.

It was a short drive from Hillbrow, across Joe Slovo Drive, then to Raleigh Street, the backbone of the area. Sharmi drove around for more than half an hour, down one back street and then another, before pulling up outside a mechanic's shop, locked up for the night. She looked around the car's interior, part sentimental, part caution. A pile of newspapers, a half-empty bottle of water, a Nando's takeaway bag. She opened the door and shut it again. She reached for the Nando's bag, pulled out the receipt and scoured it.

'Shit!' It had the address of the fast-food outlet on the N12 going east to Nelspruit, the provincial capital of Mpumalanga.

If you've left tracks get rid of them.

Sharmi screwed up the receipt and chucked it into her bag. She got out of the car, left the key in the ignition and the door slightly ajar, then walked away. No one noticed her, still less cared.

10

The police helicopter clattered in a winter-blue sky, circling above Regina Mundi church in Soweto. Its rotor blades chopped the air with all the finesse of a carpet beater. In the old days its appearance in the sky would have sown resentment among the famously resilient people below; now they looked up with an indifference that spoke volumes for the transformation that had taken place in the country. There was a far more interesting spectacle on the ground. This old church of protest, its perimeter wall and grounds hurriedly spruced up for the occasion, was the focus of a national event. From the air, the long line of shiny limousines being marshalled around it by the police looked like a brash silver and black necklace placed inappropriately around the shoulders of an ageing and much-loved aunt.

Josiah Motlantshe had chosen Regina Mundi for the funeral of his son, Lesedi, even before he had returned to Johannesburg. It was a theatrical choice in keeping with the smoke-and-mirrors world in which South Africa's new elite continued to claim a fellowship with the thousands who had longed for freedom, even if the gap between them and the rest of the country was now every bit as wide as it had been between blacks and whites. They fooled no one except, perhaps, themselves.

As each VIP party arrived outside the main gate, a minder jumped out and held open the back door of a limousine. Its occupants eased themselves out in the practised way of those who've long ago done away with the need to open their own doors, buttoning a jacket or adjusting a shawl in one fluid movement. Dark sunglasses were *de rigueur*, as if to suggest that underneath their eyes were puffy with grief.

A former head of the ANC military wing, Umkhonto we Sizwe, now a major shareholder in an Indian-owned hotel chain, stuck his fist into the air, but only briefly, reminding himself that the days when funerals inevitably turned into political rallies were fading. This was a new world. There were carefully subdued greetings between mourners, the usual raucous exchanges replaced by mutually reinforced expressions of sadness: the Motlantshes' loss was their loss too. The provincial premier lingered rather longer outside the gate than was necessary, studiously alert to the whereabouts of several camera crews that were darting, like pollinating bees, from one group to another. He had wanted to be there when the presidential party arrived (hence the full-on security in the air and on the ground) but was ushered in by one of the officials.

The British high commissioner climbed out of his car with what seemed to be a look of apology, perhaps for arriving in what was now a rather aged Jaguar (even this, one of the plum jobs in the gift of the foreign secretary, had not escaped the swingeing budget cuts back home). He wore his black tie long, with the fat end tucked into the top of his trousers, as if he'd been somewhat absent-minded the last time he'd used the lavatory. His wife, giving every impression that she would rather be back in an Islington café, marched resolutely towards the church doors but then had to wait, stranded in limbo, while her husband pretended to recognise the man talking to him.

The crowd, five or six deep, looked on. The people at the back peered through rows of beanies and baseball caps that constantly shifted one way and then the other. Headgear that had been put on in the cool light of dawn offered a different kind of protection now that the sun was getting higher. As the temperature warmed, the musty smell of morning breath and clothes soaked in paraffin smoke gave way to an altogether more pungent odour.

There was an air of expectancy, but it was the kind of anticipation you might expect in the minutes before a rock concert, not the solemnity you would associate with a funeral. What was unfolding in front of them was a soap opera, not a wake. They knew many of the characters, household names whose lives were played out in the glossy pages of tabloid magazines and Friday-night talk shows. The VIPs were there to exhibit their collective grief, but what the people of Soweto noticed, what they assumed, was how much easier it must be to carry the burden of sadness when it was cushioned by wealth and status.

Teenage girls elbowed each other, gawking at a young woman, not much older than they were, recognising her instantly from a photo feature on Lesedi's last birthday in *Destiny* magazine. The article had recounted how the party had been held at her interior-design studio (a gift from her father) in a recently reclaimed and refurbished warehouse on Main Street in Johannesburg. They remembered all the details, how Maki (that was her name) had organised the lavish event as a surprise. The magazine had described her simply as a 'friend' of Lesedi, but the girls of Soweto strained their eyes, looking carefully for any signs indicating a deeper relationship with him. Their brothers looked at Maki too, dreaming of a day when they might escort a fragrant pale-skinned woman like her. If there was any resentment among the crowd, nobody spoke of it. In truth, they took vicarious pride in this display of black wealth, ignorant of or unconcerned by how it had been achieved, clinging to the idea that it might, one day, be within their grasp too. It was like going to the cinema, being transported for a few hours into another world, suspending their disbelief.

Inside Regina Mundi, the painted cement floor on which tired old canvas shoes had once left their dusty imprint now echoed to the sound of Italian stilettos. The first twenty or so rows of hard wooden pews, darkened by generations of greasy handprints, had been reserved for VIPs, the white printed place names making each bench look like a piano keyboard. There was a strict seating plan, proximity to the front two rows denoting favoured status with the Motlantshe family, who were due to arrive with the hearse from their Houghton home.

There was a sickly aroma in the church, a mix of the scent from the huge bouquets of lilies placed at the end of every pew and the assortment of perfumes worn by guests. It made Lindi Seaton feel mildly queasy. She had planned to head for Mpumalanga that day, the day after her arrival in South Africa, but had delayed her trip to have a meeting with a researcher at the Forced Migration Unit at Wits University. In the meantime Comfort, at the BBC office, had suggested she attend the funeral.

'It will give you some idea of just how important the family is and why there's so much anger at Lesedi's death,' Comfort had said. 'I'm sending a crew down there so you can go with them. I'm sure you can stand at the back of the press area.'

The BBC team had set off early, to beat the security-check queues, and Lindi had had an hour or so to spare before even the first people started to arrive for the midday funeral service. To kill time, she had taken a walk.

The streets were lined with bungalows, each sitting in its own plot. As she walked along the dusty kerbs, Lindi had realised she could see into the front compounds, which distinguished them from the homes in the rich northern suburbs, where the walls were designed to hide wealth, if not necessarily disguise it. Here there was nothing to feel guilty about. Those who'd managed to get a foothold in the area, Rockville, were proud of what they had achieved. Here, progress up the social ladder was something to proclaim, even flaunt. In the white suburbs to the north it was different. There, the high walls were designed to conceal the legacy of easy entitlement that apartheid had conferred on its white beneficiaries.

Lindi had walked to the bottom of the street, until she came to one of the ubiquitous *spaza* shops, the roadside stalls that sold everything from soap to salt. This one, painted a gaudy purple, had once been a freight container. Who knows where it had been before coming to rest here in Soweto? She'd asked for a carton of orange juice but was told there was none in stock.

'But I've got a nice cool Coke,' the man behind the counter said, smiling at her from behind an array of plastic sauce bottles, their sides criss-crossed with a glutinous trail of their contents. Lindi settled for a can of Liquifruit that claimed to be free of additives and crammed full of goodness. The shopkeeper wiped the can with a frayed and stained cloth, which he had just been using to clean the counter. Lindi held the can well below the counter and surreptitiously wiped the top with a pinch of her dress.

'Will there be a lot of people here for the funeral?' she asked.

'Oh, many, many. A lot of people are feeling sad for that family. That Lesedi was going to be a good man, a big man.'

'I heard he was murdered.' She had learned the lesson of the taxi journey and was determined to keep her observations as neutral as possible.

'Yes, those Mozambicans killed him. There are too many in Mpumalanga. That's where they killed him.'

'Well, I hope they catch the killer,' she said, sorting through the unfamiliar ten-rand notes.

'Oh, they will catch him. They have already arrested one. But they will not stop. They are going to catch all of them and send them back to Maputo.'

Walking back towards Regina Mundi, Lindi replayed the shop-keeper's words in her mind: 'send them back to Maputo'. How many times, in how many different countries and in how many different languages had those words, 'send them back', been used? And how many people around the world had heard them and been terrified by what they meant? Those three words robbed them of their identities as individuals, as families and neighbours, even as friends. *Them*, not us. Them over there. Search them. Catch them. Arrest them. Deport them. Kill them. That was all it took: shift a people from the column marked 'us' to the one marked 'them' and everything became possible, justifiable. She found those words, spoken by the avuncular figure of the smiling, seemingly gentle shopkeeper, as chilling as anything she had read in Anton's frenetic messages or the tickertape headlines on the news channels.

11

Word went round that the Motlantshes were down the road but had been forced to wait because the presidential cavalcade was late. The hearse and several other cars had been seen parked down a side-street. Someone in the congregation leaned forward and whispered into the ear of a friend that the president had probably thought there was time for 'a quick one' before leaving the official mansion – and he wasn't talking about the leader's drinking habits. They were still sniggering when there was a collective rustle of starched fabric as, starting from the back of the church, each row of the congregation rose to its feet.

The president looked from side to side as he moved forward, acknowledging those he recognised. Those accorded the honour of a presidential nod visibly glowed in the aftermath, like disciples touched by the Holy Spirit. They looked down their row just to make sure that others had noticed their favoured status. The first lady, her hold on the title only as secure as the libidinous exploits of her husband would allow, was so heavily made-up that she seemed to be wearing a mask. Rumour had it that a bottle of gin a day left her with a morning-after puffiness to rival that of a journeyman boxer emerging from the ring – though there were some who said her husband was not averse to handing out his own face-changing pugilistic jabs from time to time. The country was divided between those who felt sorry, even embarrassed, for her, and those who said she was so addicted to status that she would put up with almost anything to cling to the privilege bestowed on her because she had once caught the wandering eye of a man on his way to the top.

When the couple had been shown to their velvet-backed seats – the benches were deemed too plebeian, not to say uncomfortable for the presidential arse – the gospel choir started up. The singers' velvet cloaks were vintage Harlem. They belted out hymns, even a Nina Simone number, said to be Lesedi's favourite, swaying so that their gowns gently floated this way and that in a delayed mimic of the singers' motions.

Lindi, seated at the very back, watched the pall-bearers enter the church, the coffin apparently floating between them. It was an elaborate affair. The hardwood coffin, with inset panels of the kind you might find in an old-fashioned London club, clinging to its heyday, was studded with fussy brass fittings, all curlicues and twists. The combination looked preposterous in this most simple place of worship, as did the pall-bearers. Their heavy morning coats made no allowance for the rising heat of a crowded church. The strain of carrying the coffin showed at first in the little beads of sweat on their foreheads, which quickly became a steady stream that moved from temple to chin, before disappearing into the soon-soaked, dull-white collars of their shirts. From her seat on the back row, Lindi watched the deliberate progress of the cortège as it passed her and moved on.

With each choreographed step up the aisle, the last pair of bearers revealed another pew on the opposite side of the church. They were about a third of the way when Lindi realised she was no longer looking at the funeral procession but at a single figure in the congregation. From where she was standing, all she could see was the back of the man's shoulder, his left ear and a partial profile. But she knew who he was, even before her brain had had time to digest the information. As he turned towards the coffin, Lindi recognised Kagiso and she only just resisted the urge to call out. She stared at him, willing him to turn. When he did, and they caught each other's eye, she felt an intimacy that belied the years they had been apart.

From that moment on the service seemed to take for ever.

The priest had to speak. His theme was fathers and sons and he only just managed to stop short of making the divine comparison. The president couldn't be left out. Another microphone was switched on so his words could be heard from the speakers outside the church. Lesedi was like a son to him, he said. He had watched him grow up.

'This is not the time or the place for anger and recriminations,' he said, stumbling on the word and perhaps inwardly cursing his speechwriter, 'but we will find those who put him in this coffin. The police have arrested a Mozambican man. But such a terrible thing was not done by one simple man.'

At this point he gazed down from the raised platform that had been built for the occasion and gave a plausible impression of a man who would struggle to find the composure necessary to complete his eulogy.

'We will find those who directed this terrible crime – not because Lesedi was a Motlantshe, not because his family helped to free South Africa. No, we will . . . we will find these underground terrorists who did this because he was a child of the new South Africa and every child is precious. They are our future.'

Josiah Motlantshe led the cheers. It was his turn next. He dabbed at his cheeks as he told the mourners how Lesedi had been a son, a friend and colleague all rolled into one and what a gaping hole there would be in his life from now on. His wife, Priscilla, stared at him, her face rigid, devoid of any emotion. Motlantshe ended by asking if anyone in the congregation wanted to add anything.

Maki stood up, the apparent spontaneity of the invitation spoiled by the alacrity with which she strode to the platform and the typewritten piece of paper she unfolded on her way there. She said she spoke for all of Lesedi's many friends who would remember him as a man who would stop at nothing to help someone less fortunate than himself. She told them of the time when the two of them – just the two of them – had been travelling in a rural area and come across a family by the roadside with an elderly woman lying on a mat. They were waiting for a bus to take the woman to hospital in the next big town.

'That was an hour's drive from where we were at the time,' she said.

Lesedi had had no hesitation in bundling the four villagers into his car and driving them to the provincial capital.

'He asked me to sit at the back so the old man could have his rightful place in the front seat. That was the kind of man Lesedi was,' she said. 'I will treasure the time I had with him and will for ever wonder what might have been.'

The press pack, cordoned off to one side at the front of the church, could barely contain itself. This was pure gold. The cameras flashed so continuously, you couldn't distinguish one burst of white light from another.

The priest took up a position just behind the coffin and waited for quiet. He gave the final blessing. He said Lesedi would be buried right there in Soweto where he belonged and that the family had requested, politely, that the interment should be private, just for the two hundred or so people who had received invitations to attend. He broke into Zulu when he said that afterwards refreshments would be served in the tent outside, and that Josiah Motlantshe had insisted that everyone was invited. There was a reverberating rumble of approval from the crowd outside, which could be heard inside Regina Mundi.

All eyes were on the pall-bearers as they performed the most challenging part of their task, lifting the coffin from the bier and on to their shoulders again. That done they began the sedate walk back down the aisle, accompanied by the choir singing the mournful and moving 'Senzenina', the old anti-apartheid protest song, now given a new meaning, a new currency, in this new South Africa.

Kagiso let the others in his pew out but stayed where he was. After the joy of his instant recognition at seeing Lindi, he was now overcome by awkwardness, like a plantation worker in front of the white madam. His hands plunged deep into his trouser pockets, he shuffled down and across the aisle, saying, 'Hey! It's great to see you.' He'd barely taken a couple of steps before Lindi was there in front of him.

'Is that it?' she asked, but didn't wait for an answer. With an abandon that was normally alien to her, Lindi reached up to Kagiso and hugged him. It was only when she realised that his arms were still hanging limply by his sides that she pulled away.

'Look at me! I'm all over you like a rash. I'm sorry.'

'Ah! No, it's me. I just wasn't sure what to expect. It's been so long and . . .' His voice trailed off.

'And what?'

'Well, we were just kids.'

'And we were like family!' As the words came out she felt the chill shadow of doubt pass over her. Perhaps it had all been an elaborate one-sided fantasy, this idea that the Seatons' generosity all those years earlier had amounted to anything more than the rich giving alms to the poor.

Kagiso didn't just see the anxiety, he remembered it, and now he understood it. He saw again the girl who'd edged her way around his friendship with Ralph. He saw the crumpling power of rejection on a face that only moments earlier had been a beaming picture of warmth and friendship.

'Let's just do that again,' he said. 'I'm such a *domkop*! First on the phone last night and now acting like some uptight white man.' He held both Lindi's hands and pulled her in. 'Welcome back.'

They started walking towards the entrance, hardly able to hear each other amid the clang and clatter of the temporary stage being disman-tled. It was a relief to be outside.

Just ahead of them, Kagiso saw Jake Willemse. In the second or two that it took him to decide whether or not he wanted to acknowledge the minister the other man caught his eye. There was nothing for it, they were going to have to talk. Willemse excused himself from the couple he was chatting with and came over to where Kagiso and Lindi were standing.

'So, it's my old friend Kagiso Rapabane,' he said.

'Minister, it's good to see you again.'

'How long is it since you left us to fight for the little man? Must be a couple of years.'

'Almost exactly. You have a good memory, Minister.'

'Eh! Man! What's with the minister stuff? We're not in Pretoria now. Call me Jake.'

'Yes, okay, Jake – this is a very good friend of mine. Lindi Seaton.'

Willemse held his hand out. 'One of his comrades in the good fight?'

'Actually, I've just arrived from London – though I was born here. I'm visiting family friends, you know, the usual stuff.'

'And what do you do when you're not seeing family and friends?'

An inevitable question for which, much to her regret now, Lindi hadn't really prepared. She wanted to make her answer sound as bland as possible. 'I work for South Trust, a not-for-profit—'

Willemse interrupted: 'I'm quite aware of South Trust. Well, I'm sure you'll find we don't need any of your help here. Kagiso, I hope you

111

have told your friend that this isn't the old South Africa she left behind.' He was looking straight at Lindi when he said this. Then he turned to Kagiso. 'My people tell me you've become quite a thorn in their side since you changed your mind about the project. Quite a turnaround from the keen young policy man I used to know.'

'Well, yes, I have been concerned about some of the land transactions that are being—'

'Look, why don't you let me worry about that, eh? I'm sure you have enough on your plate organising your little cooperative. How about actually teaching them to grow more food? That would help, not this nonsense about who owns what piece of land.' He looked around. 'Now, I must get going – I must join the Motlantshes.'

His handshakes were perfunctory.

'And you, young lady, we take a dim view of foreigners meddling in our affairs. I suggest you enjoy the abundant wonders of our beautiful country and then go home – I'm sure there are plenty of people who need your charity there. Goodbye.'

Willemse started walking away but stopped and turned round. 'By the way, Kagiso, I didn't know you were so close to Lesedi.'

'I'm not – I mean I wasn't. Our paths crossed a couple of times, that's all.'

'That's not what I heard. I gather you got on like . . .' and he turned to Lindi at this point '. . . how do you British say it? Like a house on fire. You had quite a chat, I'm told.'

'I'm not sure who told you that.'

'You know me, Kagiso. I like to keep myself informed. I suppose he told you about our wonderful plans for Mpumalanga?'

Kagiso stepped round the question as deftly as he could. 'I think Lesedi was more interested in listening to what the people had to say.'

'Ah! Of course, the *people*. Yes, we mustn't forget about them, especially since they've got such a young, intelligent man like you looking after them. And did you tell Lesedi about your – what did you call them? Your concerns?'

'He didn't need me to tell him anything. Our clients are quite capable of speaking for themselves.'

'So they're clients, are they? Excellent, excellent. I hear you were probably the last person to see him alive – apart from whoever killed him, of course. Come to think of it, it can't have been very long after you met him.'

And with that, he walked off again.

Jake Willemse's big idea – the one that had made him a favourite with business and appeared to have put him on a fast track to the top of the political ladder – was that the ruling party had been obsessed by land ownership, clinging to the idea like a badge of honour, instead of concentrating on what actually happened on the land. He'd given a speech a couple of months into his tenure in which he had questioned the policy. It had provoked quite a stir.

'Hanging on to the land is like hanging on to your virginity. What's the point?'

His audience of international bankers, mostly men, had lapped it up. He'd gone on in similar vein, mocking those who still thought grazing a few cattle on a small patch of land, or growing enough to feed the family, was a worthy goal for a modern agricultural policy. 'That is what we were doing four hundred years ago – and look what happened.'

Willemse had reminded his audience that the wealth of the city they were in – Johannesburg – had been built on what was in the land: gold. 'That was fine for the nineteenth and twentieth centuries,' he said, 'but here, now, in the twenty-first century the land itself is precious. Land is the new gold! And we are blessed with more than we need. To be worried about little bits of paper that transfer small parcels of land from a white man to a black woman, or from the rich to the poor, is yesterday's politics. You don't create wealth by passing the land between ourselves. Imagine if we had dug the gold up and just shared it out among us. No, you create wealth by realising its full potential – and that means getting in foreign investment.'

He'd come close to committing sacrilege when he'd derided those politicians who went back to their rural home, put on traditional garb, joined in ceremonial dances and delivered a speech about the pleasures of a bucolic life. He didn't mention any names but everyone knew who he was talking about – a former president who still wielded consider- able influence.

'It's all right for them. They get into their air-conditioned limos and head back to the city. And when they get there do you think they sit down to a plate of *pap* and meat, like their friends and relatives in the rural areas?' He'd left the question hanging, the rhetorical device more telling than anything else he might have said.

The speech had elicited a standing ovation. Overnight Willemse had become a darling of the international lecture circuit, that group of men and women who move from the sanitised first-class cabin of a plane to the carpeted splendour of a five-star luxury hotel without really having to touch the ground. Here was a man who was willing to think the unthinkable, to speak out against tired old dogmas. Within days, the director of the Davos World Economic Forum in Switzerland had been in touch to offer him an open-ended invitation to deliver a speech at a future meeting. Jake Willemse, it seemed, could do no wrong.

Lindi let him walk out of earshot. 'What an unspeakable little shit he is!'

'Oh! He's that, all right. He's also one of the most powerful men in the country with some even more powerful friends.'

'And what was he trying to imply? I mean about Lesedi being killed right after you saw him.'

'It's rubbish. He thinks he can frighten me.'

'Frighten you, how?'

'They're trying to pin this thing on somebody.' Kagiso waved his hand towards the church. 'Anybody.'

'But you? Hang on, let me get this straight. From what Maude said you work for a charity, right?'

'Right.'

'I looked it up, Soil of Africa. It campaigns for land reform.'

'Right,' he replied abruptly.

'Christ! Kagiso! I'm not reading out a checklist.'

'What do you want to know? You've seen the website. We campaign for land reform, not the kind that people like Willemse want. We oppose foreign ownership, we oppose our own corporations squeezing out the people who actually live on the land, and we find lawyers to defend people forced off what they thought was their land. Last time I looked, it didn't say anything about murdering people.'

114

'For God's sake! It's not me who's accusing you. I'm just trying to get my head around what Willemse was getting at.'

'I told you. He's trying to frighten me and people like me.'

Lindi took a deep breath. 'We're not really getting anywhere, are we? It's me. I still haven't recovered from the flight. All right, what *were* you doing with Lesedi?'

'He was interested in some of the work I'm doing in Malelane and he came to see me.'

'And what's all this about your making a turnaround?'

'It's a long story. First things first: let's get something to drink. I think we should take up Josiah Motlantshe's offer and have some of his refreshments,' said Kagiso.

'I thought we might go back into town. I've got an appointment at Wits later. Anyway, it looks pretty hectic in there. Have you got time?'

'Not really. I've got a lift back to Malelane later this afternoon, and a couple of things I have to sort out before that. Look, you wait here and I'll go and get us some tea or something.'

'It could take you a while,' she said.

'Watch me! Just head for the shade where all those drivers are standing around and I'll come and find you. I'll be back now-now,' he said, the old familiarity returning, a sweet memory reawakened.

Lindi watched him as he walked away. He had an easy, loping gait. He approached the uniformed marshal who was controlling the flow of people into the entrance of the massive canvas marquee. He was a good twenty metres or so from where she was but even from that distance she could sense how comfortable he was around these people, and they with him. The marshal took Kagiso by the hand towards the front of the queue. Kagiso said something to the people there, turning to look at her. They all laughed and let him in.

Once Kagiso was inside they reverted to their earlier demeanour, the nervous look of those who stand in line – fearing that nothing will be left when they get to the front. Their apprehension was not helped by the sight of those who emerged from the exit at the other side of the marquee. Lindi saw them falling about with laughter, their cheeks bulging with food, cradling an assortment of cakes, buns and cans of fizzy drinks in their arms.

Kagiso came back the way he'd gone in, the marshal making the way clear for him again. He was carrying a couple of takeaway cups with their caps on and a paper plate with some snacks. 'I guessed you wouldn't want sugar in your tea,' he said.

'You guessed right. And what, may I ask, did you say to them to make them all look at me?'

'Oh, I just told them that the white madam over there was not coping with the heat and was in danger of fainting.'

'You did, did you?'

'But what got the laughs was the guy speaking Zulu, who said something like, "Bloody typical, they've been here for hundreds of years and they're still not used to the sun."'

'I'm glad you all had a good laugh at my expense.' She prodded him in the ribs.

'Hey! I'll spill my tea. Anyway, it did the trick. So where do we start?'

Kagiso leaned down, brushed away some twigs on the grass and stretched out on the ground, propping himself up on one elbow. He looked relaxed, a man at ease with himself, quite a contrast from the tetchy awkwardness of just a few minutes earlier.

Lindi sat down next to him.

'So what's this "turnaround" that Willemse was talking about?'

'Oh! It's all a bit ridiculous, really. I suppose I was what you'd call a rising star in the ministry. I used to work for him, did a fair amount of the research on which his new policy was based.'

'What was that?'

'Basically he said arguments about taking over land were so old-school. He argued that whether you owned land or not was irrelevant. The question was, were you getting enough from it – either pay and conditions or output? Pretty much what he just said.'

'All very rational.'

'That's what I used to think, too.'

'I can feel a "but" coming.'

'But that's not really what's happening on the ground.'

'What do you mean?'

'Well, I was sent down to Mpumalanga to show the policy could work. You know, bring workers and owners together, set up farm councils, profit-share schemes, land-lease programmes. You name it, I could try it. The only rule was – don't get bogged down in arguments about ownership.'

'And it's not happening?'

'Well, it did for a few months – we had some fantastic results. And then the farmers – most of them are still white – started going off the idea. I found they were selling the land to government, exactly what Willemse said he wasn't interested in.'

'Did you complain?'

'Well, not directly to him, but to his office.'

'And?'

He shrugged. 'They sent me a very polite letter, which basically told me to keep my nose out of it.'

'Which is more or less what Willemse just said to you today.'

'Yeah. He doesn't do subtle.'

'I'd say he's got his eyes on you.'

'Oh, I don't doubt that. Minister Jake Willemse doesn't like people who interfere in his business. After today I'd say he's got his eyes on you too, Lindi. Whatever you're up to – and I assume that stuff about family and friends was bullshit – I'd be careful who you talk to and what you say in public. In fact, being seen hanging around with me probably hasn't done you any favours.'

'Since you mention it I think they're already watching me.'

Kagiso frowned. 'Really?'

'Well, they took me aside at Immigration and gave me a warning about working. I'm on a tourist visa.'

'How did they know to take you aside? It's not like they could have known you were coming.'

'Good question. Could be a couple of reasons,' Lindi mused. 'My boss, South Trust's director, gave an interview the morning after Lesedi's killing saying it was all linked to the land question. Not that he had any evidence, more of a gut thing. Anyway, after that we got a call from the South African High Commission in London. So they certainly know about us.'

'I heard the interview. They had a clip on the BBC website. What was the other reason?'

'Maybe I'm being paranoid but the morning after Lesedi's murder I got a call from an old colleague of mine, from the days when I used to work for the UK Foreign and Commonwealth Office.'

Kagiso raised his eyebrows in mock horror. 'Harry Seaton's daughter worked for the colonial masters!'

'Very funny. If it's any consolation, it was a train crash and I left in disgrace. Anyhow, this guy now works for something called Africa Rising Investments. They're private-equity turnaround specialists, though from what I can make out the only thing they're really good at turning around is the money they make. He called me that morning – it was three days ago, maybe four, I've lost track – and warned me, or South Trust, about meddling.'

'Let me guess, Africa Rising is involved in land purchases?'

'You go to the top of the class. Yes, they've done stuff all over the place – Sudan, Ethiopia and loads more.'

Kagiso looked surprised. 'We – I mean Soil of Africa – we keep an eye on people like that but I haven't come across Africa Rising doing anything here.'

'They don't exactly shout about it. They stay under the radar. That's the way they like it and that's the way their clients like it – the Chinese, the Gulf countries, whoever's paying them.'

'And Lesedi headlines are not good for business.'

'Exactly. Judging by this guy's call to me, I'd say Africa Rising must be knee-deep in some land deals here.'

'If that's the case you can assume they have a hotline to the government and your ex-colleague has surely been onto them,' said Kagiso. 'It's going to make your mission here pretty tough.'

'It's not really a mission. I'm sort of under the radar too. If I get anywhere South Trust will come here officially. For now, I just need to find out who's who.'

'How do you mean?'

Lindi looked around. The last time they'd done this, had a picnic, they'd been children watched over by Maude. She remembered the photo in her parents' hallway, the family portrait with Kagiso and Maude included. It had always seemed forced, contrived, but sitting next to Kagiso now she accepted there had been a truth to it. Lindi checked they weren't being listened to. Reassured by the distance between them and the rest of the gathering, she continued: 'The way we work is to bring opposing sides together. You know, try to get community-level talks going, influence the media, see if third parties can be brought in to mediate. But for any of that to start we need to know who the opposing sides are.'

'Well, Soil of Africa has probably done more to shed light on this filthy business than anyone else.'

'That's not strictly true, is it?' Lindi tried to keep a note of scepticism from creeping into her voice.

'We're right there working on the ground, which is more than you can say for most.'

'What about this Land Collective?'

'What about it?'

'Come on, Kagiso. Look, I'm not making a judgement or anything, but I'd say it's their campaign of sabotage that's made people sit up and listen. That's how it seemed to us in London.'

'Okay. Say you're right – you certainly aren't the first one to say that. But you want to talk to people, and that rules out the Land Collective. Talking, as you've seen, is not what they do.'

'You're not telling me you have no idea who they are? You can't help me?'

'Right now the best help I can give you is to stay away from you – and vice versa.'

'You sound quite spooked, Kagiso. Is there something I should know?'

Kagiso leaned forward and put a hand on her shoulder. 'Listen to me,' he said. 'All you need to know is just how high the stakes are. One man has been killed, and not just any man. Lesedi is like royalty here, you've just seen that. Whoever did it, if they're willing to take him out, there's no telling where they would stop.'

There was an air of finality about what he said next, standing up and brushing himself down. 'The last thing I need right now, I mean Soil of Africa needs, is to be seen helping you. We don't need any more scrutiny than we're under already.'

Lindi got to her feet, and together they started walking back towards the church. On the other side of the yard, the 'special guests' who'd been invited to the burial were just coming back from the cemetery. Some were milling around, others already piling into the leathery comforts of their limousines. There was only so much of this township thing they could take. Their chauffeurs had kept the cars running with the air-conditioning on. In the melee Kagiso spotted Willemse again. He was talking to Josiah Motlantshe.

'Look at them.' Kagiso gestured to where the two men were standing. 'Lesedi's father is mixed up in this whole thing. He's the one offering the sweeteners to the farmers. It's made to look like a government initiative but he's the main man. I'd love to know how much he gives Willemse and all the other hyenas.'

'So whose side was Lesedi on?'

'He and his father were polar opposites. All that *kak* in the church about the two of them being like friends and colleagues! Lesedi told me they did nothing but argue.'

The police sirens were wailing.

'That'll be the president on his way,' said Kagiso.

'Just one last thing,' pressed Lindi. 'Why would the Land Collective switch from sabotage to murder?'

'Who says they have?'

'Isn't that the assumption?'

'That's what Willemse and his cronies want you to think but it doesn't stack up. No one with a cause to promote would kill Lesedi. And why would they film the whole murder and stick it on YouTube, something they've never done with any of their previous acts of sabotage? The only thing that makes sense is that it creates an atmosphere of such revulsion that people are ready to give the government carte blanche to retaliate in any way it wants.'

'So you think the government sanctioned Lesedi's murder?'

'Have you got a better theory? There's billions riding on these land deals. Look how desperate they are, arresting one of the Mozambicans. They are the poorest of the poor, who will work for practically nothing because it's better than they can get at home. Why would they risk it all by killing one of the most popular men in the country?'

Lindi nodded. 'Shall we share a cab? I'm going into town.'

'No, it's better if we . . . Sorry. As I said, it's better if it doesn't look like we're working together.'

'Okay. Did I tell you I'm planning to spend a couple of days in Mpumalanga? I'm seeing the Catholic bishop in Nelspruit. And then I thought I'd go to Malelane. Couldn't we meet there?'

He shook his head. 'Least of all in Malelane! Look, I've got some things to do before I catch my lift back there. And I want to spend a couple of minutes by the graveside – I didn't qualify for an invitation.'

'So is Willemse right? You were close to him?'

'Hardly – we had only just met – but I believe he was a good man.'

'We are going to see each other again, aren't we?'

'I'll be in touch once I know what the next few days look like.'

The crowd of mourners had thinned out. The limousines were gone. The marquee was already being taken down. A few children were rummaging through the catering boxes, stacked up and ready to be taken away, searching for anything that hadn't been eaten.

Kagiso walked towards the cemetery. As he approached it, he saw a small group of people near the grave, and one lone figure next to it: Lesedi's mother. Her eyes were shut. He moved towards the grave but hesitated. Priscilla Motlantshe looked up at the noise, and beckoned him over. The two of them stood in silence on opposite sides of the grave. Neither had met the other before but they were joined together in this most intimate act of farewell. After a few minutes Kagiso walked over to her side of the grave and took her hand. 'I'm so sorry for your loss, Mrs Motlantshe,' he said.

Priscilla thanked him. It seemed to her that those were the first genuine words of sympathy she'd heard all day, and all the more touching because they had been uttered in private. She asked him if he was a friend from university days.

'No, we only really met recently,' he said. She asked where. 'In Malelane, I run a charity there.'

'What's your name?' she asked.

'Kagiso. Kagiso Rapabane.'

She nodded in recognition. 'He called me from Malelane. It was one of the last times I talked with him. Lesedi told me about his visit. He

121

told me about the good things you are doing there, he spoke very well of you,' she said.

'And the people there liked him,' Kagiso added.

'And you, what did you think?'

'Well, yes,' he responded, thrown by the direct question. 'I liked him. I was surprised. He was not what I expected.'

'Oh. And what did you expect?'

'I'm not sure, except that, well, he is . . . was a Motlantshe.'

'You mean like his father.'

'I didn't say that.'

'It's what you meant, though.' Her gaze was direct but not confrontational.

'I suppose so. I'm sorry, I didn't come here to upset you.'

She shook her head briskly. 'You are not the first one to think like that. Lesedi *was* different. He wanted to be different.'

Kagiso glanced at his watch and made a gesture of apology. 'I have to go, but there is something I . . .'

'What is it?'

'I want you to know . . . Well, I want you to know that we, I mean the charity I run, we oppose your husband's way of doing things, but it is not personal.'

'You have to do what you think is right. And if Lesedi said he wanted to help you, then I will try also. When all of this is over, come and see me. A friend of Lesedi is a friend of mine.'

12

After the funeral, Kagiso went back to his mother's house in Diepkloof, on the northern edge of Soweto. After much fussing over him by Maude, there was a great deal of reminiscing about life with the Seatons. Maude wanted a description of Lindi, scolding her son for not remembering every detail of her appearance. Then she berated him for not bringing her over that very evening. All this while she cut up a couple of chickens and prepared them for the pot. The son of a poor relative who stayed with her had been sent out for groceries and condiments the minute Kagiso had walked through the door.

Word of Kagiso's presence spread through their section of Diepkloof, aided by a couple of well-chosen calls from Maude. Before too long, Kagiso found himself in the middle of an impromptu party. There was plenty of talk about the 'prodigal' son. His auntie, no doubt prompted by Maude, wanted to know if he'd found anyone special and his nephews wanted to know what the country girls were like.

In the latter part of the evening, conversation inevitably turned to this 'business' with Lesedi. One of his mother's neighbours, a retired railway worker, became quite exercised – and drunk. He ended a dramatic speech, laced with all manner of brandy-fuelled expletives, with the conclusion that he'd known all along that no good would come of all these protests about land. The irony was not lost on Kagiso. A nation that had been born of protest was now tiring of it. But he knew that the old man, the neighbour, probably spoke for many South Africans. Collectively, they were spent. A quiet life was what they wanted after the tumultuous achievement of freedom. Not for the first time he wondered if he was out on a limb.

The following morning, Kagiso woke up much later than he'd planned. By the time he shuffled into the living room, the only communal room, there was not a single trace of the previous night's revelry. Maude was sitting at the table, a pair of spectacles pinched over her nose, staring at a pile of papers. She started to get up, pushing down on the table with both hands. Kagiso touched her shoulder and told her to stay seated. She seemed suddenly frail. He noticed her ankles were thick. He brought two mugs of tea to the table and sat down next to her.

The papers in front of Maude related to a pension the Seatons had set up for her before they left and which they had continued to fund years after they left South Africa.

'They want to stop sending me the pension,' she said weakly.

'Who? Harry and Helen? That can't be right.' Kagiso frowned.

'No! It's the company.'

'Let me see.' He read the letter through and explained that the insurance company no longer wanted to send monthly statements by post automatically. It would be done online, unless customers expressly asked to stay on the postal system. He imagined some bright young thing coming up with the plan, oblivious to the pre-internet generation for whom this particular product had been designed. Maude sighed with relief, her mind put at rest by his confident assurances.

That matter concluded, Maude had a number of chores for Kagiso. Every time he finished one she seemed to have another waiting. He wondered if she was inventing them as she went along – a mother's ploy to keep her beloved son close to her, even if only for a few more minutes. In the end Kagiso decided he would take the overnight train, via Pretoria. Maude beamed, like a child with an ice cream, when he told her. She immediately set about making a cake for him to take to Malelane. No amount of protest would stop her.

In fact, he didn't regret the delayed departure. He needed respite. The meeting with the others in Hillbrow, his argument with Sharmi, the reunion with Lindi, bumping into Willemse again and the funeral itself, all of it had unnerved him. He needed the time and space to think, above all to understand how an idea hatched in the edifying glow of idealism had been transmuted into this uncontrolled and ugly sequence of events, like the scientific perfection of nuclear fission turned into the hateful vengeance of Hiroshima.

When they used to plan their sabotage it was only ever one operation at a time. Success or failure was judged according to whether or not that particular mission was accomplished. Kagiso realised he had never really stood back to look at the whole, or to see how each act had set off its own chain reaction. It was like knowing the ingredients in a recipe but never understanding what happened in the mixing and making. He – they – had wanted others to follow where they had led, but had assumed their new supporters would merely replicate their own actions. He'd never thought that some might want to reinvent the campaign, to go freelance.

But his biggest miscalculation had been to underestimate the lengths to which those who stood to gain most from the sale of land to foreign interests would go, their power and determination. He understood that now. Kagiso could see that he and the others had never tried to get inside the minds of the profiteers and middlemen, the financiers and farmers. For every action there is an equal and opposite reaction. Is that how it went? Einstein, Newton – he couldn't remember. It seemed what was true in physics was truer still in the world of politics and money-making. Of course they were going to hit back. Of course blood would be spilled. How naive he'd been.

Back in her Greenside guesthouse, Lindi called Anton in London.

'Hey! How's it feel to be back home?'

'The weird thing is that it *does* sort of feel like home – even after, what, twenty years.'

'You know what they say. You can take the girl out of Africa, but you can't take Africa out of the girl. How are you getting on?'

'Did you tell anyone I was coming down here? Did the High Commission call back or anything?'

'No – and yes. I mean, yes, the High Commission did call back. And, no, all I said was that at some stage we might want to get involved. No great secret, it's what we do.'

'When was that?'

'It must have been some time on the day you left. What's with all the questions?'

Lindi raised an eyebrow. 'It's just that they seem to know I'm here.

A lot of questions at the airport. Then yesterday, here at the guesthouse, there was a taxi parked outside. The receptionist thought it was for me but I hadn't ordered one.'

'I told you, this is big. These people, whoever they are, they're playing for high stakes.'

'What – do you really think I'm being tagged or whatever they call it?'

'It's possible. You want me to come down?' Anton asked, rather too eagerly for Lindi's liking.

'I'm not saying I need help. I'm just letting you know what's going on.'

'Okay, okay. But just say the word.' Sensing her irritation, and eager to keep her on the line for a full report, he changed the subject. 'What's your take on things so far?'

'Well, I've had a real stroke of luck. Turns out the son of our old housekeeper – I've told you the story – he runs an outfit in Mpumalanga that supports black farmers.'

'What's it called? I'll look it up while we're talking.'

'Soil of Africa. He rules out the whole Mozambican thing.'

'That was bloody obvious from the start.'

'Hang on – I'm just taking you through this bit by bit. My contact at the Wits Migration Unit says there'll be plenty of work for us on xenophobia once all this has died down. The other thing he's adamant about is that the killing had nothing to do with the Land Collective's campaign of violence.'

'Who's this? Your Wits person?'

'No, Kagiso, the guy from Soil of Africa.'

'How would he know? Okay, I've got it. His name is Rapabane, right?'

'Yeah, that's him.'

'Joint irrigation scheme with neighbouring white farmer, a *bosberaad* between commercial farmers and smallholders, nice colour photo and all that . . . Hmm, pretty standard stuff.'

'What are you on about?'

'I'm looking at your friend's website. I wouldn't rule it out, the Land Collective I mean.'

'Kagiso thinks killing Lesedi Motlantshe is so counter-productive no one in their right mind would even have considered it.'

'I'm not so sure. Shit happens when you're in a war.'

'Yeah, but this is not a war.'

'It is for the Land Collective. Look, back in the struggle, we had all those qualms about what was a legitimate target and so on, but every now and then somebody would go off the rails and we'd have a PR disaster. It's the same now. I doubt if this Land Collective thing is anything like as organised as we were.'

'I think Kagiso reckons it could be the government.'

'Why?'

'Well, he didn't give me the low-down, but he says Lesedi was a good man and that is why he wanted to talk to the people at Soil of Africa on the day he died. He wanted to make a difference.'

'And that was enough for the Pretoria boys to knock him off? It's possible – anything is possible. Look, I wouldn't put it past those bastards but it's a long shot, no pun intended. I'd keep an open mind. Don't rule out the Land Collective.'

'I'm not ruling it out but getting to them could be tricky. I asked Kagiso and he thinks it's impossible.'

'How much do you trust this guy?'

'Kagiso? He's like family.'

A snort at the other end of the line. 'That was twenty years ago. Time passes, things change – *people* change.'

He said it. She feared it. Never mind that Anton was at his patronising best: what if he was right? In her mind, Lindi reran meeting Kagiso just a few hours earlier. Perhaps she'd been naive. She cringed with embarrassment at her words – *He's like family*. Now the words sounded hollow. It wasn't as if she hadn't had those doubts herself.

'What are you suggesting?' she responded tersely.

'Something is not right,' Anton said. 'Look, if Kagiso's the champion of the landless, which is what it says on their website, then he's got to know more about the Land Collective than he's letting on. Either that or he's just another naive charity worker who's out of his depth. I know which one I think is more likely. If he's serious about land reform, he's got to know about the Collective. He's just not sharing it with you.'

'Why would he do that?'

'Who knows? But I don't like it.'

Sharmi Meer had time to kill. She was now what the social workers might call a woman of no fixed abode. Her car wasn't the only thing she'd abandoned. She'd left her apartment too. She wandered back to Yeoville and to the mechanic's shop. As she'd hoped – and expected – the car was gone. It was probably replated and repainted by now.

She wasn't normally sentimental about possessions and she was surprised by the pang of loss she felt as she stared at the kerbside where she had last seen the Beetle. The last thing she'd done before stepping out of the car was check the odometer: more than 150,000 kilometres. Sharmi remembered the journeys, all those kilometres, especially the one back to Johannesburg with Kagiso a couple of days after they'd first met. It was like looking in the rear-view mirror of her life. It had been a journey with such promise, at least that's what she'd hoped, a journey that might have changed her life. It had done that, all right, but only for the worse.

She'd thought she could walk away from the events of that journey and she very nearly had – that was until she'd met Kagiso again. The sense of betrayal had come flooding back. It had been almost palpable. First the memory of it, then the compulsion to get even.

Now, as Sharmi stood in an outdoor market in Yeoville, absently running her fingers through a rack of embroidered shirts from Ghana, she knew how hooked she was on competing with Kagiso. Their relationship had become increasingly destructive, eating up their time and energy in a clash of wills that served no greater purpose than its own vicious cycle.

But she was free of it now. She'd found a way to have the last word. That would be her next move.

She took the phone from her hip pocket. It was the one that was supposed to be used only in an emergency. She looked at the contacts list: just three numbers, no names. She could hear the lecture from Kagiso. *Don't keep the numbers on your phone: commit them to memory.* Even if she did call Kagiso, Sharmi couldn't think what she would say to him. If it had been Two-Boy, that would have been easy. She'd tell him she loved him, yes, loved him like a sister, and she'd ask him not to be lonely and to take care of himself. With François, too, it would be simple: one of those it-was-good-while-it-lasted calls. She realised it wouldn't bother her one way or another if she never saw him again. But it was different with Kagiso. She knew the call would be about an ending, but she hadn't yet worked out what kind.

13

It was Josiah Motlantshe's casual announcement that he would be travelling again that galvanised his wife into action.

There were many things in their lopsided marriage that irked Priscilla Motlantshe, but which she was resigned to tolerate. However, the thought that her husband could so quickly pursue the business deal that had been interrupted by Lesedi's death seemed shocking, even by his standards.

In some ways, his many affairs – which he could barely be bothered to conceal these days – were a relief to her. She had long ago ceased to harbour any passion for her husband. She remembered their first time. Her physical response to him, the sheer pleasure of allowing him into her body, had been so deeply entwined with her admiration for his political courage. The years of separation, when he was incarcerated on Robben Island, had made no difference. If anything it had intensified her desire.

Looking back, she knew all that had begun to wither the day he'd cut his first big business deal. She didn't begrudge him the money, or the achievement, but she'd seen how the energy and intelligence that had once driven his activism began to feed an appetite for wealth. The apartment in Sandton, with its incumbent (indeed recumbent) mistress was a relatively new development. The fact of it angered her far less than the idea that he thought she was stupid enough not to know about it.

Over the years, she had found a rationale that allowed her to tolerate his voracious pursuit of money and those who could help him make more of it. There were plenty of people who admired his ascent of the corporate mountain, viewing it as proof that black men were every bit as commercially gifted as the white men who had for so long had the field to themselves. Priscilla didn't really buy into that particular conceit – at least, not as far as her husband was concerned – but it gave her a kind of cover, a suit of armour she could wear in the days when she used to accompany him to endless rounds of cocktail parties.

She found the new black elite hard to swallow. It was not their money but the way they made it. There were millions of black families in the emerging middle class, who had worked their way honestly to a suburban home, a new car, a decent school for their children and a holiday abroad. For them the promise of freedom had come good, and Priscilla admired them. It was the others, whose wealth came from political patronage and racial preferment, she abhorred: it wasn't what the 'struggle' had been about. There they were, those ample women, tottering around on heels designed to carry the weight of some Italian waif. It had always struck her as comical that after years, decades in fact, of ridiculing the white madams and their endless, often futile commitment to physical rearrangement and disguise, those black women should pursue the same hopeless cause with such vigour.

She could forgive the young ones who had grown up with this exhibition of wealth and knew no better. It was their mothers Priscilla felt sorry for. Women who had once embodied the fecund resilience of African femininity tried to squeeze themselves into a mould that churned out the primped and pampered white women who lunched on salads in their gated communities and thrived on the inherited status of their husbands.

Priscilla had taken her cue from an elder stateswoman of the struggle, Albertina Sisulu, who stood her ground, resolutely hanging on to the values that had earned her respect in life and reverence in death.

The men were no better, she thought. Once, they had argued the merits of public ownership versus private provision, railed against a system that placed greater emphasis on the value of a share than on the welfare of an individual. Now they competed on a new plain. Brands replaced ideology. The party cadres who had once exhorted their members to share out the wealth of the country to all who lived in it now shared it out among themselves. The most expensive watch, the newest car, the biggest house – they accumulated it all without the slightest sense of irony. And her own husband, Josiah, was the finest exponent of the new art of self-aggrandisement.

She could put up with all of that. She had no choice, except the one-way ticket to isolation that a divorce would trigger. Josiah had threatened her with that prospect more than once, pointing out that he had the power to make sure the girls would stay with him. She wasn't going to give him that chance. And he knew it. So they lived their separate lives, an arrangement founded on a sort of truce that gave Josiah licence to do whatever he wanted outside the home but gave her the right to decide what went on inside it – and that included bringing up the children.

Any hope Priscilla had had that the death of their beloved Lesedi might, just for a while, draw the family together had evaporated at the end of the funeral ceremony, just a few hours earlier. Josiah had seen her and the two girls into the car and said he would join them later. As the chauffeur eased the car out of Regina Mundi's gates, Priscilla had watched her husband climb into the back seat of Jake Willemse's official limousine.

Priscilla and the girls had made the journey back to their Houghton mansion in silence. Her daughters had disappeared upstairs as soon as they arrived home. A couple of minutes later she'd heard the canned laughter of a TV show, another rerun to which her daughters could mime the script. She'd called one of the house-workers, a distant and destitute relative, and asked her to take two mugs of hot chocolate to the girls. She'd gone into the kitchen and seen that the cook had left a meal for them. When the maid came back downstairs, Priscilla had told the girl to put the food away and take the rest of the evening off.

It was eight in the evening. Priscilla had just buried her only son – and lost a companion. She was alone.

She made herself a cup of tea and sat down at the breakfast bar, the polished black granite reflecting a featureless outline of her head and shoulders. She stared at it. There were no distinguishing marks, not even enough to show she was a woman, let alone a mother. Just a shape. An empty, dark shape.

Lesedi had been a toddler when Josiah was jailed. His release years later was barely noticed, coinciding as it had with the release of such anti-apartheid luminaries as Walter Sisulu and Ahmed Kathrada. Priscilla remembered the years when Josiah was behind bars as among the happiest she had known. She never tired of telling people she was ready to wait for him, whether it was one year or a hundred.

In the absence of the father, mother and son developed an uncommon bond. They were friends. It was a relationship that survived the disruption of Josiah's return to the family – which Lesedi had found difficult to cope with – and strengthened as the couple's estrangement became permanent. Lesedi was Priscilla's link to a past when morals mattered more than money. She might have given up on her husband but she had clung to Lesedi, hoping for the day when he would make his own mark on the world.

Now Priscilla recalled the conversation she'd had with Lesedi on the day he was killed. In fact, there had been two conversations. During the first, he'd been in ebullient mood, energised by the meeting with farm workers in Mpumalanga. That was when he'd mentioned Kagiso Rapabane. Lesedi had been full of admiration for the man, saying he wished he could do something as useful as that. Apparently he'd promised Kagiso that he would intervene on behalf of the farm workers.

'Dad won't like it but I'm determined that we do this deal differently. It's a disgrace what's happening,' he'd said, his voice full of fire and indignation.

She'd listened with a mixture of pride and fear. Pride in his instincts, fear for what would happen when he confronted his father. She'd tried to prepare him for rejection, saying he needed to think carefully before he talked to his father.

The next call was markedly different. She'd known something was wrong the second she'd heard his voice.

'I've just had a row with Willemse,' he'd said. 'I couldn't reach Daddy so I called Willemse and told him that the whole thing stinks. I'm not afraid to lift the lid on this whole business and he knows that.'

She'd asked him what the minister had said.

Her son had tried to make light of it. 'Oh, just a lot of shouting and stuff. He can't touch me.'

She'd asked him if the minister had threatened him.

'No, just going on about what was at stake for Daddy and so on. Said I shouldn't meddle in stuff I didn't understand.'

And then Lesedi had uttered the words that had left her cold. 'But I do understand, Mom. I've got all the information – the deals, the bribes. I've got it all somewhere safe.'

Just the memory of those words brought her up sharp, as they had done when she'd first heard them. She'd seen Lesedi for what he was – a boy in a man's world – and she'd feared for him. She had ended the conversation there and then, saying they should talk more when he got home. He'd told her not to wait up as he had one more meeting with the community worker, Kagiso, before he set off for Johannesburg. It was the last time she'd spoken to her son.

A few minutes later she'd taken a call from Jake Willemse. His tone had been silken civility, his message anything but. *Your son should get himself a proper job*, he'd intimated in a barely veiled threat, *instead of interfering in government business.* 'He really will get into all sorts of trouble if he carries on like this.'

He'd stressed the word 'government' as if it were sacred ground, a place for the gods, not mere mortals like Lesedi. He'd ended the call by saying he'd have to tell the boy's father. This was the conversation she'd relayed to Josiah when he'd called from Dubai.

Priscilla heard a key in the front door and looked across the vast open-plan living room to see the security guard let Josiah in. Even at this distance she could see he'd been drinking. In some men alcohol dispels the gloom and lifts the mood. In Josiah it made him combative and aggressive. He'd never touched her in anger but the threat was always there.

'Vusi! Hey!' he shouted. 'Where are these people?'

'I gave them the evening off. I thought we'd want to be on our own.'

'You thought what?' he barked.

'I said, I thought it would be better if we all had some time to ourselves. Shall I call the girls?'

'No, leave them. Get me a drink,' he said, as he entered the hallway toilet, leaving the door open.

Priscilla poured out a large measure of Johnnie Walker Blue Label and walked over to the fridge.

'No, no, leave the ice.'

'I'm just getting myself some ginger ale,' she said. She noticed that his fly was still open. There was a drip mark on his trousers. He kicked off his shoes and fell onto the white leather sofa, which gave out a hiss as his full weight sank into it.

It was then that whatever tiny vestige of a relationship Priscilla still shared with Josiah disappeared. True, they were no longer man and wife in a conjugal sense, but there had been moments, if few and far between, when she might look across a room full of people and see Josiah, vigorous and animated, and remember why she'd once felt as if her life could never be complete without him at her side.

Now the memory of that feeling had disappeared for good. Priscilla didn't need to will it away: it simply vanished, expunged from her life story. She felt as if she'd witnessed a death right there, in front of her, at that moment. For she could no longer see the man, just a corpulent and vulgar body.

'I'm going in the morning,' he said.

'Going where?'

'I have to meet those fellows in Dubai. They're still there. Kariakis persuaded them to stay until I get back.'

If a man is to be judged by the company he keeps, then Priscilla Motlantshe rued the day her husband had met George Kariakis. He was pre-eminent among a whole new class of middlemen who had emerged to service these new land deals. Suitable land had to be identified, local officials sounded out, wined and dined, and legal obstacles overcome – more often than not with a secret hefty contribution to the bank account of whichever official could change the rules.

After some poor press in the wake of the first few deals, these consultants – ever quick to spot a new opening – had started offering a public-relations service too. Kariakis's latest PR offering purported to show what conditions were like for a group of workers in southern Sudan after their farm – formerly state-owned – had been taken over by a private company based in Dubai. The brochure made it look like a holiday camp. The residents had running water in their homes, lunch breaks under canvas awnings in the field, and a community club where they relaxed in the evenings. Children were filmed queuing to see the company doctor for a check-up, and a young European volunteer was shown giving English lessons to a class of eager women. It reminded

Motlantshe of the black-and-white films the apartheid government's Department of Public Information once produced. A whole generation of whites was persuaded that apartheid South Africa's black population was 'the happiest on the continent'. Same technique, new audience.

In the beginning, this new 'carve-up' of Africa, as academics and activists alike were calling it, was dominated by that breed of merchants who had always trawled through the continent, sniffing out the prospect of money-making with an unerring nose for a quick deal. Lately, more conventional players – international banks and private-equity firms – had been attracted to the business, drawn in by the oversize profit margins, like a pack of hyenas moving in on a kill. But in a business where personal contact was the key they often seemed flat-footed. And the undisputed 'land king of Africa', as the *Financial Times* had dubbed him, was George Kariakis, a half-Greek, half-Lebanese trader whose family had long-standing, if dubious, links with several African leaders of the old school – the ones who still found it difficult to make a distinction between the national coffers and their own bank accounts, especially the ones they held offshore.

'I'll go and pack some things for you,' she said. 'How long will you be away?'

He didn't bother answering. Priscilla walked to the stairs, one heavy step at a time, carrying the dead weight of a failed marriage. Packing her husband's bag took no time at all. She'd done it often enough. All she had to do was take the ironed and folded clothes from the cupboard and place them in the bag. There was a time when she had chosen his outfits with care, looking at which ties would go with which suits. Now she pulled off the first ties that came to hand and left the suits in the dry cleaner's cellophane wrapper.

She walked out into the upstairs hallway and checked the girls' bedrooms. They were both fast asleep. She envied their escape from a day of howling emotion and eternal loss. From where she was she could hear Josiah snoring, slumped on the sofa. She couldn't be bothered to wake him and cajole him to bed. Those days were over.

Priscilla went into Lesedi's room. Sitting on his bed she pulled his pillow towards her, settled it in her lap, and remembered the boy who would sit there, eyes staring at her in wide-open innocence, as she told him stories about his father and the other freedom-fighters. She lifted the pillow to her face and breathed deep, sucking in what remained of him. She had had such dreams for him. But the mother who had once known every crease and dimple on her child's body also knew that the innocence that had been so endearing in the boy had been a weakness in the man.

She blamed herself. She had armed him with idealism, but that alone was not enough to withstand the greed and guile of the world around him. Looking back, she realised that she had tried to make of Lesedi all that she had once hoped his father would be. And she had succeeded. But what good was idealism when it lay beaten and dormant in a corpse? The thought filled her eyes with tears, not the reflexive kind she had shed in public earlier that day at the funeral, but a convulsive outpouring that came from somewhere deep inside her. Priscilla cried for her son, but she cried for herself, too, for she knew that a part of her had died that day.

She buried her face in the pillow and waited for the pain to dull. And when it did, it was replaced by something else: a mother's desire to make sure her son had not died in vain.

14

The cab driver jammed the car into an impossibly tiny space outside Park station, between the bollard on one side and a VW Kombi on the other. Lindi opened the door, stuck her head through the gap, then corkscrewed the rest of her body out, but in the process snagged her rucksack on the door handle inside.

'Don't pull, don't pull,' shouted the driver. 'You are going to spoil the car.' He leaned over from the front seat and freed the strap. It was still too bulky. Lindi reached in and pulled out the two-litre bottle of water from the webbing, then tugged the rucksack free. She hadn't even started and already she was exhausted. Never a good sleeper, the overnight flight a couple of days earlier and lying awake, rerunning the previous day's encounter with Kagiso till well after midnight, had left her feeling enervated.

Meeting Kagiso hadn't gone anything like she'd planned or hoped. There had been something awkward about it, something unsaid in their conversation. She was still wondering whether it was simply the passage of time, or something else. It was a little after six in the morning. The cup of coffee she'd been promised by the housekeeper at the guesthouse had failed to materialise in time. She was aware of the first signs of a dizzying pang of hunger.

The combination of Park station and the adjoining Noord Street, a terminus for the city's minibus taxis, make for one of the busiest transport hubs on the continent. After the croissant-and-cappuccino civility of Greenside, where she'd stayed for the last two nights, this was Africa in all its impressive tumult – even at this time of the day.

Lindi waited for the driver to get her bag out of the boot. He sat where he was and told her through the half-open window that she should get it herself. It had been a mistake to pay him before she had got out. Lindi lifted the overnight case and put it on the ground. She was about to shut the boot, but instead pulled the case handle up and started walking in the direction that most other people seemed to be going. She didn't look back, but the sound of the driver cursing gave a satisfying lift to a morning that had already offered its fair share of challenges.

The earliest vendors were already selling an assortment of street food. There were bloodless and dimpled strips of tripe fizzing on a grill. The man cooking picked a piece off the fire, doused it liberally with piri-piri sauce and blew on it before putting it into his mouth. The sickly-sweet smell of rice and mince, cooked over a hissing gas camping stove nearby, reached Lindi and smothered her appetite. Others were unpacking their wares. In a couple of hours they would be selling everything from fake Rolex watches to shoelaces and polyester corsets.

Two of them caught Lindi's eye. Their chatter – loud and ebullient – was in a language she didn't recognise at first but then realised was a version of French. One had the tell-tale facial tribal markings still evident on some of the more elderly migrants from West Africa. They were playing their part in the great conveyor-belt of trade, unnoticed in the official statistics, which distributes wealth from Africa's teeming and wealthy cities to its forgotten and poor villages. The meagre profits from a few weeks outside Park station in Johannesburg would, in the wonderful alchemy of pavement commerce, be transmuted into a corrugated-iron roof over a mud hut somewhere in the Bandiagara Hills of Mali.

Inside the station Lindi and the other early-morning travellers were like fish swimming against the current, quickly swamped by commuters coming the other way, disgorged by one of the arriving trains from Johannesburg's township hinterland. It made her think of the Hugh Masekela hit 'Stimela', a favourite of her father. The Afro-jazz classic, with Masekela's inimitable sound effects mimicking gushes of high-pressure steam and whistles, evoked the old journey of rural labourers drawn to Johannesburg's gold reef – and all too often to a life of dissolution in the city's migrant hostels. More than two decades of majority rule had yet to rid the country entirely of that particular remnant of the old order.

Lindi realised she was in the wrong place and looked for signs for the long-distance bus terminus. She spotted an elderly porter. His shirt collar hung around his scraggy neck.

'Follow me,' he said, and started to shuffle back towards where Lindi had come from. He stopped just before the entrance and pointed to one side.

'Just over there, madam. You see the soldiers over there? Go past them.'

'Do the buses to Mpumalanga go from there?'

'Mpumalanga? You're not going to Cape Town?'

'No, I want to go to Nelspruit.'

'For the Kruger Park?'

'No, no, I just want to go to Nelspruit,' Lindi said, struggling to disguise her irritation.

'Only these Mozambicans are going that way now. Watch them – they are going to steal your things.'

'I'm sure I'll be fine,' she said, and walked towards the group of soldiers. The presence of troops in the city centre was highly unusual. They were there to help a police force now stretched to the limit.

There were about six of them. One of the soldiers eyed her. Lindi realised how incongruous she was in this place. She was white and she was a woman alone. She'd spotted a couple of backpackers earlier, sitting on the ground, slouched against a wall. Batik-trousered, dread-locked hippies, Anton would have called them. British, judging from their accents. The soldiers were moving on, except the one who had been watching her.

'You are going where?' he said, as she approached.

'To get a coach ticket,' she said.

'To where?'

'To Nelspruit.'

'What business have you there?'

'I'm visiting a friend.'

'You're from where?'

'London in UK,' she said, with as much finality as she could muster.

'Okay, thank you.' He nodded and moved off to join the others.

There was an entirely different atmosphere in the long-distance coach terminus, Park City Transit Centre. Instead of the purposeful coming and going in the Metrorail station, where people were fleet of foot and travelling light to a day's work in the big city, here they were burdened with possessions, people taking what they could and heading out of town. It was the difference between those keen to arrive and those desperate to leave.

Bulawayo, Mutare, Maputo, Harare, Lusaka – the destination boards reminded her of childhood days when she and Ralph would pore over the family atlas and imagine adventures in exotic places.

There was a long queue in front of 4A, the departure gate for the 8 a.m. coach that went to Nelspruit in Mpumalanga, then on to Komartipoort, the border crossing into Mozambique. She was glad the BBC office manager had advised her to make a reservation. She still had to collect her ticket.

There was an even longer queue outside the Translux ticket office. It started with a semblance of order in front of the fingermarked glass partition at the counter, then fanned out. There must have been a couple of hundred people, perhaps double that – Lindi couldn't tell. And more of them were joining by the minute. Somebody's luggage, a heavy-duty plastic bag, was being passed, like a crowd surfer at a concert, towards the front. She was nearly knocked over as a young man was ejected from the queue by two women. Lindi didn't have to speak Shangaan to understand that their vocabulary was both colourful and robust. It was now 7.15: she had less than forty-five minutes.

She was thinking about trying to push through the crowd when she felt an arm reach over her shoulder to shove the man in front of her out of the way. He tripped over the luggage on the floor and fell against some of the others who, in turn, threw him back upright. It was the soldier again.

'Move! Move!' he shouted at the crowd, and then, 'Follow me,' to Lindi.

There was a moment, just a millisecond, when Lindi thought she ought to protest – but she needed that ticket. People looked on sullenly as the soldier carved his way towards the front of the queue, Lindi in his wake. As he emerged at the very front, the man who was next in line at the counter turned round instinctively to hold his place and pushed back, realising too late who the queue jumper was. The soldier grabbed him by the neck and shouted, 'Get out, get out of here!'

'I'm sorry, *baas*. I'm sorry. I just want my ticket. I have waited since three hours.' The man was pleading.

'You can wait some more. Go to the back.'

'Look, that's really not necessary,' said Lindi. 'I can wait.'

'No, these people have to be taught a lesson. They are causing trouble here in South Africa.' He turned to the man again and barked, '*Voetsek*. Fuck off, man! Okay, madam, you can get your ticket now.'

The soldier rejoined the rest of his group. They were pointing at the man, bent and crumpled under the suitcase he was carrying on his shoulder, and laughing. Lindi heard the murmur behind her. She knew what they were thinking: white skin, straight to the front. Same old story.

At the departure gate, one of the uniformed staff from the coach company called out for those who held reservations. Lindi was the only one. She was escorted through to the bus and given the front seat where there was extra leg-room.

Outside there was a growing commotion. One of the cases had burst open as the bus conductor had flung it into the hold, spilling the contents back out onto the pavement. He shouted at the owner as she and her two children tried to gather up their possessions. Lindi saw the fracas unfolding from her seat. She was struck by what the woman had chosen to cram into her bag, which was all too publicly on display. Lindi felt as if she was peeping. The bulk of it was children's clothing, and there were some exercise books. One of them lay open, a child's deliberate handwriting sitting on each line of the ruled paper, the letters lined up, like starlings on a power cable. There was little that seemed to belong to the mother: a bar of soap, some medicines, a saucepan, several packages of dried pasta, and another with salt.

Lindi wondered what the woman had decided to leave behind. There was nothing sentimental here, no photos, no frivolity. It was a survival kit. It reminded Lindi of the radio programme back in Britain that asked famous guests to compile a list of the music they would like to have if they were to be stranded on a desert island. Participants were also allowed to take a luxury. On the last edition she'd listened to, the actress had asked for an endless supply of her favourite scented candles so she could while away the balmy evenings in a mist of lavender or some such. In this suitcase, there was no thought of luxury, just the grinding certainty that making it from one day to the next would be hard enough.

The coach filled quickly. The woman and her two children were the last to get on. The mother had bundled some of her possessions into a cloth. She looked down the bus for spaces. She saw that the one next to Lindi was free but motioned to the children to keep walking. Lindi looked down the aisle. The woman had found the last two seats and had one of the children on her lap. Lindi leaned forward and asked the driver to tell the woman there was a seat free next to her.

'Ah. No, it's okay, ma'am. They are fine like that.'

'But it's going to be hours.'

'These people are used to it.'

Lindi got up and started walking down the aisle.

'One of your children can come and sit next to me,' she said.

The mother looked ahead and caught the driver's disapproving expression. Just a few moments earlier he had abused her for not packing properly and wasting his time.

'I will keep them here, madam,' she said.

Lindi felt marooned halfway down the bus. To walk back to her seat on her own would be to hand victory to the driver. She looked at the elder child, the boy sitting next to his mother. 'Come with me,' she said. 'I've got something for you in my bag. You can have some and bring some to your sister.'

The boy looked up at his mother. She stared at Lindi, a trace of fear in her eyes. There had been so many decisions to make in the last few days, matters of life and death, and now this one, the simplest of them all, seemed beyond her. Lindi held out her hand to the boy. He took it gingerly, as if he might come to some harm. Together they walked back to Lindi's seat. She sat down by the window, rummaged through her rucksack and found one of the energy bars she always carried on long journeys.

'Now, what's your name?'

'Paulo Simbini.'

'That's a lovely name. And how old are you, Paulo?'

'I'm eight years.'

'And what is your sister's name?'

'She has a South African name because she was born here.'

'And what is her South African name?'

'It's Britney.'

What were they thinking of, the parents, when they chose a name with its antecedents in American pop culture? Britney was only the latest in a long line of children saddled with names that owed nothing to their family's culture but carried the migrant's hope that what you called a child might somehow ease its journey in a foreign land. Lindi revisited her old hang-up about her parents' decision to give her a Zulu name. Perhaps they, too, were like travellers hoping their child would grow up in a new and different country, one that had put racial separation behind it. She unwrapped the snack and broke it in half.

'This half is for you, Paulo. I'll keep it safe while you take this one to Britney. Okay?'

Paulo got back just as the coach eased out of the terminus, heading out past Benoni and the eastern suburbs on the N12 highway.

'Do you have a South African name?' he asked.

'Yes, I do, it's Lindi.'

'That's a nice name.'

'Thank you, Paulo. My real name is Lindiwe but all my friends call me Lindi so I want you to call me Lindi.'

'Are we friends?'

'Well, I hope so. We've got quite a few hours together, so we can get to know each other.'

'Where do you live?'

'That's a long story. Do you know where UK is?'

The boy shook his head. 'Is it a big country?'

'No, but some very famous people come from there.'

'Like who?'

'Well, let's see. I bet you like games, I mean like football and athletics.'

'Yes, it's my favourite on TV.'

'So you've heard of Mo Farah?

'You mean the one who runs very far?'

'Yes. He's from my country. And Manchester United, you've heard of them?'

'Wow! Are they from your country too?'

'Yes, they're all from UK. That's where I live.'

'Cool! I'm going to race in the Olympics when I grow up. I'm the fastest boy in my class.'

'I'm sure you'll be faster than Usain Bolt one day. Do you remember him?'

'There's a picture of him in my school. My mom says I have to work very hard to be the best. She says one day she's going to buy me *takkies* just like Usain Bolt used to wear.'

'And what's your mom's name, Paulo?'

'Anastasia. But her boss calls her Anna. I think it's because they don't like Mozambican names.'

'I'm sure it's just because it's shorter. You know, like I said my real name is Lindiwe.'

Paulo was quiet for a moment. Then: 'They don't like people from Mozambique,' he said. 'My dad told my mom that they were killing Mozambicans. It was his secret but I heard him tell my mom. That's why he told us to come on this bus.'

'There are just some very silly people, that's all. The police will catch them and you'll soon be able to go back home.'

'I don't want to go back home. There are angry people there.'

'I tell you what, let's talk about something else. What else are you good at, apart from running?'

'I'm a very good drawer. I could show you but my books are in a bag.'

Lindi opened her rucksack again. She found her notebook and one of her pencils languishing at the bottom – she was a compulsive writer of notes in the margins of books. 'Draw me a picture,' she said. 'And if it's really good I might have something else for you and Britney.'

'What should I draw?'

'Anything you want. Have a little think. You've got loads of time.'

Lindi made a bundle of her denim jacket and used it to cushion her head against the window. She was tired. She was also frightened. Not for herself but for the people around her. Perhaps for the first time since she had landed in South Africa she felt she had a measure of what was happening around her. The conversation with Paulo, the boy's simple acceptance that his family, his people, were unwanted, had discomfited her – because it was true. In the last hour or so she had seen it for herself.

An incipient malice was spreading. She'd lost count of the number of times she had come across the casual animosity. There was the street vendor at the previous day's funeral; then just this morning there had been the soldier and the bus driver. Even the ageing porter, with his off-the-cuff warning about watching out for her things. Together, these encounters had crystallised Anton's warnings and Kagiso's fears. What had he said the day before? *This thing is running out of control.* That was how he'd put it. She felt now, as the rhythmic vibrations of the bus numbed her into sleep, that she understood exactly what he'd meant.

Lindi knew there was menace in the air even before she opened her eyes. The smell of burning, acrid and invasive. She sat bolt upright, instinctively grabbing her rucksack. There was a moment's relief when she realised the fire was outside, but her groggy mind registered a new threat. The bus was swaying from side to side. Outside, a mob of about fifty people, youths, were pushing against the side. They worked in unison, taking advantage of the bus's swinging momentum to effect an even greater movement with each successive shove. Lindi pulled away from the window as another fist pounded on the glass. They were screaming, mouths open, like snarling dogs.

Lindi looked to her left: Paulo was gone. She got up and saw that he was back with his mother, his face pushed against her chest. From where she sat, all Lindi could see was row upon row of faces, each of them etched now with their own version of fear. For every man, woman and child, a different way to communicate horror. Some of the children had begun to cry.

The women were gathering their possessions. A couple of the men were arguing with the driver, who was now standing in the aisle next to the door. Still the bus rocked from side to side.

They were in Middleburg, first stop on the route. Lindi could see the Translux office. In front of it, a crowd of people, fighting each other to get to the front. It made the Johannesburg queue seem positively ordered by comparison. Those at the back couldn't see what was happening ahead of them but Lindi could. The security grille at the ticket office was down, and behind it a man was gesticulating to the desperate passengers. He was waving them away but they persisted, some of them shaking the grille as if they meant to tear it down.

Lindi saw a youth approach the back of the crowd. He had a bandana across his nose and mouth and what looked like a metal rod in his hand. He grabbed one of the bags that was lying on the ground. A young woman turned round and made a lunge for it but the youth slammed the rod down. The woman reeled away, her mouth open in a soundless scream, her body doubled up and her crippled left hand tucked under the other armpit.

The bandana boy dragged the suitcase towards the fire where about a dozen youths – some of them looked no more than in their early teens – were stoking the flames. He was about to throw the bag onto the blaze when one of the others stopped him. Whatever was said between them drew hilarity from the others, now hovering around the suitcase. One came forward with a hammer with which he repeatedly struck the locks on the bag. Within seconds it burst open and the youth pounced on it. Bits of clothing were flung out of the huddle towards the fire. Then, like a magician who reveals his trick, one of the youths emerged from the group, his arms held out wide. He was wearing a brassiere across his chest. The others fell about laughing, grabbing at other garments. One of the gang put a pair of knickers over his head; another tied a cloth around his waist. What was left they hurled onto the flames. The suitcase buckled, then caught fire, emitting a thick plume of black smoke. Somebody pointed to the coach and the gang regrouped. They started swaggering towards it.

The passengers, who'd seen the mayhem unfold, suddenly realised they might have been watching their own fate foretold. Lindi felt a tightening in her chest.

'Drive the bus,' one of the passengers shouted. Others took up the call.

'No, I have to go and check with my office.' The driver looked terrified, the arrogant authority of a couple of hours earlier replaced now with wide-eyed fear.

'This is not my problem,' he said. He looked at Lindi. 'Madam, we must go. It is not safe for you.'

Lindi understood, with a clarity that surprised her, that this was one of those moments that would define her. She had a choice to make, now, immediately. Take a stand or walk away.

'I am not going anywhere and neither are you,' she said. 'If you open that door you will be responsible for whatever happens to these people.' She struggled to control her voice. 'Get behind the wheel and get us out of here.'

The gang had arrived at the bus. They were grabbing the door. She was standing toe to toe with the driver. There was an explosive crack behind them and a scream from one of the passengers. A window had been smashed and one of the mob was poking his hand through the shattered glass.

'Do it *now!*' she yelled, and firmly pushed the driver towards the cockpit.

He turned on the ignition and revved the engine, scattering the crowd outside. The driver kept his left hand on the horn and the coach lurched forward. The exit was blocked by another vehicle, a minibus that had obviously been ransacked. The driver pulled the steering wheel around and the bus climbed a traffic island in the centre of the road, leaning so precariously to one side that a shout went up from the passengers. He put his foot down hard on the accelerator and the bus bounced back onto the tarmac. They were clear of the terminus. Another hundred metres and they would be on the open road.

Lindi went up to the driver.

'Get on your phone. Talk to your office and tell them what's happened. Ask them to make sure the police are at the next stop before we get there.'

She returned to her seat. There was total silence in the coach. Lindi felt cold and clammy; she realised she was trembling uncontrollably. She pushed herself back into her seat and gripped the armrest. Her eye caught the notebook she'd given Paulo. It was lying on the floor. Lindi picked it up. The image was unmistakable. The Ponte building on fire. Stick people leaned out of the windows with speech bubbles coming out of their heads. 'Help, help,' Paulo had written in his precise hand.

At the bottom of the building a figure was lying flat on the ground. Next to it she read two words: 'my father'.

Lindi shut her eyes. She had to stop herself crying.

The route further east was clogged with traffic. It seemed as if every minivan and taxi was heading towards Mozambique. She'd been told fares to the border post at Komatipoort had doubled, then trebled in as many days. Everything from armchairs to mattresses had been strapped onto roof racks, dwarfing the vehicles beneath them. At every major intersection on the N4 there was a crowd of people, arms held out, pleading for a lift. The coach driver, surly and silent since Middleburg, would slow down as he approached them, wait till they started gathering their bags and bundles, then accelerate away. He would glance at Lindi with a smug satisfaction, as if he was getting his own back for the earlier humiliation of being told what to do by a woman.

There were a number of checkpoints where passengers were being made to get off the bus, stand in line and be searched. Lindi was waved through all of them until the coach was pulled over at the last check-point before Nelspruit. A policeman ordered everyone off, then spoke to the driver, who flicked a look at Lindi as he answered. The policeman turned away slightly as he spoke into his walkie-talkie. Another officer walked over to the bus, flicking through a clipboard. His eyes settled on Lindi.

'So you want to be friends with these people, eh? You have to be searched just like them. We are going to do it over there.' He pointed to a windowless prefabricated shed some twenty metres away.

'I have nothing to hide but please get one of your women officers to do it,' Lindi said firmly.

'They are busy.'

'Then I will wait.'

Lindi watched as each of the other passengers on the coach was checked and allowed back on board. She had seen a couple of uniformed women chatting to each other.

'What about those two?' she asked the officer in charge.

'Ah, no, they are very busy. Just wait your turn.'

'The rest of the bus is finished. All of them are back inside.'

'That's because they are not proud white women like you. I can search you now or you can wait.'

Passengers from vehicles behind the coach had been allowed past her. The coach driver had leaned out of his window and told her he would have to leave her behind if she carried on with her nonsense. Some of the other passengers had started to call out to her. She looked up to see Paulo, fear and anxiety written all over his face. She knew she couldn't hold out any longer.

'Oh, so you are finally ready,' the officer said, as he swaggered over to Lindi. 'Let's go,' he said, pointing to the shed. Lindi turned to look at the anxious faces on the coach. She started walking, following the officer.

She hesitated. The officer pushed her in and shut the door. There was an overpowering smell of cheap beer and stale food. It was pitch black. The contrast with the outside couldn't have been greater. Lindi turned round and tried to get past the man. He grabbed her arm and swung her back. She tripped and hit her head on the back wall. She was sweating profusely, her heart pounding. She filled her lungs, trying to regain her balance. Her eyes adjusted to the darkness. Two or three steps and the officer was in front of her. She felt his beery breath.

'If you make this difficult, we are going to make it difficult for you.' He was smiling. 'Just do as I say and you will be back with your friends now-now'

'I will be reporting this to your superiors,' Lindi said, unconvinced, even as she spoke, that it would make any difference.

'You can talk to anybody. We have a terrorist situation here and we have orders to be very strict.'

'Do I look like a terrorist?'

'I don't know till I have searched you. Now, hold out your arms.'

He put his hands around her shoulders and round her armpits, allowing his thumbs to settle over her breasts. He was looking her in the eye. Lindi grabbed his wrists, but it made no difference. His arms were like a clamp.

'We're just doing our job,' he said. 'Sometimes we are supposed to ask the women to take their clothes off. I can do it now if I want to,' he said, still staring at Lindi and moving his hands down her body. He ran his hands along the waistband of her knickers, which he could feel through her linen skirt. (What on earth had made her wear a skirt? She regretted the choice.) Then he pushed hard between her thighs, before carrying on down to her ankles.

'Turn around.' He was breathing harder. Lindi didn't budge. He reached up, held Lindi by the hips. She tried, again, to get out of his grasp. It was useless. He forced her round and pushed her hard against the wall. Lindi tilted her head sideways – it was the only way she could breathe. He started running his hands up Lindi's legs. This time he reached under her skirt.

'No,' she screamed, and started banging her fists against the timber wall.

'No one is going to hear you. And no one is listening. You understand?'

He stood up, leaving his right hand between her legs. 'Now I have some questions for you. So what are you doing with these people?'

'I'm not *with* these people. I'm just travelling on the same bus,' she screamed at him.

Lindi felt his finger as he worked it under her pants. She felt sick and retched. The man pulled away from her. Lindi turned around and, without thinking, she spat at him. He slapped her, slashing her cheek with his nails as she tried to evade the blow.

'I have to charge you now for assaulting a police officer. You are going to be in big trouble.'

It was the last thing she needed. She had drawn attention to herself. She thought through her options.

'Look, I should not have done that. I apologise.'

The officer moved closer to her again. 'So what are you going to do for me? I have to have some compensation.' That smile again. That foetid breath again. He placed his arms above her shoulders. 'We can try again. This time you can enjoy it.'

'Look, those people have been waiting for me. I've got some money in my bag. It's in the coach. Let me go and you can have your compensation.'

'The driver told me that you are defending them, those Mozambicans.'

'That's because they have done nothing wrong. You should be helping them, not harassing them.'

'Don't tell us how to do our jobs in South Africa. We don't need people like you here. You are a troublemaker. We can send you back to your own country.'

Lindi ducked under his arms. He didn't stop her, just looked at her with disgust and spat, 'Okay, go and fetch your money.'

He followed her out. She made a dash for the coach, which she was relieved to see was still there. Once inside she found her wallet and pulled out fifty rand, then another fifty. She decided to stay in her seat and beckoned the police officer to come on board the bus.

'Come out! You have to come out,' he shouted.

'I'm staying where I am. If you want the money you have to come and get it.'

Resistance at last. Only a gesture but it felt good all the same.

The officer turned around. The man in charge was back. He looked at the driver. 'You can go now.' As the coach pulled away, Lindi looked at the officer. He pointed at her and drew a finger across his neck.

Lindi was furious: she had become the centre of attention. The officer had made sure of that. It wasn't her fault. She told herself she hadn't had a choice. But now what? For all she knew her presence on the bus was being conveyed from one police post to the next. She had to get below the radar. She thought about calling Anton, but what could he do? She was on her own. There had been a time when the thought might have unsettled her, crippled her confidence. Not now, not any more.

First things first. Lindi decided to change her accommodation in Nelspruit. A private B&B outside the city was probably wisest. She pulled out her phone and turned it on. Glancing at her emails, she saw Anton had already been in contact – he had sent a web link to Radio 702. It was reporting that the violence was spreading, much of it in Mpumalanga Province. Hundreds of homes belonging to Mozambicans had been ransacked and their belongings burned. The plumes of smoke she'd seen twisting out of virtually every town they'd passed began to make sense.

Back in Johannesburg, the death toll at Ponte City was not conclusive but was rising. The report said the final count would almost certainly be in the dozens. Mozambicans had been asked to report to their local police to have their identity documents checked, 'for their own safety'. Huge queues had formed outside the stations. Anyone with connections to Mpumalanga Province or who had been there in the previous few days was pulled aside. Radio 702 quoted a number of Mozambicans saying the police had asked for money before releasing them. Anton's email had been characteristically robust: *If we don't make a breakthrough soon there won't be a conflict to resolve, just bodies to bury.*

15

Lindi went back inside her room at the Mirabel Guesthouse, careful not to let the insect screen slam shut. She needn't have worried. As far as she could tell there was no one else in the place. She'd been sitting on the stoep for about half an hour, catching the last of the sun as it floated down towards the serried ranks of citrus trees on the adjoining estate. Her room was unremarkable, apart from a solid stinkwood *riempie* bench, its rawhide thongs stretched and sagging. Lindi had been reluctant to put her bag on it when Mrs Venter, the landlady, had shown her to the room.

'Don't worry, it's carried a lot of heavier weights than that,' she'd said. 'It belonged to my great-grandfather. I'm told he used to sit on it most of the day, smoking his pipe, after they brought him back from Ceylon.'

Her voice had trailed away with those last few words, as if the incarceration of Boer prisoners of war on that Indian Ocean island was an injustice she could still feel.

Lindi saw her dress and underclothes on the floor. She thought the shower had cleansed her but she felt again the revulsion in her guts. She swallowed hard. She checked her rucksack, made sure the torch was working, topped up the half-empty bottle of water from the tap in the corner of the room and went into the kitchen. She'd declined the meal that was on offer and had asked, instead, for a light snack. Under a wire-mesh cloche she found several pieces of fried chicken, pumpkin fritters, a quadrangle of what looked like a custard pie and a saucer of honey – she found out later that it was a dip for the fritters. There wasn't a salad leaf in sight.

Even at the best of times, Lindi was a rather mechanical eater. She ate because she needed to rather than because she enjoyed it. Going out for a meal was about the company, the food a sideshow. Left on her own of an evening, as she often was back in London, she was happy with a tub of hummus, sticks of carrot or celery and a boiled egg. Now she ate a piece of chicken, which she enjoyed more than she expected, and a couple of the fritters, but left the tart untouched.

'Good homemade Afrikaner *melktert*,' Mrs Venter had said. Lindi made a mental note to come up with an excuse for not trying it.

She went outside to the stoep again and was glad of the jumper she had put on. Even here in the low-lying east of the country the evening temperature had dipped. The sun, which had now slipped below the horizon, still managed to illuminate the sky with its purple-orange after-burn but its power was spent. She sat on the cane sofa again, the cushions still moulded to her shape.

She had a few minutes before Father Petro de Freitas was due to pick her up. The Catholic bishop in Nelspruit, whom she had met earlier in the day, had introduced her to Father Petro.

'He's the man you should be talking to,' the bishop had said. 'They flock to his masses because he speaks Shangaan, their language.'

Father Petro had said he would take her to meet some migrant families.

Lindi shut her eyes. She felt she hadn't really dealt with the day's events, just reacted to them. And that wasn't enough: she couldn't sleep or rest easy until she had properly absorbed the day. Even as a child, when the Seatons were on a family holiday and Lindi and Ralph had had to share a room, it had annoyed her, the way Ralph would simply turn over in bed and fall asleep even after the most exciting of days. Harry would invariably find her wide-eyed and exasperated when he did his lights-out check, so he'd taught her a trick to deal with it.

'Shut your eyes, not tight-tight, just let them droop down, down.' She could hear his voice, deep and warm, as if it were yesterday. 'Now imagine a long, long, long train.' He would always repeat words, stretching them out so that they were at once sonorous and soporific. 'I think it's a steam train. See all those carriages it's pulling? Take everything that's happened today and put each one in a different carriage. In they go, one by one by one by one. When they're all in safely, tell the engine driver he can pull away. Now watch the train go.

Slowly, slowly, slowly. It's going, going. You can hardly see it now, just a little puff of smoke far away. It's going to go round that bend and into that tunnel. There goes the first carriage, then the next . . . and there's the last. It's gone, the sleep train is gone.'

Lindi employed a version of her father's trick now: a carriage for each segment of a day that had begun in the dawn calm of Greenside and the journey here to Mpumalanga.

Paulo Simbini had refused to come back to sit with her after the coach had pulled out of Middleburg. And who could blame him? His picture, with the body lying prone at the bottom of a burning Ponte City, was still in her notebook, a rebuke to her it'll-be-all-right-in-the-morning reassurances.

Unlike those frenetic childhood nights when the whole point of the exercise was to fold away the day and see it disappearing, she realised she didn't want to forget this one. Every part of it, from the cussed early-morning taxi driver who'd taken her to Park station, the casual prejudice she'd encountered there, the terror of Middleburg, even the assault, all of it helped to form a graphic reassurance that she was right to be here. It was the difference between understanding an injustice on paper and feeling it in your bones.

Lindi had come to South Africa because Anton had wanted her to, but she would stay because she – not just Anton – thought it was the right thing to do. The equivocation, the weighing up of competing arguments, the things that had always made her the careful but dependable one seemed to have gone. She noticed the change in herself in an almost physical way. For once she had been forced to rely on instinct and she'd found the experience liberating. She imagined it was like being high on some drug. She was free – free of herself. She felt good about herself, and wondered if she'd ever really known the feeling before.

She saw a car turn off the main road. Its lights caught the trees and cast shadows on the walls of the stoep. As it dipped and swerved to avoid the ruts in the gravelled lane, the shadows came together, then drifted apart, like dancers at a ball. A man got out of the vehicle. At first she didn't recognise Father Petro without his cassock.

'You've come in disguise, I see,' she said, walking up to him.

'Like they say, God works in mysterious ways. Did you get some rest? You've had a hell of a day.'

'I had a bit of a nap out here a while ago. Actually, I feel pretty good.' Lindi smiled, climbing into the passenger seat as Father Petro got back into the car. Inside it smelt of fuel. 'I'm no mechanic but do you have a leak?'

'A leak? Ah, no, that's just some spare gas I've got in the boot. Apparently none of the tankers got through today. Do you mind if I smoke?'

Lindi was about to say that might not be such a good idea but decided against it. In any case, by the look of the ashtray the question was purely rhetorical. 'So what's the plan, Father Petro?'

'Oh, just call me Petro. Everybody else does, except the bishop. He's a bit old-school – is that how you say it?'

'I'd say that just about sums him up, yes. I didn't like the way he started off this afternoon by asking why they had sent a woman to do a man's work.'

'I think he feels you may not be ready for this.'

She shrugged. 'Well, I am so let's go. And, anyway, what do you mean "ready for this"? What's the "this"? That's what I want to know.'

Father Petro steered the car with his left knee, nudging the wheel this way and that, while he used both hands to shield the lighted match. He barely checked the main road before he turned left, back towards Nelspruit.

'Lindi, I don't have the answer you're looking for. But I know these people. I have faith in them and when they tell me that it's impossible Lesedi was killed by one of them, I believe them,' he said, the cigarette flicking up and down between his lips as if it had a life of its own.

'But there must be tens of thousands of Mozambican farm labourers here, many of them illegal. You can't vouch for all of them.'

'No, I can't. That is true. But look at it this way,' he said, as he swung the car out into the middle of the road to overtake a tractor pulling a trailer loaded with sugarcane stalks but only just avoiding a vehicle coming the other way. 'Bit late for them to be carrying the cane around. Now what was I saying?'

'You were about to say why you believe what the Mozambicans have been telling you.' Just before you tried to kill both of us.

'Ah, yes. I was coming to that. Look, there are two issues here. First, the anger about land being sold to foreigners. That is a real problem and it's done over the heads of local people. But it doesn't affect the Mozambicans. The new owners are going to need labourers, and these people will work for almost nothing. They are the poorest of the poor.'

'That's just what a friend of mine told me,' Lindi said, recalling her conversation with Kagiso outside Regina Mundi.

'Well, your friend is right.'

Father Petro fingered the breast pocket of his shirt and found another cigarette.

'Do you want me to light it for you?'

'Thank you.' He took a sideways glance at her, smiling. 'I think you're frightened I'm going to crash the car, my sister.'

'Oh, I wonder why you'd think that,' replied Lindi, tartly.

'Don't worry, we're doing God's work. Nothing can happen to us.'

'You said there were two issues. What's the second?'

'Did I say that? Two issues? Let me see.'

Lindi wondered how frustrating it would be if his sermons were anything like this.

'Yes, I have it. The second issue is this Lesedi fellow. He was not greedy like his father. People here know that. On the day he died he was here in Mpumalanga, apparently to listen to people. So why would they kill him?'

'Yes, I heard he visited a charity on the day he was killed. Soil of Africa. Do you know it?'

'Yes, I know it well. It's run by an interesting fellow. He used to work in government and then he switched sides.'

'Kagiso Rapabane. He's the guy I was just talking about.'

'I see you have done your homework, sister. Yes, I know Rapabane. We have done some work together on this land business. He's a good man, a brave man to take on the government like that. He's made some enemies.'

'Enemies?'

'The people who are making millions out of these deals. You see, when I say something, they just call me a foolish priest. But Rapabane, well, that's different.'

'In what way different?'

'People listen to him because they know he used to work for government. And the guys in Pretoria don't like that. They think of him like Judas – he's a traitor.'

'Do you think he's in danger?'

'Rapabane? Some people kill for ideology, some for religion. With these people it's money.'

'Have you told him?'

'I tell him I pray for him.' The intensity of her questioning prompted him to ask how she knew Kagiso.

'Oh, our families go back a long way.'

'How so?'

'His mother was our house-worker. It sounds cringe-making but really they were more like family.'

'Cringe what? I don't know this word.'

'It just means I'm embarrassed to say it now.'

'Sister, you don't have to be embarrassed. In those days, that was the only relationship a white person could have with a black one. If you were kind to Rapabane's mother, you were doing something that did not even occur to many white people in this country. Well, here we are, the bright lights of Nelspruit.'

They drove past the coach park and Lindi remembered that that was the last time she'd seen Paulo, his mother and sister. The boy had waved to her tentatively. Where was he tonight? In whose bed was he sleeping? Would he ever, as she had glibly promised him, see his Johannesburg home again?

'Wait here and I will find the man who is going to help us.'

Lindi watched Father Petro walk across the car park towards Laeveld Plaza, then along a row of shop fronts. She noticed for the first time that he had a limp. Most of the businesses were closed for the day. Father Petro went into Raja Wholesalers, one of the few that were still open. Lindi got out of the car and looked around to see where the music was coming from. A single speaker, the size of a packing chest, stood guard outside Music Warehouse, just behind their car. The volume had been set to rise above a car park full of shoppers; now the distorted decibels cracked the air. Under a sign saying 'Now Playing' she saw the CD cover artwork for *Rev Vusi Gama and the Zion Messengers*. Lindi looked back towards Raja Wholesalers. No sign of Father Petro. She went into the music shop.

'Howzit?' Lindi had picked up South Africa's universal greeting.

'Ah, it's okay,' said the youth behind the counter.

'It's very quiet.'

'Everybody has gone home. They are worried about what's happening.'

'And what's that?'

'You're not from here?'

'No, I'm just travelling.'

He scratched the side of his nose. 'Then you have to be careful. There are some thugs around here. They are looking for Mozambicans.'

Lindi knew the script. She didn't need another run-through. 'Where are they?'

'Which ones?'

'The Mozambicans.'

'They have left their homes because these *tsotsis* destroyed some of them.'

She nodded. 'And what about the police? Haven't they tried to stop it?'

The young man chuckled.

'What's so funny?'

'You don't know our police, ma'am. They are too lazy. They don't care because people don't like the Mozambicans. They say they are taking all the jobs. This afternoon the police were laughing with the thugs. Just here in front of the shop.'

'So where are the Mozambicans?'

'They are going back to their country. Many of them are there in the church.'

Lindi saw Father Petro come out of Raja Wholesalers. 'Okay, good evening. I'm going to meet my friend.'

'That man, the priest? Father Petro?'

161

'You know him?'

'Everybody knows him. He's a nice man but . . .'

'But what?'

'Ah, no, it's nothing.'

'What were you going to say?'

'No, I mean he's a good man but he likes these Mozambicans.'

'That's what a priest is supposed to do, isn't it? Look after people when they are in need,' Lindi said.

'You're right, ma'am. But that's why the police and the *tsotsis* don't like him. He is protecting them. The church where they are staying, it's his church.'

'Is that right? Well, I'd better get going.'

'Good evening, ma'am.'

Lindi walked across the car park. She met Father Petro in the middle. 'You didn't tell me you had Mozambican families in your church.'

'So you've caught me, eh?' He was smiling.

Lindi marvelled at his equanimity. So this is what faith is about, she thought. Lindi was not religious, but in Father Petro's presence she could begin to see how liberating it must be to hand your fate over to someone or something else. 'Couldn't we just talk to some of the people in your church?' she asked.

'I thought about that but I'm not sure it's a good idea. The police are hanging around outside the gate and always asking questions.' He still had a broad grin across his face. 'I'm afraid nobody has told those stupid fellows the story of the shepherd and his flock.'

'The chap in the shop said the police don't like you.'

'He said that? Well . . . how do you say it? I'm not on their Christmas card list but we get along fine. We understand each other.'

'So why are they hanging around outside your church?'

'They want to go in there and start scaring people, asking their stupid questions. They think I'm hiding someone. Lindi, I'm a fool but not so much, eh?' He nudged her.

'But from what I've seen today, if they really wanted to go in, a church gate or whatever isn't going to stop them, is it?'

Lindi noticed a vehicle turn into the car park. Its lights were set on full beam. It swung round and started coming towards them at no more than walking pace. They were lit up, like actors on a stage. Father Petro turned but stood his ground. Lindi reached out to him.

'Don't worry, let me talk to these fools,' he said.

The white *bakkie* swerved just a couple of metres away and pulled up beside them. The driver wound down his window. 'So you have a new friend, Father.' The man still had his sunglasses on.

'You know me, Officer, always happy to help strangers.'

The driver turned his head towards Lindi, though she couldn't really tell whether or not he was looking at her.

'You must tell your new friend to have a nice time in our province and stay away from these Mozambican rubbish people. It's not her business.' He started winding the window up again but stopped when it was two-thirds of the way. 'And, Father, you also must be careful. There are a lot of *tsotsis* around tonight.'

The *bakkie* pulled away.

'If he was trying to frighten me, he succeeded,' said Lindi. 'That was sinister.'

'Don't mind them,' Father Petro said. He put a hand on Lindi's shoulder. 'They can't harm you. You have your British passport, the best insurance policy.'

'And what about you, Petro? What do you have?'

'Ah! That's a good question, my sister. I have nothing that I can show you but I have my belief – my belief that everyone has some good in them. Even those bastards! Jesus, forgive me.'

He lit a cigarette, sucked deeply, and held his breath, savouring its gift of herbal relief.

'Those guys hate because they don't know love, not real love. And the Mozambicans, they think they have lost everything, but nobody is telling them they have kept the most important thing. Their dignity.'

He let the smoke drift out, now bereft of its potency. 'You think I am stupid, yes?'

'No, Father, I don't. I think secretly I might even admire your faith.' And Lindi wondered why she had just called him plain 'Father' for the first time. It struck her that Father Petro de Freitas's faith was just about the most certain thing she had encountered in the last forty-eight hours of flux.

Her adult life had been built on those things you could measure, on goals and outcomes, on research and evidence, on argument and persuasion. They were tools good enough to describe what was happening, a prop to justify a decision, but none of it could help her give it any meaning. Lindi leaned over and kissed his cheek. 'You're a good man, Petro,' she said.

'And, you see, I get the girls too!' He laughed.

'Now don't be cheeky or I'll have to take it back. Petro, you ought to know something before we go any further. I think all that was meant for me. I'm pretty sure I'm being followed – they seem to have had their eyes on me from the moment I arrived in SA. Ever since I got here I've been warned about meddling. And today at the Nelspruit checkpoint I was given a hard time. It wasn't random.'

Father Petro's seemingly perpetual smile was gone. 'Is there something you are not telling me, sister?'

'I don't want to make your life any more complicated than it already is.'

'Oh, don't worry about me. I'm used to complicated. What else can it be when you stand in the middle, God on one side and his flawed people on the other, eh? Have you told me everything about your mission here?'

'Well, as much as I can. I don't mean I'm hiding anything, I just don't know much.'

'Your organisation, South what-what, is it linked to these people doing the sabotage?'

'Absolutely not! But I do want to find them, find someone who represents them. I'm a bit like you. I'm in the middle too. That's what we do, try to get two sides talking to each other.'

'So maybe that's their plan. They are hoping you will lead them to these people. You must be careful. Whoever you meet will be added to the list of suspects.'

'Where does that leave you?'

'Me? I'm already a suspect. They don't understand me. I talk to everyone, no matter who they are – you know, the good, the bad, the ugly, I talk to them all. But, for sure, we must be careful, you and I. Do they know where you are staying?'

'I don't think so. I had a reservation at a hotel but I didn't show up. I took a taxi to Mirabel's.'

'But they know you are with me.'

'So what happens now?'

'Well, we were supposed to meet someone at Raja's, someone who says he'd heard rumours about what happened to Lesedi, but when the man came apparently the police were at the shop.'

'Looking for him?'

'No, they are not that clever. I asked Patel, he's the manager there, to deliver some mealie-meal to the church this morning and they saw his van at our compound so they came round this evening, asking him why he was helping the Mozambicans. Now Patel has got nervous. He has to keep the local officials sweet or they make life difficult for him.'

'Damn! Is there any other way we can reach this guy? I'm not here to play detective, but the more I know about who's doing what to whom, the better.'

'According to Patel, this man, he used to work for the family at a business they have in Malelane and apparently he saw something or heard something on the day that Motlantshe's boy was killed.'

'Did Patel say what he'd seen? His employee, I mean.'

'No. He sounded pretty vague. Just something about a couple of strange faces in town, a car he didn't recognise. These are small places – everyone knows everyone.'

'Do you know where he is now?'

'Patel told me he's gone back to Malelane. I have his number and I spoke to him from the shop. I don't want to use my phone till I get there. These idiots are not so organised, but why take chances?'

Lindi looked at her watch. It was still only seven thirty but the deserted streets made it feel much later. Back in London, people were only just getting home from a day at work. 'It's not too late. How far is Malelane? Couldn't we go there?'

'Well, I was thinking about it. It's fifty, maybe sixty klicks from here. About an hour's drive.'

'If we set off now . . .'

'I don't think that's a good idea, especially after those jokers turning up just now. I think we need to be separate. Anyway, if we turn up together it might – how do you say it? – freak this guy out. He's nervous enough already. If I can persuade him, I'll bring him back and we can meet very early tomorrow somewhere around here. If not, I'll find out what he knows.'

'I'd rather come with you.'

'I understand. But this way is better. Let me speak to Patel. We need to get you back to your guesthouse quietly.'

They walked over to Raja's Wholesalers. Sanjit Patel, dressed in a pair of dark blue, sharply pressed trousers and a light blue shirt with a button-down collar, saw them coming and started walking to meet them outside the shop. He was on his phone. He shook hands with Lindi while still talking. They listened in to one side of the conversation.

'Okay, chief. No problem. I'll send someone around now, now . . . Eh? . . . Of course, man. Only the best for you . . . No, don't worry. That's what friends are for . . . Okay, chief. I'll see you soon.'

'Let me guess, that was Morotse,' Father Petro said, then, turning to Lindi, 'He runs the premier's office here. Hey, I forgot. This is Lindi Seaton from London, this is Sanjit Patel. He is . . . the mover and shaker of Nelspruit.'

'So pleased to meet you.' He held out his hand again. 'Father Petro is teasing me all of the time.'

'Patel, you have your car?'

'It's behind the shop.'

'Good, good. Listen, I've got a couple of things to do and sister here will be on her own. How about you take her home, give her some of Mrs Patel's famous biryani? I'll call by later.'

'Sure, sure, it will be my pleasure.' He turned towards the counter at the back of the shop. 'Jacob! Call madam, tell her I'm bringing a guest home. Jacob! Where the hell is that fellow? Hold on, I'm coming just now.'

'What's going on?' Lindi half whispered, as Patel walked away.

'Everything is fine. I'm just being careful. Those chaps may be hanging around. If I take you to the guesthouse they might follow us. You go to Patel's, stay there for a couple of hours. Our friends will get bored – they'll be getting drunk somewhere by then. I'll pick you up later. If I'm going to be late I'll phone and Patel can take you home.'

166

Father Petro looked at Lindi and saw the doubt in her face. 'Sister, you don't like my plan?'

'It's not that. Why didn't you tell him where you're going? You obviously don't trust him.'

Father Petro made a face and tapped his nose. 'How do you say it? Need-to-know basis?' He laughed.

'I think I'm about to have a sense of humour failure.'

'What?'

'Never mind. What about Patel? He must know what you're up to.'

'He thinks I'm just going back to my flock in the church. I didn't tell him anything about going to Malelane.'

'You're sure about him?'

'He's okay . . . I think he's okay. He's a good man but he's in a bad place so he doesn't like to take sides. So we are not going to test him. He will show you off to his wife, you have a nice dinner and then we start again in the morning.'

Sanjit Patel came back. 'My wife is very much looking forward to seeing you, Ms Seaton.'

'Okay, my friends, I'd better get going. Now, Patel, you take care of our guest.'

They watched Father Petro de Freitas drive out of the car park.

'My car is in the back, Ms Seaton. Give me a couple of minutes. Let me just lock up and I'll be with you.'

Lindi heard him as she walked out to the back of the shop. The suave soft-spoken elegance was gone. He was barking out instructions to the workers who were still in the shop. One came to the delivery bay, opened a steel box fitted to the wall and turned a switch inside it. It unfurled the steel shutters, which came down sedately, except for the occasional jerk, like a mechanical hiccup. Just before it fell below her eyeline, Lindi saw Patel make another call on his mobile phone. A couple of minutes later he came out with the staff. One pulled down the final shutter manually. He locked that too and gave the keys to Patel.

'Good night, sir,' they said in unison.

'Six o'clock sharp-sharp,' he said. He didn't return their farewell. He turned to Lindi. 'Okay, Ms Seaton, we're ready.'

He opened the passenger door and Lindi sat down, cosseted in supple leather. Patel got in on the driver's side. He turned on the ignition and they glided away. 'Can I offer you a drink?' he asked. 'There's a hotel on the way back to my house.'

'No, thanks. I'm really looking forward to meeting your wife – and her famous biryani.'

'So how do you know Father Petro?'

'Oh, we just met this afternoon. I was visiting the bishop.'

'You work for the Church, Ms Seaton?'

Lindi thought about asking him to be less formal, but decided to leave things as they were. 'No, I work for an organisation in London. It's called South Trust.'

'I'm sorry, I've not heard of that one. Of course we know about the UN and Save the Children . . .'

'Well, we're very different. We don't go around giving food or money.'

'Oh, very good, very good,' he said. 'So you're interested in the Mozambicans.'

'Actually, I'm interested in what led to the situation with the Mozambicans.'

'I don't follow. You mean Lesedi Motlantshe's murder?' he asked.

'Well, not even that, really. Though I suppose the murder may be a part of it . . .'

'Part of what?'

'The reason I'm here is to find out what's going on with all this selling of land.'

'Oh, that is very straightforward. There is nothing to find out. Everybody knows what's going on.'

'If everybody knows, why doesn't anyone try to stop it?'

'Look, Ms Seaton, I don't think you know Africa like I know it. My family has been doing business here for generations. My great-grand-father started off in Tanzania. Then one of his sons went to the Congo, another to Kenya and so on. Now I am here. Everywhere we have been it is the same.'

'The same in what way exactly?'

'The big people just look after themselves. Always. That is what is happening here. It is no different,' he said.

'South Africa is not exactly Congo.'

'You're right. There is more money to steal here.'

'That's a bit harsh!'

He shook his head. 'People saw what Mandela did when he was around and they say South Africa will be different. But they forget that before Mandela there were other good men in Africa. Nkrumah, Kenyatta, Nyerere. They all started off with wonderful words and ideas but it was the people around them. Look what happened to their countries.'

Patel pulled up outside a walled compound and pressed the horn. Ancient eyes looked through a grille in the metal gate before it began to roll away along a track in the ground. The man, wrapped up in several layers of clothing, raised his arm in a desultory salute. Patel ignored him.

Patel continued. 'South Africa is the same. Hundreds of years ago African chiefs were selling their own people to the slavers. Now they are selling the land.'

A couple of Alsatians came bounding up to the car. Patel ignored them, too. He didn't get out.

'And where do you come in, Mr Patel? You just watch it all happen.'

'I make my money. I pay my staff. The rest, I send it out. What more must I do?'

'You don't ask any questions?'

'Why should I? I know the answer already. This is Africa.'

'But how does sitting back and watching Motlantshe come here, buy up the land and sell it off to foreigners help?'

'You think this is Motlantshe? You think he can do all these deals on his own and just keep the money to himself?' Patel turned the engine off. 'Ms Seaton, you need to know this whole stinking business goes all the way to the top. Those chaps in Pretoria are getting their cut. Motlantshe is just the deal-maker, the man in the middle.'

'But the figures are all published.'

'Oh, yes, they publish the figures they want you to see. The government got all these farms around here for nothing. Why didn't the farmers shout and scream, eh?'

'You tell me.'

'Because our friend Motlantshe went round afterwards and paid them off.'

'What's in it for Motlantshe?'

'The land is not sold outright to the foreign players. It is kept in a holding company, fifty-fifty. Motlantshe gets fifty, the foreigners get fifty.'

'How do you know all this?' Lindi probed.

'Because I make it my business to know. That is how we Indians have survived in Africa. When the money starts rolling in, Motlantshe gives the big boys their share and everyone is happy.'

'Except the people who get thrown off the land they've lived on for generations.'

Patel got out of the car and walked around to Lindi's side. She had already opened the door but Patel held it for her. 'Look, Ms Seaton, I know you don't like people like me. But I deal with Africa as it is, not Africa as it should be. You think I like to send a case of Johnnie Walker to that bastard tonight? But if I don't, what happens? They find some problem with my papers and then I pay even more. It is okay for Father Petro. He is always talking to God, but I am dealing with men.'

They walked up the few steps to the front door, which opened as they approached. Aadashini Patel had been waiting for them. She pressed her palms together and raised them.

'This is my wife,' Patel introduced them. 'Ms Seaton is visiting for a few days.'

'I'm sorry to barge in on you like this. And I've come empty-handed, too.'

It was a pleasant enough evening, all the more so given the culinary efforts of a dutiful wife for whom providing a family meal was a defining role. Lindi felt a sense of solidarity with the woman, a need to make a show of her appreciation, something, she sensed, which was lacking in the Patel household. She asked for recipes she knew she would never try out and Aardashini obliged with enthusiasm and in painstaking detail. But all the while Lindi had her eye on the clock and her mind on the job. There came a point when she could no longer keep up the charade of ardent interest in the finer points of Indian cuisine.

'I wonder what's keeping Father Petro,' she said, affecting as nonchalant a manner as she could muster.

'Let's see, what's the time?' replied Patel. 'Oh, yes, nine forty-five. Father Petro never stops but it is late even for him. Let me call him.' There was no answer. He gave it another fifteen minutes before trying again. It went straight to voicemail. Lindi felt the need to take charge before there were any questions about exactly what he could be doing.

'Listen, he did say to me that he was tired, and if it got too late he would just see me in the morning. I'm really sorry, but could you give me another lift?'

'Of course, no problem at all. We could go by the church and see what he's up to. It's only a little bit out of the way.'

'No need for that. To be honest, I'm shattered. I was up at five this morning. I just need my bed.'

When they pulled up outside the Mirabel Guesthouse, Patel came round to Lindi's side of the car.

'Look, what we were talking about before in the car, you know, about the corruption and so on. Please understand, I care about this country. I do what I can, but if you don't play the game their way you're finished. End of story.'

'I understand. I'm sorry if I sounded like I was judging you.'

'Good night, Ms Seaton.' Patel got back into his car. 'And you be careful. This is not a game they're playing here.'

Lindi woke up with a start. Her phone was ringing. She grabbed at it but dropped it on the floor. It landed screen side up. Two thirty in the morning.

She picked it up and pressed the green button. She recognised Patel's voice straight away.

'Ms Seaton, I am afraid I have some bad news. Father Petro has been in a car crash. It's bad, very bad.'

16

Kagiso arrived in Nelspruit at 4 a.m., having taken the overnight train from Johannesburg. He was glad he'd spent the previous day, the day of Lesedi's funeral, with his mother.

Nelspruit was the nearest mainline station to Malelane, Soil of Africa's home. Kagiso had done the journey many times before and knew he'd have to wait no more than an hour or so before the first taxis to Malelane started plying the route.

Nelspruit station resembled a vast covered dormitory. Every wall and pillar had someone slumped against it; bags and blankets were strewn over every available patch of floor space, in front of shop windows, under staircases, even the approaches to the toilets.

In one corner the Red Cross had set up a stand. He noticed a message board with dozens of photos pinned to it – people who had become separated from their families, many of them children.

He walked out of the station and started along Voortrekker Street towards the city. He was heading for Mama K's. It was the last café to close at night and the first to open in the morning. Kagiso rented a room in a property owned by the eponymous Mama K – Khethiwe Shabangu – in Malelane. The pain of parting with his money when he went to see her to pay the rent was always eased by the ample meal he got in return. Ma Khethiwe was as generous as she was well proportioned. She was large, buxom, sensual, the kind only Africa produces: women who have no desire to hide what they see as nature's gift. If Ma Khethiwe was there, he knew he'd be set up for the day. He was in luck.

'You are working too hard, child,' she said, putting down a plate with two thick slabs of airy white bread, covered with margarine and jam. 'These other fellows,' she was pointing at two uniformed men slumped at an adjacent table, 'they are security guards, they working all night. But you, you supposed to be resting before you go to the office.' She'd already stirred three heaped spoons of sugar into the milky tea (out there in the sticks, anything less and you might be accused of mimicking 'white' habits). Kagiso leaned back on the plastic chair, which gave way disconcertingly till his head rested on the wall behind. He shut his eyes.

He had spent much of the train journey awake (sleep was impossible in 'sitter class'), turning over the events of the previous forty-eight hours and trying to quell his anxiety. No, not anxiety: fear. That was what it was. It wasn't fear for his personal safety, though he did worry about that too, but something bigger, more amorphous and sinister. He was frightened by the magnitude of what was unfolding all around him, and knowing that he was at the centre of it, even if he'd never intended it to be that way.

There it was, the seed of his discombobulation. Till the Hillbrow meeting, Kagiso had been able to make a distinction between his two lives. It was the only way he could make it work. How could the man from Soil of Africa ask a farmer to walk the road of reconciliation and shared endeavour if that other man, the one who plotted and planned, was also at the table? He now understood the conflict. In his heart Kagiso liked being the former and hated having to be the latter.

He remembered the time when he had helped to organise an end of harvest *braai*, South Africa's version of a barbecue, on a farm right on the border with Mozambique. It was the first year of a profit-sharing scheme that Kagiso had helped put together. The area had been blessed with good rains and a bountiful crop. That evening, as a blood-orange sky had turned purple, as shadows grew longer and fainter till they just seeped away into the soil, one of the migrant workers had brought out his *mbira*, a traditional hand-held musical instrument, a finger piano, as some called it.

Kagiso had sat on the edge of the group, entranced by this vision of a different future. The farmer and his wife, Afrikaners both, sat near the fire. On the other side of the circle their children huddled next to the housemaid and some of the workers' children. An old man, rheumy eyes staring into the embers, pulled at a *zol*, a home-made cigarette spiced with the comforting fragrance of *dagga*. Women spread polyester blankets over their bare legs and young men shared the last few bottles of beer. Calloused thumbs plucked at the metal tines of the *mbira*, shaped like the flat handles of tablespoons, and picked out a tune that had been written in another century in the great language of the coast, Swahili. Nobody understood the words but all were moved by the ballad, the lament of a young suitor who knows he will not wed his angel, his *malaika*, for want of good fortune. Kagiso had looked across at the farmer and was sure he'd seen the man's eyes well up with a tenderness so far removed from the caricature of his people. The morning, he knew, would expose again the starkness of his country's struggle to find a middle ground between great wealth and great poverty but, for that evening, under that deep and star-studded African sky, Kagiso let himself dream, yes, dream, of another country, one in which hope triumphed over despair and idealism scored a victory over cynicism.

Now the man who believed in idealism and persuasion was about to be eclipsed by the saboteur, who resorted to the insidious power to destroy. It was the unsettling effect of being defined by your least attractive feature.

And what about the others? Kagiso remembered how often they had talked about what to do if there was a danger of discovery, about how they would continue to be able to get messages to each other, how they could carry on their work. They'd discussed the mechanics of clandestine activity but, he realised now, it had never occurred to them to ask each other how they might *feel*. None of them had any idea of how the others might react.

What if one of them was pulled in? The trust that comes with friendship, the certainty of a shared enterprise, they had taken for granted. But now, separated and alone, each of them had to find his or her own reason for staying true. Stripped of the borrowed purpose of the Collective, each would be left to discover whether what drove them was conviction or something less, just a good idea at the time.

François, still the white boy eager to prove he deserved to be a part of this new South Africa. He wasn't really fighting for the future, he was fighting against his past. Kagiso tried to envisage François again, but now imagining him without the balm of friendship, which soothes out the blemishes and deficiencies of character. What was he, really? What did he represent? Maybe he was just another of those privileged liberals who fight other people's battles comfortable in the knowledge that their own position is secure, the ones who are unable, or unwilling, to understand that the favoured status bestowed on them at birth might be part of the problem.

Two-Boy, restless, bored, looking for something that might replace the tedium of a career and the stupor of his battle with the bottle. He hadn't been searching for the Land Collective, he'd needed a diversion, something to replace the previous thing that had excited his interest. He'd found Sharmi. He'd followed her.

So it all came back to Sharmi again. Two-Boy wasn't the only one who'd been drawn to her, enticed by the sheer, gravitational force of her personality. It had happened to Kagiso, though he'd resented it at the time. Her conviction had seemed like a rebuke, a judgement. Even then, before the Land Collective, Sharmi had known you had to take sides. She understood that theirs was a country still divided between rich and poor, white and black, and that she was not going to stand in the middle. She wanted victory; compromise was like coming second. He'd been close to her, and it had left him feeling exposed.

Kagiso realised he'd never confided in any of them, or they in him. What had looked like intimacy was nothing of the sort. In fact, all the arguing and debating was a substitute for intimacy. Like a loveless couple, who fear the hidden threat of silence and inactivity, they had kept themselves busy. So long as there was another target to identify there was no time to tell François that he would respect him whether he was a co-conspirator or not. So long as there was another message to intercept, there was no need to help find something else to excite Two-Boy's brilliant but delinquent mind. And so long as they had the next mission to consider, there was no time to tell Sharmi he'd like to revisit their past, to make sense of it.

His phone rang. With some relief he saw it wasn't one of the others on the back-up number. Kagiso looked at his watch. Still only five thirty in the morning. He answered the call. It was a colleague from Soil of Africa.

'Howzit, Stride? What's up, man?'

'Ah, no, I was just wondering if you're back today.'

'Come on, Stride! It's five thirty and you calling me for that?'

'Sorry. I couldn't sleep. So you still in Jozie?'

'Yeah. I'll probably stick around for the day and get back tomorrow.'

'Okay. Call when you get here. Sorry to wake you up, man.'

'That's okay. See you.'

The lie was instinctive. In the time he'd worked in Malelane he couldn't remember a single occasion when anyone at Soil of Africa had called him to check on his whereabouts.

The sound of morning talk radio coming alive through the speaker hanging on a nail in the wall behind him startled Kagiso.

Mama Khethiwe called to him: 'Is it too loud for you? The news is coming.'

'No, it's fine. I was just thinking of something,' he said.

'I been watching you, child. Since you came in you been thinking. What you got to be thinking so hard for?'

'Ah, no, it's nothing important.'

'You got woman trouble? That or money, they the only two things get men worrying.'

'No woman, no trouble,' Kagiso said. 'Just like Bob Marley.'

'Like who?'

'The singer Bob Marley, he actually said . . . It's nothing . . .'

'Then it's the money. You lose your job or what?'

'I've still got my job. I'm just tired.'

Kagiso looked at his watch. Nearly six o'clock. RiseFM's signature tune came through the loudspeaker.

'Good morning, *sawubona, goeie more*! Wherever you are, whatever you speak, welcome to RiseFM, the rhythm of Mpumalanga! I'm Jonny . . . and I'm Patricia. Hey! We're cooking up a great breakfast show for you . . . But first let's get the latest news from Celi Dube. What have you got, Celi?'

'Hi, guys. Well, there's really only one story – and it's the one that's been dominating the airwaves since last week. Mpumalanga's police chief says they are getting closer all the time to finding the man who killed Lesedi Motlantshe. Lieutenant General Jackson Sibande told a packed news conference at his Nelspruit headquarters last night that it's only a matter of time before they find their man. Sibande told journalists that detectives believe an underground network of terrorists was responsible for what he called the cold-blooded and cowardly killing. He said they're just a step away from catching the ring-leader.'

'Did the police chief say where they are looking?'

'No, Jonny. All he would say is that their man is somewhere between Jo'burg and Mpumalanga. He's on the run and dangerous. Those are the words he used.'

'Hey, Celi. Does this ring-leader have a name? Are we going to see an e-fit?'

'That's just the question we asked the big boss, Patricia. Lieutenant General Sibande says they know their man and they'll release more details soon, probably in the next couple of days. One other thing, guys. The police chief said they're working on the theory that this gang might be getting some outside help.'

There were a couple of other news items. The local energy company was threatening to cut off supply to a township where half the residents had failed to pay their bills, and Mpumalanga's recently crowned beauty queen had left her husband for the businessman who had sponsored the pageant.

'Tch, tch. She is a foolish woman,' Mama Khethiwe said, turning the volume down again. 'That man is going to get tired of her and throw her out. Then she will be begging her man to come back. So these killers are underground, eh?'

Kagiso marvelled at the way she switched seamlessly from the mundane to the momentous. 'That's what they say. Do you believe them?'

'Ah, I don't know, child, but it is like the old days, before you were born. The police they were always saying underground this and underground that.'

'But they were the good guys. Mandela, Slovo and Maharaj, they were the freedom-fighters.'

'So you know your history, eh, Kagiso? But these people who did this thing to the Motlantshe boy, they are just thugs.'

'You are right but . . .' Kagiso's phone rang again.

'Eh! You big man now! Getting calls this time of the day.'

Kagiso looked at the screen. 'It's only my mother,' he said. 'Mama, you calling early-early.'

'Leave the mama. What are you doing?'

Kagiso could tell his mother was either concerned or angry, probably both. 'Is everything okay?'

'Everything is not okay,' Maude said. 'Some men were here just now. They say they from the police.'

'Where are they?'

'They just gone now-now. I just closed the door. Are you in trouble?'

'No, no, I'm not in trouble.' Kagiso saw Mama Khethiwe glance at him. He turned away from the counter and tried to speak more quietly. 'What did they want? Did they say?'

'This line is very bad.'

Kagiso had to raise his voice again. 'I said what did they want, the police?'

'They said they want to talk to you. Mfana, please tell your mother what is happening.'

'Nothing is happening, Mama. Lesedi Motlantshe was at our office the day he died. So the police are just checking. I've spoken to them already . . .'

'Why didn't you tell your mother about this?'

'Because there is nothing to tell. It's just routine.'

'Just what?'

'Routine. They have to check everything. Look, I'm going to call them. I'm sorry they have worried you. Let me sort this thing out. Okay. Bye.'

Kagiso turned around and caught Mama Khethiwe's eye. He could see there would be questions. But he needed to think first. He started walking towards the door. 'I'll be back,' he said, looking towards the counter. 'I'm just going to make some calls.'

'Why you want to stand in the road for? Go to my room in the back here.'

Khethiwe Shabangu pointed to a door at the side of the café. Kagiso hesitated.

'It's okay,' Khethiwe said, conveying with an almost imperceptible nod a sense of complicity.

For Kagiso, a man habitually inclined to the solitary and for so long forced to be secretive, this invitation to trust from someone with whom he had an amicable, but hardly intimate, relationship seemed more like a test than a decision. He stood in the doorway. What had been a deserted street just a couple of hours previously, when he'd left the station, was now beginning its daily transformation into what it was designed for: a place to buy and sell. Across the road, a delivery van branded with the unmistakable and ubiquitous red and white colours of Coca-Cola, came into view, its cargo of bottles tinkling against each other, like a glass symphony. The first office workers were appearing, the ones who turned on the air-con and loaded the photocopier paper trays, so that others could get straight down to the business of making someone else rich. Kagiso turned back into Mama K's and headed for the side door.

'It's quiet there,' Mama Khethiwe said.

His eyes had barely adjusted to the windowless room when his phone rang again. He checked the number. It was Elizabeth 'Sissy' Masango, Mama Khethiwe's niece, with whom he shared the bungalow in Malelane.

'Sissy, what's up? It's so early.'

'I wanted to call you before but I couldn't.'

'What do you mean? Is anything wrong?'

'Kagiso, I'm frightened. Some men came to the house. They went everywhere – they're looking for you.'

'Are you there now?'

'No, one of them is still there. I told him I must go to the shop. Kagiso, you must come back and tell them to stop all this. I don't know what is happening. What have you—'

'Stop! Just wait.' Kagiso was as firm as he could be without shouting. 'Look, Sissy, you know me, I have not done anything wrong. You have to trust me. I'm going to sort this mess out and I'm going to come back, but first you have to do something for me.'

'You have to tell them to go, I want them out of the—'

'Listen – listen to me. First, do they know you are calling me?'

'No. That's why I came out of the house.'

'So where are you?'

'I'm at the church.' Sissy Misango was a fervent and regular member of the Mountain of Fire and Miracles Church. It was where she'd got the extra chairs on the day Lesedi had visited Soil of Africa. You could see the church from the Soil of Africa office.

'I want you to go over to my office and ask Tobias – you know Tobias, the night watchman – ask him if anything has happened there.'

'I'm not going there. The police are there.'

'What? Now?'

'Yes, many of them, and their cars.'

'What are they doing?'

'They are talking to people from your office.'

'Do you recognise any of them?'

'You mean the police?'

'No, I mean my friends from work.'

'Tobias is there and that other one, the one who is coming to the house sometimes.'

'Stride?'

'I think so. I don't remember his name.'

'And he's talking to the police.'

'Yes.'

'Okay, Sissy. There's just one more thing. What time did the police come to the house?'

'In the night. I don't know what time.'

'What? One hour ago, two, what?'

'In the middle of the night.'

Kagiso took a deep breath, a moment just to compose himself. 'Now, look, Sissy, I know this is very frightening but I want you to know that nothing bad can happen to you. Just tell anybody who asks that I am in Jo'burg. And don't tell anybody that you have spoken with me.'

'But I want to speak to my auntie. Is she there?'

'Yes, but I will speak to her. You're not to speak to anyone. Do you understand?'

'Yes.'

'Good. And, Sissy, maybe you should just leave your phone somewhere safe in the church.'

'In the church, why?'

'Well, in case the police start asking you if I have called you or something and they ask to see your phone.'

'Kagiso, this is something bad. All this lying and stories and what-what.'

'I will explain everything to you. You'd better go back. One more thing, turn off your—'

She'd gone. Yet another person he was going to have to trust. One by one they were working through the people he knew. He had to warn Lindi.

Lindi was sitting upright in her bed, her knees tucked under her chin and her arms folded tight around them. She'd been in that position since Sanjit Patel's call. That was over two hours ago. Now the first light of the day was peeping through the curtains. She still couldn't believe that Father Petro, the avuncular soul she'd met less than twenty-four hours previously, was dead. The tears were gone now. All that was left was the thought of him praying, laughing and coughing his way through life.

Patel had said he would call back once he'd found out exactly what had happened.

Her phone rang. It was an unknown number. She was on to it before the ringtone began its second cycle.

'Mr Patel!'

'No, this is Kagiso.'

'Oh, sorry, I was expecting another call.' And quickly added, 'I'm so glad you called.'

'Who's calling you this early?'

'Long story. Something terrible has happened. If it's what I think it is.'

'Lindi, what are you talking about?'

'I'm sorry, I'm sorry. There was this guy, a priest, who was helping me – you know, helping me to meet people and so on – and, anyway, he's dead now.'

'Dead? What's his name?'

'He told me he knew you. Father Petro de Freitas.'

'Jesus! I knew him pretty well. He used to be there at the meetings

I organised between farm labourers and owners. They trusted him, especially the Mozambicans. How did he die?'

'I don't know exactly. That's what I'm waiting to hear. Apparently he crashed in his car. I don't feel good about it at all. I was with him yesterday when he sort of got a warning from these dodgy-looking blokes . . .'

'Dodgy? What do you mean?'

'Dodgy, suspicious . . .'

'Why do you think they were suspicious?'

'Christ! Kagiso, I don't *know*, I'm just trying to explain that the whole thing feels wrong. They just looked thuggish to me.'

'Lindi, listen to me. Something *is* wrong. Big-time. You've got to be really careful.'

'What's happened – what's happened since we met at the funeral?'

'We can't discuss this on the phone. Who are you waiting for?'

'A local businessman.'

'Be careful.'

'I didn't like him at first but I think Father Petro trusted him.'

'Don't trust him. Don't tell him you've spoken to me. Don't tell him anything you don't have to.'

'Shit. Shit!'

'What's up?'

'I think that other call I told you about is coming through. I'll call you back.'

Lindi was just too late. The caller had hung up. She checked the number of the incoming call. It was Sanjit Patel's. She was waiting to see if he'd call back when the phone bleeped to signal a voice message.

'Stay where you are. I'm coming over.' That was all he'd said.

She called Kagiso's number.

'It's me,' she said. 'I missed his call but he left a message. Just told me to stay where I am because he's coming to see me.'

'How long will he be?'

'I don't know. If he's coming from town, from his shop, about fifteen, twenty minutes, give or take.'

'You've got to get out of there.'

'Why? What are you talking about?'

'If you're suspicions about Father Petro are right, these people are going to want to talk you next.'

'What people? I haven't done anything.'

'Yes, you have!' Kagiso was practically screaming. He was silent for a few seconds. 'Lindi, you knew Father Petro and you know me. In some people's eyes that is enough to make you a suspect.'

'They've had their eyes on me since I got here. What's changed?'

'There isn't time for this. You must do as I tell you or we must end this call and not meet again.'

'Jesus! I need to know what's going on.'

'No time, I've got to go.'

'Wait, wait. I'm not happy about this – but, okay, how long would it take for me to get to Malelane?'

'I'm not in Malelane.'

'I thought you were going there after the funeral. Are you still in Jo'burg?'

'No, I'm in Nelspruit. I got in on the overnight train.'

'In Nelspruit! But so am I. I'm in a little B&B just outside—'

'Don't tell me,' he cut her short. 'Have you got a car?'

'No. I was relying on Father Petro.'

'Is there anyone who can give you a lift?'

'I don't know if the landlady's around. There's a farm shop next door, I chatted to the guys in there a bit yesterday and they seem to be around already. I could ask them for a lift.'

'Do it. Tell them it's urgent, that you've been called back to Johannesburg. Ask to be dropped off in town. Then go to the railway station. Walk down Voortrekker in front of the station till you see Mama K's. When you get there ask the woman whether there's a bathroom you can use. I'll tell her to expect you. Got it?'

'I don't like this one little bit. What's the businessman going to think when he gets here? If he isn't suspicious now, he certainly will be when I do a disappearing act.'

'It's a risk you'll – we'll have to take. The alternative is that he turns up with some of those thugs.'

'God, what is going on, Kagiso?'

'Time's running out. I promise you one thing. I'm with the good guys.' Silence. 'Lindi, if you want to change your mind I'll understand. This isn't your fight.'

'I'm already packing. I'm coming.'

'And, Lindi, just turn your phone off. At least till we decide what's happening.'

'Kagiso, you're wrong about one thing. This is my fight, too.'

'See you.'

17

Anton Chetty hadn't heard from Lindi since she'd sent a brief email describing a 'horrendous' journey to Nelspruit, giving details of her meeting with the Bishop of Mpumalanga and the introduction to a priest who was going to take her to meet some Mozambican farm workers. Rather cryptically, she'd added that the priest – apparently a great champion of the Mozambican community – seemed to have some 'inside' knowledge about Lesedi's murder. Anton had expected a fuller account in the evening, as had been the case on every other night she'd been away. But last night there had been no email.

He was, as usual, in Saleh's café, sitting at his favoured spot by the window. He pulled at his silver goatee, the uncharacteristically groomed beard that sprouted from his ebony skin, as he flicked through the British newspapers on his iPad. He checked his phone yet again. No missed calls. No reply to the email he'd fired off early that morning either.

Anton browsed his 'favourites' list and found the Land Collective web page. There hadn't been a new entry since the day after Lesedi's murder when he, she, whoever, had defended the Mozambicans. Still nothing. Why would they fall silent at the very point when their words might galvanise supporters into action? But what supporters and what action? Anton realised he'd taken quite a lot for granted. He'd infused the Land Collective with motives and ideals that were his own inventions. He'd taken a vicarious interest in whoever wrote the statements, finding in this nameless, faceless individual someone who might actually complete the mission he had so conspicuously failed to finish.

But what if this person was a charlatan whose only purpose was to cause chaos for its own sake? He'd met a few of those in his time. Not for them the heavy weight of responsibility, the obligation to create something better. It's enough to destroy. He now imagined whoever it was sitting back, watching the beloved country devour itself. Anton had been pinning his hopes on finding whoever was behind the Land Collective's statements, assuming he, or she, would hold the key to ending the violence, and realised he'd put his faith in an apparition, a product of his own imagination.

He'd been flicking through several other South African news websites and one line, five words, caught his attention. It was a headline in a bold font: 'Priest Dies In Car Crash'. Mentally, he lined up the sequence of events he feared: he hadn't heard from Lindi; Lindi was due to meet a priest; a priest had died in a car crash; Lindi had been in the car with him; she, too, was either dead or injured. He read on, scanning whole lines at a time, dreading some mention of a passenger. But there was nothing. Police said their work had been hampered by the fact that the car had caught fire.

That did it. He pulled out his phone and dialled Lindi's number. The line was dead.

18

Kagiso imagined the café filling up. He could hear the morning commuters, mostly men, giving their orders, flirting with Mama Khethiwe, and her typically robust but endearing replies. It wasn't her slab-like jam sandwiches or milky teas that drew the same people to Mama K's day after working day. It wasn't the hot lunchtime pies or steaming *pap* with mutton curry either. There were plenty of other places that offered all that. They came because Mama Khethiwe had a way of fortifying their souls, too, preparing them for a day of labour. Her café was like an outpost of their homes, a last chance to feel cared for and respected before they steeled themselves for hours of being told where to go, what to do and how to do it.

He began to worry that Lindi would look conspicuous when she arrived and tried to see her through the eyes of the people on the other side of the door. One of the many unexpected consequences of political freedom was the inclusion of South Africa on the backpacker trail. In the early days, these young, almost exclusively white, travellers had been something of a talking point. Their interest in 'black culture' had been a refreshing contrast to the fearful disdain that had been drilled into most of the local white population. But now the dishevelled tourists, who seemed to carry their life's belongings on their backs, were barely remarked on, except for the numerous complaints about how little money they had to spend. He guessed Lindi would be counted among their number and felt reassured.

He waited.

Any minute now, Lindi would walk through that door and be drawn, irrevocably, into his life, a part of it that even his mother did not know about. There'd been so many decisions he'd had to make since the sabotage had begun – he'd agonised about all of them.

Countless times he'd found himself still awake at dawn, fighting a private battle between what his activism propelled him towards and what his conscience warned him against. And yet this latest decision – to confide in Lindi and break the cardinal rule of the cell – he had taken on the run.

Lindi could feel the clammy dampness of her shirt under the rucksack.

She'd been surprised by how readily the farm-shop owner had let her have a lift with the delivery van. 'Don't you worry, ma'am,' he'd said. 'We'll make a plan, get you on your bus now-now.'

She'd done exactly as Kagiso had suggested, telling the man she'd had some bad news and had to return to Johannesburg. She'd left enough money to cover her overnight stay at the Mirabel and said she'd call Mrs Venter later in the day.

She was dropped off at the bus terminus, and as soon as the van was out of sight she walked, in fact it was more like a run, to the railway station. Her phone started ringing. She recognised the number, Sanjit Patel's, and remembered to turn her phone off.

The perspiration was only partly down to the physical effort of rushing around with her luggage. In the space of that short phone call with Kagiso she'd stepped into utterly uncharted territory. She'd acted on impulse and now fought against the inclination to reprimand herself for not being more wary.

Lindi walked for a few minutes on what she thought was Voortrekker and had to turn back. A pedestrian pointed to what looked like an alley – which South Africans call a service road – and told her that if she cut through it she would come out on Voortrekker.

She hadn't checked out of the Mirabel properly; she hadn't given any sort of explanation to Mr Patel; she hadn't discussed any of this with Anton. Every omission amounted to a risk, the kind of impetuosity that she'd never understood when she'd seen it in others.

And now she was walking down a back alley to meet . . . to meet who? She barely knew Kagiso – Kagiso the boy, perhaps, but not Kagiso the man. She had fashioned a person, a fully fledged character, out of no more than the threadbare fabric of a memory.

She emerged onto Voortrekker Street and almost immediately saw

Mama K's a little further down on the opposite side of the road. Lindi stood still.

Commuters walked around and past her. She hardly noticed them. She'd reached a point of no return.

Kagiso heard footsteps. Then a crack of light fanned out across the room as Mama Khethiwe held open the door. 'Your friend is here,' she said. 'Why you sitting in the dark?'

She reached in and pressed a switch by the doorframe. A dim, naked light came on. They were in a storeroom. There were sacks of mealie-meal and rice on the floor, and one wall was lined with the café's other raw materials – bags of sugar, tubs of jam and a drum of cooking oil.

'I'm coming to talk to you when the customers have gone,' she said.

Lindi walked in and waited for the door to close behind her. The rucksack sat high on her shoulders, making her seem smaller than she was, as if a gentle push might topple her.

'Let me help you with that.'

'I can manage it.' Lindi swung the bag into the corner of the room, by the door.

'You're angry.'

'Oh, I wouldn't say that. I'm absolutely thrilled. It's not every day you get to abandon all your plans and traipse all over town without knowing why you're doing it.'

Kagiso looked bemused. The British proclivity to deploy sarcasm like an attack dog in a verbal skirmish was largely lost on African ears.

'I've left a trail of people with questions about where I've gone and suspicions about what I'm up to. That, Kagiso, is not why I came to South Africa and you'd better have a really good reason for why I'm standing here now.'

'You didn't have to come.'

'You didn't give me a bloody choice!'

'It's not too late. You could leave now.'

'Oh! Please!'

'You're the one who said you wanted to meet again.'

'That's cheap, Kagiso. That's beneath you.'

191

Lindi turned her back on him and went to where she had dumped her luggage. She pulled out her water bottle and took a big swig. When she turned, he was slumped against the far wall, where the sacks of mealie-meal and rice were stacked. He looked up at her. He'd taken his spectacles off and his eyes glistened, catching the light.

'I'm sorry,' he said, just a whisper. 'I'm in trouble, Lindi. I'm exhausted and now I have dragged you into this mess.'

'You need to tell me what's going on,' she said.

'I'm not sure where to start.'

'Like they say, you could start at the beginning. But before that I really do need to use the loo.'

'The what?'

'The loo, the toilet. I'll be back in a jiffy. Then you'd better tell me how much trouble I'm getting myself into.'

'That's what I'm worried about. You may not like what you hear.'

'We'll see. Is it through the café?'

'Yeah. It's round the back. Just ask Khethiwe. She'll give you a key.'

Kagiso stood up and rubbed his face, hard, as if to wake himself from a dream. For the first time in months, perhaps even years, he'd let his guard down. He felt like a prisoner who'd just been released, pleased to be out but unsure how to navigate his way through his new-found freedom. He heard the door knob turn.

'That was quick . . . Oh, sorry, I thought it was my friend.' Even in the dim light he could see that Khethiwe Shabangu had a face like thunder. She shut the door with purpose and stood there with her hands on her hips, like a bully about to do violence. 'What's going on?'

'Funny, that's just what my friend wanted to know before she left the room.'

'Funny? You think I'm smiling? Eh? No. Because I can smell trouble and it is right here in this room. Who is that woman? What does she want?'

'It's got nothing to do with her.'

'Then who?'

'I owe you an explanation . . .'

'Don't be explaining anything. I want the truth, child. You mixed up in something bad? This Lesedi business?'

'What makes you say that?'

'I'm a woman. You not the first man to try to hide something from me. I see your face when the radio start talking just now.'

The door behind Mama Khethiwe opened. It was Lindi.

Khethiwe stretched out an arm and held the door. 'Wait.'

'No, let her come in. She needs to hear this. She's a good friend.'

Lindi walked in and stood next to Khethiwe.

'Okay, let me do this properly. Ma Khethiwe, this is Lindi Seaton. She's from UK but her family are from South Africa and they were very good to me and my mother. Lindi, this is Khethiwe Shabangu. She owns my digs in Malelane and she's been like my aunty ever since I moved east.'

Khethiwe looked unconvinced. Lindi held out her hand, which the other woman took as if she were handling stolen goods.

'This may take a while. Do you want to sit down?' He was looking at Ma Khethiwe and gesturing towards the large drum of cooking oil. She shook her head.

'Who's looking after the shop?'

'The boy has come. He's there.'

'Lindi, you going to sit down?'

'No, I'm fine.'

'Look, I'm taking a risk telling you and you're taking a risk listening so now's the time for you to . . . to be sure you want to go through with this.'

Nothing. They remained silent.

'Okay, I'll give it to you straight. The police are right. There is an underground group and I am part of it.'

Ma Khethiwe covered her mouth with a hand. Lindi moved to the corner of the room where she'd left her rucksack.

'But they are absolutely wrong about Lesedi's murder. I had nothing to do with it.'

'Underground. Like they were telling on the radio just now,' Khethiwe said.

'Yes, we have been working to stop this selling of the land to foreigners.'

'Christ!' said Lindi. 'Don't you think you should have told me earlier, back in Jo'burg? No wonder I'm a bloody suspect. I'm not here officially, I'm meant to be into conflict resolution, and here I am, wandering about with an underground activist.'

'I tried to tell you, Lindi. I told you we should not be seen together. There's still time. You could get out now.'

'Thanks for the offer but I think it's just a little late to bail out. How many of you are there?'

'I can't tell you, Lindi. I shouldn't be telling you anything. I'd be putting other people at risk.'

'So how the police find out about this underground thing?' Khethiwe was getting back into her stride. 'They catch some of them?'

'I don't think they have caught anybody. It's too risky for me to try to contact any of them.' He turned to Khethiwe. 'I think that stuff on the radio about being one step away from an arrest could be a bluff. They're close but I don't think they're that close. We've been careful.'

'Hang on, Kagiso. If they don't have any proof, why are we standing here talking like this, like thieves?'

'Look, they are after me. That much is clear. But which "me" are they after? Kagiso, the Soil of Africa man who is a thorn in their side, or Kagiso, who is a member of Land Collective and co-conspirator in a campaign of violence? I think it is the former. It's part of their prop-aganda, shift the blame onto anybody but themselves, like they started off blaming it on the poor Mozambicans.'

'But if it's you as head of Soil of Africa you could take them on. Soil of Africa is legitimate. You've done nothing – nothing illegal.'

'It's not just a question of what I do, it's what I know. Lindi, remember at the funeral Willemse telling me how I was the last person to see Lesedi alive and how he heard we'd got on very well?'

'Like a house on fire, was his expression.'

'Who is this Willemse?'

'You know, that Coloured minister.'

'The one making all those speeches and what-what! I don't like him. He likes to listen to his own voice too much.'

'That's him. You've got it in one.'

'Anyway, what were you going to say?'

'On the day he died, Lesedi came to Soil of Africa in Malelane and met a whole bunch of local people. I think he was genuinely moved by what they told him about the evictions and so on. But it didn't stop there. After he left us he called Willemse, told him about meeting the people at Soil of Africa and exactly what he thought of the whole land-sales business. Apparently he'd told Willemse he wanted this deal, the Mpumalanga one, done differently. "Above board" was the way he put it.'

'How do you know all this?'

'He told me. He called me back and said he wanted to meet me urgently. He didn't want anyone else around so we met on the road. In the morning, at the meeting, he'd been full of life. When I met him that second time he was scared, nervous. Willemse had threatened him. Told him he didn't know what he was getting into. Said his father would end up in jail. Lesedi had hit back – said if his father was jailed, he'd make sure Willemse joined him there. He told me he had all the details. He said he could have emailed it to the papers right there and then if he had wanted to. He said he knew where the skeletons were buried.'

'It still doesn't mean they can actually pin anything on you, Kagiso,' she said. 'As far as I can make out, this is a fight between Lesedi, his father and Willemse.'

'Wait, I'm not finished. Willemse had asked him, Lesedi, if he'd discussed going public with me. Lesedi had said yes. It was a lie. When he left the first time all he'd said to me was that he would do his best for the people. But he said he was so angry with Willemse he'd told him I knew all about the deals, how farmers were being bribed so they would keep quiet.'

Lindi pressed the sides of her forehead with her fingertips. She was beginning to understand just how deeply Kagiso was implicated.

'Apparently Willemse had said Soil of Africa was finished – I was finished. Lesedi told me Willemse was a thug – that was what he called him - and he was worried for me.'

'Worried for you?'

'That's what he said, Ma. He said Willemse would stop at nothing. You see, as far as Willemse is concerned, I'm now on the list of those people who know how the deals are done and who's doing them.'

'I'm sorry, but it still doesn't make sense. Willemse could have had you picked up at the funeral. If your take on what Lesedi said is right, why did they pass up the chance to pull you in?'

'I've been wondering about that, Lindi. Maybe they thought they could take care of me later. Get everything lined up, link me to the sabotage, make a big deal of my arrest, full media fanfare. Their immediate concern was to make sure no one started to ask whether it was an inside job, a government-backed assassination. They had to make sure the blame was pinned on somebody else, anybody, as quickly as possible. And they succeeded. The Ponte on fire, the lynching of Mozambicans – it's all going to plan.'

'I'm not sure about this, Kagiso. You're the one who hasn't got any proof. All this is assuming that Willemse was behind Lesedi's death. Would he really bump off the son of a man he's doing business with?'

'That man would kill his own mother for money.' Khethiwe was now sitting on the drum of cooking oil. 'Those people in Pretoria, they are all snakes.'

'You're right. I don't have any proof. But one thing is for sure. I'm not going to find any if I get pulled in. They've been to my mother's place during the night and . . .' Kagiso remembered that he hadn't told Khethiwe about the raid on her house in Malelane. He was looking at her now. 'I took a call from Sissy this morning, just a few minutes ago.'

'Oh, please, please, that child is not involved in this!'

'No, she isn't, but the police have been searching the house.'

'What? The police have been in my house? I have to call that girl.' Khethiwe was making for the door.

Kagiso moved towards her. 'You can't. Please don't do that,' he begged.

'You get that child into trouble and now you want to tell me I mustn't speak to her. Eh? Is that what you are saying?'

'She's not in any trouble because she knows nothing, but she will be if you start calling her. The police are still there.'

'In my house?'

'In your house, at my office.'

There was silence, as if the same thought descended on each of them simultaneously. Lindi gave voice to it. 'Presumably it's not going to take them long to work out Khethiwe owns this place as well. They'll be wanting to question you next. Your niece Sessie may—'

'Sissy, her name is Sissy.'

'Sissy almost certainly would have had to tell them the house was yours, Khethiwe. Kagiso, did you tell Sissy that you were here?'

'No. She doesn't know where I am. I told her to tell anyone who asks that I'm in Jo'burg. But you're right, they'll be coming here next.'

Lindi and Kagiso both looked at Khethiwe. The question was implied but was there nonetheless. Why would Khethiwe get involved?

'What? You think I'm going to help them, the police?'

'It's just that, with your house being raided and all—'

Khethiwe didn't let Lindi finish. 'You think that is going to scare me? Listen, madam,' she spat the word, made it sound like filth, 'when your parents were sitting in their fine houses we were being beaten and jailed. You think those boys in the police are going to scare me?'

'That's not fair, Khethiwe. Lindi's parents were—'

'It's okay,' Lindi said.

Resistance came naturally to Khethiwe. It was a state of mind that was practically inbred, as it was in so many of her generation. They and their forebears had spent so much of their time resisting or thinking of resisting that it had become a default setting. It was a rebellious temperament that had been quelled since the end of apartheid but was resurfacing now that the future the likes of Nelson Mandela and Desmond Tutu had promised appeared to be receding.

For Khethiwe it was not Kagiso's cause that worried her but what he might have done in its name.

'There's only one thing I need to know. Look at me, child,' she said, turning to Kagiso. 'You swear, like I am your mother, that you not involved in this killing of the Motlantshe boy?'

'Ma Khethiwe, I swear. You think I could do such a thing? Anyway, like I said, Lesedi was ready to help us. Why would I kill him?'

'It's all right, it's all right.'

'The first thing we have to do is get out of here,' Kagiso said.

'We've got to get out of Nelspruit, that's for sure. For all we know Patel has already talked to the police . . .'

'Patel? Who's Patel?'

'You know, the businessman I was supposed to be meeting this morning. The one I mentioned on the phone. I think he's probably okay but—'

Ma Khethiwe interrupted their duet. 'Patel? An Indian? Those fellows, they are only interested in making money.'

'Well, I'm not sure about that. I did think he was a bit creepy to start with . . .'

'Crippy? What is that?'

'Sorry, Khethiwe. Creepy. It means suspicious, I thought he was suspicious but—'

'Look, whether he's suspicious or not we just can't take any risks,' Kagiso said. 'It's time to move. Maybe back to Jo'burg?'

Lindi shook her head. 'There are checkpoints everywhere. They were searching vehicles when I came yesterday. Most of the buses and cars were coming this way and they were full of Mozambicans and their bundles.'

'They were taking money,' Khethiwe said, as if it were a matter of fact, like conductors checking tickets. 'These people, these Mozambicans, they're scared. They going to give all their money to get to the border. The police are getting rich.'

'Maybe that's a safer bet,' Kagiso said.

'What?'

'Maybe you and I should get out, go over.'

'And then what?' said Lindi. 'What you've got to do, what we've got to do, is prove that you had nothing to do with Lesedi's murder, and that he was ready to expose the land deals. You're not going to do that sitting in Mozambique, on the other side of the border.'

'She's right.' Khethiwe was beginning to warm to Lindi. 'But you have to get out of here now-now.'

'Okay.' Kagiso stood up with the look of a man who intended to take charge. 'Here's what we'll do. Let's head to Komatipoort – it's a small place, a border town, perfect to get out if we have to.'

He looked at Lindi. 'I know it a bit, I've passed through it many times for my work. It'll be pretty chaotic with all these Mozambicans and that should work for us. We've got to assume they, the police, think

I'm still in Johannesburg. Let's stay the night in Komatipoort and work
out what to do.'

'How do we get there?'

'There are taxis going there always,' said Khethiwe. 'I know one of
the drivers very well. I can ask him to take you.'

'No, no. We've got to be more random. But there is one thing you
can do for us, Ma. We need a new SIM.'

'A what?'

'A new phone number. There's a Stax back up towards the station.
Just say you need a new phone. Get the cheapest, most basic one they
have. They'll ask you what sort of deal you want. Say pay-as-you-go.
You can tell them it's a gift for a relative or something. Don't use a Stax
bag. Buy some bread and oranges and stuff and put the phone in with
them. Go to the taxi rank and I'll look out for you. Lindi, you and I'll
go there separately. You need to change your clothes, and if you've got
a hat, put it on. At the taxi rank just say you want to go to Mozambique.
Komatipoort is the last stop on the SA side. Aim to get a taxi leaving
in about forty-five minutes. I'll be watching, I'll try to get on the same
taxi but don't look at me or talk to me. If we get separated, just head
for a café or bar in Komatipoort and I will find you.'

Lindi was transfixed, no longer really listening to what Kagiso was
saying but how he was saying it. In an instant, she had seen why others
might follow him.

19

Priscilla Motlantshe had not gone to sleep on the night after the funeral. She'd left her husband, drunk and dead to the world, and gone upstairs to Lesedi's room. She'd stayed there, lying on his bed, clutching his pillow. She had gone through her last conversation with him over and over again. It was as if she were trying to fashion a different ending, like a storyteller wanting to leave her audience feeling happy and wholesome.

If only she'd done something different at the time. She could have confronted Jake Willemse. Or told Josiah everything when she'd called him and asked him to come back to South Africa. Could she really have prevented his . . . She could barely bring herself to acknowledge what had happened. Immediately after Lesedi's death, and before the funeral, her friends had told her not to read the papers or go to the websites that were reporting the details. But the visions kept crashing in. They had invaded her mind, filling it with horror and doubt. In the end she had persuaded one of her relatives to tell her what had happened. Even that sanitised version had left her gasping, drowning in a tide of pain that she felt as keenly as if the wounds had been inflicted on her own body. She'd barely eaten anything since then, nibbling at food when the girls had had their meals.

At the funeral she'd had a sensation that she wasn't really there. She'd gone through the motions and emotions without being conscious of what she was doing. She'd felt as if she was on a different plain, in a state of emotional limbo, somewhere between life and death. And then, when Josiah had announced his business plans, it had been like a shot of adrenaline: she had been catapulted back into the real world.

That had been two days earlier. Now Priscilla Motlantshe was alone in the house, except for the staff. She sat on the edge of the vast bed that she and her husband used but no longer shared. Not for the first time, she reminisced about how much simpler, more intimate, their lives had been when all they could afford was a mattress on the floor.

The girls had gone back to school, their first day since their brother had been killed. The head teacher at the American International School, where the children of South Africa's burgeoning middle class and the offspring of the country's growing expatriate population came together, had assured her that the school counsellor would be on hand to help them through what would be a difficult few weeks. Before he'd left, Josiah had said, rather grandly, that they could take as much time off school as they wanted. Priscilla had let it pass. She knew different. She knew that routine would bring its own comfort.

As for herself, Priscilla knew that the old pattern – allowing Josiah to get on with his life so long as he didn't bring it into the home – had to stop. She had to come off the fence and take sides. And she'd decided that if the consequence was the unravelling – final and irrevocable – of her marriage to him, it was a price she was willing to pay. Anything, she decided, was preferable to allowing Willemse, whom she'd never trusted, to get away with being responsible for the death of her only son. She'd convinced herself that he was to blame. Hadn't Lesedi implied that Willemse had threatened him?

Once in the last couple of days, when she had hit the nadir of her emotional collapse, she had even thought her husband might have been involved. She had rejected that. Josiah was many things but he was not a murderer.

Whatever Lesedi had known, she was going to make public. In all the enervating confusion of the last few days that was the one thing she had got right, the one thing she'd been sure of. All she had to go on was Lesedi's fateful boast – 'I do understand, Mom. I've got the accounts, the files, the letters. I've got copies of it all.'

Immediately after that call with Lesedi Priscilla had gone to his room and searched it from top to bottom. She'd imagined a stash of papers – nothing. In the end she'd grabbed his laptop, the cables and the satchel in which he usually carried it. She had acted on pure instinct. He was always using the thing. Perhaps that was where he'd kept his secrets.

She stared at the laptop now, having retrieved it from a cupboard in the guest wing of the house. Priscilla had no idea what to do with it. She had never used a computer in her life. And even if she knew how to turn it on she didn't know what she was looking for.

She needed help. It dawned on Priscilla that almost anyone she could turn to would be someone who was beholden to Josiah. That was how it worked. Like a contemporary version of the ancient kings and chiefs, who had held sway before the onslaught of the settlers, Josiah had dispensed his patronage far and wide. In return he received unquestioning allegiance. There was no one she could trust.

But perhaps there was someone Lesedi had trusted. The charity worker, the man Lesedi had seen on his last day. Lesedi had been full of admiration for him. She remembered now that she had met him briefly at the funeral. Kagiso, that was his name. Kagiso Rapabane. Now she wished she'd quizzed him more carefully. At the time it had seemed enough to know that she had met someone Lesedi had found for himself, and someone who seemed to respect her son for what, rather than who, he was.

She had to find him. She needed a phone number. Priscilla covered the laptop with a pillow and walked across the upstairs hallway to Lesedi's room. She looked at the cardboard carton on the desk: it was no bigger than a shoebox. On the lid someone had written 'Personal Effects' followed by a number. No name, just a number. The sum total of her son's life reduced to a standard-issue police box. She hesitated. She hadn't wanted to open it until now.

Priscilla took the lid off carefully, as if she were dismantling a ticking time bomb. The silver chain and cross, a gift to mark his confirmation, was cold to the touch. What was it doing in here? Why wasn't he allowed to take it with him? Priscilla imagined rough hands in some dingy police room ripping the chain off her son's neck. She shivered. There were some coins, his handkerchief, still neatly pressed, his sunglasses, his watch and his car keys. Priscilla looked at the silver fob. She remembered Lesedi getting it made to his design. On one side there was a miniature engraving of the family, on the other an extract from Nelson Mandela's famous speech from the dock. It was a facsimile of the handwritten document he'd seen in a museum, barely legible to the naked eye but perfect in every detail.

'It is an ideal for which I have lived. It is an ideal for which I still hope to live and see realised. But if need be, it is an ideal for which I am prepared to die.'

Even Mandela's corrections were there. Lesedi had had it etched in Germany, a laser-something, he'd said.

But there was no phone.

Priscilla sat down in front of the desk. She wondered whether the police had kept it or whether Josiah had taken it. She thought back to the funeral. The Premier of Mpumalanga, Jeremiah Mhlanga, had given her the box personally. He'd made quite a show of it. The police had wanted to keep all of Lesedi's things, he'd said, but he'd insisted that they hang on only to what was essential to the investigation. The box had sat on her lap on the journey back from Soweto and she'd brought it up to this room that very evening. Josiah had been too drunk when he'd got back and he'd left first thing in the morning. The Mpumalanga police must have kept the phone. They had all Lesedi's contacts, including, she presumed, Kagiso Rapabane's number.

Priscilla decided to call the Premier of Mpumalanga. What would be more natural than a grieving mother enquiring about how the hunt for her son's murderer was going?

'Jerry, it's Priscilla here.' She flipped from English to Zulu and back again, thanking him for taking the time to attend the funeral. 'I know this is a very busy time for you, with all these Mozambicans being killed and what-what.'

'Ah, no. I always have time for a Motlantshe. And how are you, my dear?'

'Oh, Jerry, I am a mother without her son. I want to see punishment for those people who took him away from his mother.'

'We are working day and night to find him.'

'Who? You know who it is? Josiah told me it was the work of some underground people.'

'Yes, yes, Josiah is right. By the way has he left for Dubai?'

'Oh, you knew he was going there?' You are all in it together. The words formed in her mind. She was probably the last person to know about her husband's return to the Gulf. 'So who is this person you are looking for?'

'The police tell me they are following every lead that they have.' Priscilla noted a change of tone: the avuncular had been replaced by the official. 'There is some chap Lesedi met just a few hours before he was . . . before he was murdered.'

'And are they close to catching him?'

'The police say he has disappeared. He has not been to his office or home in Malelane. His mother in Soweto says she has no idea where he is. The police say he is on the run, he must have something to hide.'

'Okay. Jerry, I know you will push these people to catch whoever took Lesedi. You will tell me if anything happens?'

'Of course, my dear. You will be the first person to know. Oh, and, Prissy, if this fellow contacts you, you must let me know, eh?'

Nobody had called her that for years, not since their Soweto days when Josiah and his fellow activists would sit round her kitchen table demanding more of her stews. He must think I am simple, Priscilla thought. Just by evoking the familiarity of my old nickname he thinks I am going to give him everything he wants.

'Why should he contact me? He doesn't know me.'

'Ah, no, we, the police, think he was trying to befriend Lesedi. Did Lesedi speak to you before – before he . . . Did he say anything about meeting someone?'

'No, no. He used to tell me about all his friends but I don't remember him mentioning anyone new. Okay, Jerry, I have to go. Let's talk again when Josiah is back.'

Priscilla was glad she'd made the call. She knew she had to reach Kagiso before Mhlanga and his people did.

20

Kagiso woke up with a start. He must have fallen asleep almost as soon as the taxi pulled out of the rank in Nelspruit. They were crossing Crocodile River, the wheels of the minibus hurdling the ramps where the tarmac met the bridge. He was on his own. He prayed that Lindi was in a taxi ahead of him. Kagiso was sitting in the front of the cab and instinctively checked that he still had the bag that Ma Khethiwe had given him. The driver had insisted he take the seat next to him, not with the 'smelly' Mozambicans crammed into the benches at the back.

The lush, irrigated plantations around Nelspruit were mostly behind them. Ahead, the landscape opened up: untamed scrubland framed by a line of hills, their contours masked by a diaphanous haze. Dotted here and there were the bare-branched *umsinsi* trees, though Kagiso always preferred their colloquial label, lucky bean tree. He was no naturalist, and what little he did know about the flora and fauna in this part of the country came from the hand-me-down knowledge of the night watchman at Soil of Africa.

Tobias had never left Mpumalanga and his only foray into Nelspruit, to work as a janitor in an office block in his twenties, had left him with a lifelong revulsion for the city. He was now in his sixties, that was what he said, though Kagiso suspected he might be quite a bit older. One of Kagiso's favourite rituals was to sit with Tobias on the veranda once he'd locked up the office for the day. They'd share a cigarette; it was the only time Kagiso ever smoked. He remembered Tobias telling him that the appearance of the flame-like flowers of the *umsinsi* in early spring was always a sign to begin planting the crops. Tobias used to say that as children they would hear the pods on the trees bursting and rush to collect the beans, which were supposed to bring good luck. Kagiso thought he could do with some of that now.

If Kagiso needed reminding about what was at stake he had only to listen in on the conversations going on behind him in the minibus. All the other passengers were Mozambicans. He had picked up enough Shangaan, the dialect of Tsonga used across the border, to understand half of what was being said and make a credible guess about the other half. The stories had become depressingly familiar: people dragged out of their homes and 'necklaced', the chilling euphemism for being burned alive with a flaming tyre placed over the head; properties ransacked; sons beaten and daughters raped; insults from one-time neighbours; and, always, the indifference of the police.

The journey to Komatipoort took about an hour. The taxi pulled up beside a market and was immediately surrounded by people, all of them shouting in a mixture of Shangaan and broken English.

'Move away! Get away! Take your filthy hands off my taxi!' the driver was screaming, in a clumsy Shangaan. 'I'm not going to your fucking country. I'm going back to Nelspruit.'

Kagiso resisted the urge to remonstrate and stepped out of the cab onto the road. He stood still for a moment to get his bearings. He noticed the rusting caravan on the opposite side of the street from the market, still sitting lopsidedly on a deflated tyre on one side and the wheel rim on the other. It was the Feelgood Hair Salon – he'd gone in for a cut once. The barber sat outside, spilling out of a camping chair. He was asleep, despite the noise.

Kagiso walked behind the minibus, pushed his way through the crowd and towards the market. Perhaps Lindi would be there.

It was as if a tornado had whipped through the place. He couldn't distinguish one stall from another. He should have known. The traders here were all Mozambicans. They wouldn't have stood a chance. One of the stallholders was picking over what was left of his stock: second-hand denim – that was his line of trade. He stuffed what he found into a large plastic bag. He poked at something on the ground with a stick and lifted several brassieres, the cups nestling into each other. He stared at them with apparent disapproval, as if he'd found some weeds in his vegetable patch. He looked over to where the undergarment stall had been, just a couple of metres away, and flicked the brassieres over. Kagiso walked on but stopped when he realised he was standing on shattered glass. This was where the herbalist and traditional healer sold his potions. Some of the jars were still intact, their shrivelled contents giving little clue as to whether they were once vegetable or animal. Further on, there was nothing left of Ngowane Cash Loans, except a charred sign. The till was on the ground, its cash drawer protruding, like a spent dog with its tongue hanging out.

His anxiety about Lindi deepened. He hadn't anticipated the chaos in an area where ethnic Mozambicans usually outnumbered everyone else. The thugs must have been bussed in. He headed towards the main street, his strides getting longer and quicker. The number of people milling around made it difficult to place the landmarks he remembered from previous visits. And then he saw what he was looking for, Café Dona Flora. He'd been there a number of times and was sure it was the kind of place Lindi would have felt comfortable in. But there was no sign of her. Perhaps she'd got a later taxi. What if she'd never got out of Nelspruit?

As he came out of the café, Kagiso noticed that the Spurs fast-food outlet was shut, its burglar bars pulled across and a private security guard in front of it. He kept walking. The shop and café at the BP garage was full of people but it had long since run out of anything to serve or sell. He moved on. A glimpse of white skin in the crowd. Kagiso rushed over, pulling people out of the way, like a swimmer struggling against the tide. He burst through, calling for Lindi, only to find the woman as shocked as he was surprised. She was an American Peace Corps volunteer. Kagiso apologised and said he was looking for a white woman.

'Well, all the whites have locked themselves in their homes or left town so if she's out you shouldn't have a problem finding your friend. She'd sure stick out in this crowd.'

Kagiso turned away and then, as an afterthought, asked the woman if she was okay.

'I'm fine. The guys who did all this have moved on. They took some money off me but basically they were only interested in the foreigners – well, the Mozambicans. I'm just waiting for a couple of other volunteers and then we're out of here. But thanks for asking.'

He was running out of road. It was less crowded at this end of the street. He didn't know this part of town. Kagiso looked down a side-street and saw a sign for the Ling Wong Sporting Tavern, on a board painted in the Coca-Cola livery. He left the dazzling light of a winter afternoon and entered the building.

It took a moment for his eyes to adjust to the dinginess. A TV, placed on a shelf just a couple of feet below the ceiling, was showing a boxing match. The commentary appeared to be in Afrikaans, though the sound was so distorted it was difficult to tell. A man sitting beneath it stared at Kagiso. He lifted a bottle of Castle beer to his lips and held it there as if he were kissing it. There was a brass chandelier in the centre of the room, fitted with multi-coloured bulbs. The bar was straight ahead of him. It was surrounded by iron bars that rose towards the ceiling. A sign on the wooden counter read: 'No weapons, no braking bottles, no fighting'. Someone hadn't bothered with an English dictionary. A Chinese couple peered at him. Kagiso went up to them and asked if they'd seen a white woman. The man pointed to his right. There was a wooden screen, with a sign hanging from it that said 'Private. Club Members Only.' Kagiso went round it and saw Lindi.

'Of all the gin joints in all the towns in all the world he walks into mine!'

'What?'

'*Casablanca*, the film. Oh, never mind.'

'How can you joke?'

'I'll let you into a little secret, Kagiso. It's called putting on a brave face. It's either that or damsel in distress, which is what I'm feeling like inside.'

Kagiso sat down next to her and put an arm around her shoulders. They stayed that way for a minute or two, neither of them wanting to break the magic of reunion. It was Lindi who spoke first.

'As much as I'd like to nuzzle up in your arms all day, hadn't we better come up with a plan?'

'First things first. Have you had anything to eat?'

'Good luck with that. I had a look on the way here and all the cafés are either closed or out of food.'

'I'm sorry. I just didn't think anywhere so near the border would be affected like this. Was your journey okay?'

'It was fine. One or two people asked what I was doing and I just said I was a teacher in a mission school and wanted to get out of the country. I think they may have some pies and stuff behind the counter.'

Kagiso came back to the table with a plate of food and two bottles, one Coke, the other Sprite.

'What do you fancy?'

'I'll take the Sprite, thanks. What's in the roll?'

Kagiso peeled back the fluffy white bread and exposed a thick slab of meat, unnaturally pink, the colour of tongue. 'Polony,' he said.

'God knows what's gone into that. It looks quite disgusting.'

'It is, but you'd better have a bite. Something tells me we're not going to be dining out tonight.'

'Talking of which, where are we going to stay?'

'I've just asked Mr Wong – or is it Mr Ling? I'm never sure how it works with Chinese names. He says he's got a room in a building another block down the road. I said we'd take it.'

'Okay, now you've taken care of your stomach, can we talk about what we're going to do?'

'I was thinking about it on the way here. I've got to contact Lesedi's mother.'

'His mother?' Lindi looked sceptical. 'What's she got to do with this?'

'It's just a feeling I've got. I think the key to all this is to find out whatever it was Lesedi had on Willemse. We've got to assume that's what got him killed and why they are now after me. Remember, Willemse thinks Lesedi told me everything.'

'Yes, but what makes you think his mother knows anything? And even if she does, why would she tell you? You're the number-one suspect, the man who killed her beloved son. One thing you can be sure is that Willemse and his mob have rammed that point home.'

'Like I said, it's just a feeling. Look, remember when we met at the funeral? After the service, when everyone was leaving, I went over to the graveside . . .'

'Yeah, I remember.'

'Well, Lesedi's mother was still there. She told me she'd spoken to Lesedi on the day he died. Apparently he'd told her about me and the good work we were doing. She told me to keep in touch once everything was over.'

'And you think Lesedi might have told her what he knew.'

'It's a possibility. Priscilla Motlantshe is old-school. She's not like all the others – she's not like her husband. I think she's where Lesedi's idealism came from.'

'I guess it's worth a try,' Lindi said.

Kagiso placed his hand on hers. 'I think it's all we've got,' he said. 'Let's get out of here and then we can work out how I'm going to do it.'

By the time they walked out of Ling Wong's Sporting Tavern the sun was beginning to drop. The air was rich with wood smoke, rising from the many fires that had been lit. Around each one a cluster of people were taking a rest on their way back to Mozambique, reversing a journey that had begun in hope and was ending in bitterness.

They made the short walk to the building where Kagiso had rented the room; he carried Lindi's rucksack up to the first floor. The place had the feel of a hostel. There was a pin-board with various notices covering where to take the rubbish and in what state the occupants were expected to leave the communal kitchens and showers.

'I asked them for a room with its own bathroom,' Kagiso said. 'It was an extra fifty rand for the privilege.'

The room looked clean enough, though it seemed as if the previous occupant had only just walked out. There were books on the desk in front of the window: the *Lonely Planet* guide to South Africa; a well-thumbed paperback copy of Ben Okri's *An African Elegy*, and a pile of exercise books stamped Mbokwane Secondary School. There was a curled fax headed 'What to do in an emergency'. On a side table there was a counter-top fridge, a kettle and a jar of coffee. Kagiso opened the fridge, revealing some milk, a half-empty can of peaches and a slab of cheese.

'I bet this room belonged to a volunteer,' Kagiso said, plugging in the phone charger. 'I saw one of them – she was waiting for her friends near the market. Mr Ling Wong didn't waste any time filling the room, did he? I bet Peace Corps paid for the room months in advance.'

Lindi shouted back from the bathroom, 'Well, she certainly got out in a hurry. She left half her toilet things here.'

'Have you got any money? I said I'd pay once I'd seen the room.'

Lindi walked back into the room. 'How much do you need?'

'A couple of hundred bucks should do it.' Kagiso unbuckled his shoulder bag and checked his laptop and cables. 'It's a long shot but I'm just going to check if the internet café I know is still in business. He used to stay open quite late.'

Lindi walked over to the door. 'How long before I should start getting worried?'

'I'll be back in half an hour, max.'

Lindi fished around in her rucksack and laid some fresh clothes on the bed before going into the bathroom. She couldn't remember when she'd last had a shower. It must have been Johannesburg. That was two days ago. And here she was now, in a small town in the back of beyond and a million miles from her mission to South Africa. She felt a pang of guilt. Anton. He must be beside himself. She must contact him. She decided to wait till Kagiso was back before turning her phone on again.

As the water warmed up it seemed to melt away her anxiety. Far from being weighed down by the precariousness of her situation, Lindi felt exhilarated in a way she had not experienced for a long time, perhaps ever. Her skin was alive to the luxurious caress of a thousand droplets. It seemed she could feel every one of them individually, and on which part of her body they landed. She allowed herself to stand still and enjoy the sensation long after her ablutions were complete. Eventually and reluctantly she turned the tap off, pulled back the shower curtain and wrapped a towel under her arms. She went into the bedroom.

She pulled on some knickers and was shaking out her hair when she heard the door click open behind her. She looked at the long mirror to the side of the desk and saw Kagiso reflected in it. 'I'll wait outside,' he said.

'It's all right, come in.' He shut the door, placed his bag on the floor. Lindi watched his every move in the mirror, a twitch of a muscle in his neck. His eyes locked on hers in the reflection. She let the towel drop. He was standing behind her. Lindi stayed where she was, reached back and took his hands. She pulled him in and folded his arms across her body. She could feel his pulse, smell his earthy presence, a mixture of a day on the run and wood smoke. She placed her hand on one of his. She watched him in the mirror, saw how he splayed his fingers, making way for hers. And then, gently, almost imperceptibly, Lindi pushed his hand up till she felt his fingertips touch her breasts.

Lindi sat up. She looked around the room, taking in every detail, as if to savour the time and place. The neon light in the bathroom was still on and it cast a silvery, moon-like sheen on everything. She turned round. Kagiso was asleep, one half of his face catching the light, the other in the dark, a portrait in symmetry. She resisted the urge to touch him, to feel again the silkiness of his body and rekindle the desire with which she had sought him. She found her clothes on the floor. There was a chill in the room. She got up and draped Kagiso's denim jacket over her shoulders. It was like being embraced by him again. It was a little after midnight.

Kagiso had said he'd found some bread and, quietly, like a thief in the night, Lindi peeled open his rucksack. As she pulled out the bag of rolls she noticed that the power icon on Kagiso's laptop was blinking drowsily – he hadn't shut it properly. She took it out and placed it on the desk. She hesitated for just a moment but, emboldened by the intimacy of the last few hours, she lifted the lid even further. There was a single, untitled page open. She began to read it:

Friends, I have not been able to write for a few days and I'm not sure when – or if – I will get another chance. I AM A WANTED MAN. Whatever happens to me or my comrades OUR CAMPAIGN must not be stopped. We must see it through to the end so that South Africa's

SACRED LAND, where generations of our people have toiled and sacrificed, can be RETURNED TO ITS RIGHTFUL OWNERS. We must do this to HONOUR THE MEMORY of LESEDI MOTLANTSHE. I can tell you now that he died because HE WAS ON YOUR SIDE. He was the son of a rich man but he was A CHAMPION OF THE PEOPLE. On the very day he was killed so brutally he told me he was against this ROBBERY. He was ready to join the fight and EXPOSE THE POLITICIANS who are SELLING OFF OUR BIRTHRIGHT so they can live like kings.

'It's not one of my best. I was in a hurry.' Kagiso was sitting up, the muscular curve of his shoulder reflecting the light.

'I was wondering when you were going to tell me.'

'You guessed before I told you at Ma Khethiwe's?'

'Actually, it was something Father Petro said to me that got me thinking. He called the Mozambicans the poorest of the poor, and I remembered you'd used the phrase when we met at Regina Mundi.'

'How does that make me the writer?'

'Last night, after I'd heard Petro had been in an accident, I suppose I felt I needed something to cling on to, something to make sense of the mess, and I found myself going through all the entries.'

'And?'

'There it was again, the same phrase, "the poorest of the poor".'

'I was never very good at it. At least I won't have to write many more of them.'

'What do you mean?'

'One way or another, this whole thing is going to be over soon. I want it to be over. I feel my life has been on hold. I've neglected people, hurt people.'

'Like who?'

'Oh, the list is a long one.'

'You could have told me right at the beginning, when we first met.' It was not a reproach, just a statement.

'Lindi, I have spent so long living a secret, never being sure who I could trust. I was going to show you, to tell you. But you had other things on your mind.' He was smiling.

Lindi went back to the bed. She leaned over and kissed him, first his shoulder, then his neck. She laughed softly.

'What's so funny?'

'I was thinking of Anton.'

'You make love to one man while thinking of another! My mother warned me about women like you.'

'Well, he did tell me to find the man behind the Land Collective statements.'

A flash of levity, then the reality. Just the mention of Anton's name was enough to bring her up sharp. 'I've got a plan,' Lindi said.

Two-Boy was on the night shift. He looked at the electronic clock on the wall. It was that no man's land in the relentless 24/7 working cycle, too late to be a part of the previous day but too early to herald the new morning. He often volunteered for this shift, which others were only too willing to relinquish. It was one way to deal with his insomnia. He felt the call-alert buzzer in his hip pocket. It was the other phone. He walked out of the open-plan Data Management and Technical Resources room at SABC and took the stairs down two floors. As he headed to the terrace outside the empty staff canteen he pulled out the phone and checked the screen. He didn't recognise the number. There was no voicemail.

He was seized with indecision, wondering whether to call back or not. He hadn't spoken to any of the others recently. The last conversation he'd had was with François a couple of days after they'd met at Hillbrow. François had said he thought the security people were on to them. He'd said that Sharmi seemed to have disappeared. He'd checked with mutual friends and not a whisper from her. He'd driven past her place in Melville a couple of times and her car was never there.

'She always parks that Beetle of hers in the same place, outside the bottle store,' he'd said. 'It's not there any more. It's fucking spooky.'

Two-Boy had checked with a couple of the reporters in the newsroom. As far as they knew, the only person the police were looking for was 'that do-gooder' in Mpumalanga. They'd heard that his digs in Malelane had been raided and the police were keeping an eye on anyone he was known to be close to, friends, workmates – there was even a stake-out at his mother's house.

Two-Boy found Sharmi's silence most disconcerting. He was closer to her than he was to the others. She was all hard edges and sharp words with Kagiso and François but had adopted him: a lost cause to save was probably how she saw him. Most women didn't give him a second thought, didn't get past the unlaundered clothes and the drinking. It didn't seem to matter to Sharmi and he was grateful for that. She was an inveterate breaker of rules and, over the last few years, had been in touch with him more than the other two, ignoring the admonition about communications within the group being kept to a minimum. Sometimes she'd send him a message with nothing more than a smiley. He was worried about her. Her petulance at the last meeting in Hillbrow was uncharacteristic, even by her standards. What the hell was all that about? If François was right, and she'd taken fright, she might do anything.

Each to his own. That was how it felt to Two-Boy and he hated it. If he hadn't known it before, he knew it now: he needed someone to tell him what to do. He needed a drink. He looked at his watch. Still only eleven thirty. He'd been in the office for an hour.

The phone vibrated in his hand. Two-Boy looked around nonchalantly. Just a couple of smokers getting their fix. It was the same number. He pressed the green button.

'It's me.'

Two-Boy recognised the voice immediately. 'Howzit, man!' It was all he could do to stop himself blurting out Kagiso's name.

'Can you talk?'

'Yeah, it's late, man, where are you?' Two-Boy regretted the question as soon as he'd uttered it. It was careless. He realised how unnerved he'd been by the last couple of days.

'I need a number.'

'What kind of number?'

'Mrs Motlantshe's cell phone.'

'Are you mad?' Two-Boy was conscious that he'd raised his voice. He checked to see if the smokers had noticed. They'd gone. 'You can't call her.'

'Just do it. Send me a WhatsApp with the number. One more thing. In the next couple of days I might need you to do your magic with a computer. I'll call you again.'

'Okay, okay. But can't you just tell me what this is—'

'I'll tell you when I can. Listen – don't make any mistakes.'

The line was dead. The call had lasted less than thirty seconds. The elation he'd felt just a few moments ago dissipated as rapidly as it had come. He was angry. As much as he tried to tell himself that Kagiso was right to be circumspect in their conversation, he couldn't help feeling he was being taken for granted. Christ! This wasn't the army. *Do as you're told and don't ask any questions.* He thought about getting a drink. Just a quickie. A couple of places he knew were open even at this hour. He could be back in the office in less than half an hour. Two-Boy hesitated but then went back into the building.

By the time he reached the lifts he'd decided where he'd start. He remembered a feature the weekly magazine programme, *Out and About*, had run on Priscilla Motlantshe. 'Married to the Struggle' – that was what it was called. It was about the wives of that first generation of activists and how they'd coped while their husbands fought the good fight. SABC had broadcast the report just before the last election, an unsubtle reminder of how the ruling party had delivered freedom. All he had to do was find out who the reporter was and the rest would be easy.

Anton Chetty was nursing a second bottle of red when the call came. What was the time? Late. He must have fallen asleep.

'Before you say anything, I'm sorry I've not been in touch.'

It took him a few seconds to gather his thoughts.

'Anton?' Lindi snapped.

'Yes, yes, I'm here.'

'Are you on your own? Who's that with you?'

'It's just the TV,' he replied, reaching for the remote.

'Where are you?' she pressed.

'I'm at home. Never mind where I am, where the fuck are you? What you playing at, girl? Your phone's dead, no answers to emails.

Meanwhile I'm sitting here reading about houses getting torched and people getting hacked up. All I know is you were going to see a priest and then that very day a priest gets killed.'

'You mean Father Petro? What do you know about him?'

'It's on all the websites. Anyway, it's pretty bloody obvious. Apparently he was protecting Mozambican families.'

'Look, Anton, I can't talk for long. I'm—'

'Two days of nothing and you can't talk for long!'

'Stop it! Shut up – just listen to me for once.'

Anton was dumbstruck. He felt like he'd been slapped by his own child.

'I'm sorry,' Lindi said, picturing him for the first time as a vulnerable and ageing – yes, ageing – man. 'I want to explain everything but I can't do it now. First, I'm in touch with the Land Collective. I'm with the one who writes the group's statements.'

'You found him! That's fantastic, girl.' Anton was regaining his equilibrium. 'Who is it?'

'It turns out you were . . . he's . . .'

Anton heard another voice in the background.

'I'm sorry. I'd better not say. The point is this. He's being accused of murdering Lesedi Motlantshe and they're wrong.'

'Hang on, you're with someone from the Land Collective and he is telling you they have nothing to do with Lesedi's killing?'

'Yes.'

'And you believe him?'

'Yes, I do. Anton, I don't really have time for this.'

'Just hang on a minute, my friend.'

That 'my friend' told Lindi that Anton was about to be anything but friendly.

'You've known this guy for one day, two days max, and all of a sudden you take everything he says at face value? How do you know he is not lying? I would if I were in his position – which, I don't need to remind you, is a tricky one indeed. What's happened to you? Not like you to be jumping in at the deep end.'

'I'm not sure how to take that. Nothing has happened to me. The fact is you're there and I'm here and I'm making the call. There's more to this than I can tell you on the phone. You'll just have to trust me.'

'Well, you're not making it any easier, keeping me in the dark.'

'I'll explain everything back in London . . .' Anton strained to hear Lindi's muffled voice as she said something away from the receiver. 'I really can't stay on this line for much longer. Here's the deal: Lesedi was about to spill the beans on the land sales and that's probably what got him killed.'

'Hold on, hold on. I sent you down there to see if we could get people to talk to each other, not to get involved in conspiracy theories. You're telling me Lesedi Motlantshe, son and heir to one of South Africa's richest men, was about to go all radical on us? Come on, Lindi!'

'Anton, I've got to hang up soon. There's proof of what Lesedi was up to and I need your help to get it. It'll settle this whole mess. Now you've *got* to do as I say.'

Silence.

'Anton? Are you there?'

'I'm listening.'

'I need to meet Mrs Motlantshe, Lesedi's mother. Don't ask why, I just do. The trouble is I can't just walk up to her front door. I've got to arrange to meet her somewhere.'

'What am I supposed to do? Just call her and say, "Hey, Mrs Motlantshe, you don't know me from Adam but I'm calling from London and, by the way, I want you to meet a colleague of mine"? For Chrissakes, Lindi, this isn't a game.'

'I think I know that rather better than you. Here's what you have to do. Call my father.'

'Your father? This is getting more ridiculous by the minute.'

'Anton, if you don't stop interrupting I'm going to hang up. Tell my father he has to call Mrs Motlantshe – I'll give you her number in a minute. He must remind her that he interviewed Josiah and he's sorry to hear of their sad loss. He must tell her that his daughter is in South Africa and has a message from a man Lesedi met on the day he died. She must meet me at Francis Xavier Church tomorrow morning. I'll be there by ten. Tell her that her son had some information he wanted to make public. She must bring any papers that he kept, maybe his phone or a laptop, maybe a key to a safe where he might have hidden something he wanted kept secret. Most important, she must not tell anyone.'

'Why don't you call your father yourself?'

'Because I don't want to use this phone any more than I have to. This call has already gone on for too long. Don't try to call me back. It'll be turned off. Anton, trust me. I know what I'm doing.' Lindi read out the numbers. And then, as an afterthought, 'Tell my parents I'm fine.'

'Hello, is this Mr Seaton?'

There was enough in those few words for Harry to know that the caller was South African. His heart pounded. They hadn't heard from Lindi in three or four days. He'd wanted to call her but, incredibly, it had been Helen who'd dissuaded him, saying Lindi was probably just busy. But he knew, both of them knew, it wasn't like her not even to send a text message. The only difference between them was that Helen was better at hiding her concern. And then, just this morning, even she had relented. It was the green light he'd been waiting for. He'd called her number over and over again and every time it was the same: 'The number you have dialled is unavailable.'

'Yes, this is he.'

'This is Anton Chetty from South Trust and I've—'

Harry didn't let him finish. 'What's wrong?' Helen heard him and moved closer, threading her arm through his. 'We haven't had a word from Lindi for a few days. It's most unlike her.'

Helen tugged on his arm and whispered, 'Let him speak.'

'She has been very busy.'

'So she's okay?'

'Oh, she's absolutely fine.' At the other end of the line Anton was struggling, struggling to find his bedside manner. It was a useless endeavour. He didn't have one. His range of conversational skills went from blunt to rude. He relayed Lindi's instructions. 'So you got that, Mr Seaton?'

'Call me Harry. Yes, I've written down the numbers. You approve of this?'

'I'm sorry?'

'All this cloak-and-dagger business. It's your idea, is it?'

'It's actually your daughter's idea.'

'I'm sorry. I didn't mean to sound as if I was accusing you. It seems like quite a mess down there and, well, I'm not sure Lindi knows what she's involved with.'

'Listen, Harry. You and me, we're in the same boat. It's time we let go. Lindi is her own woman.'

Just before sunrise the next morning, Kagiso looked around the room, checking they'd left nothing. Lindi was in the bathroom. They had decided to keep moving, to work their way back towards Nelspruit where they'd arranged to meet Khethiwe Shabangu and her driver for the final leg of the journey to Johannesburg.

They'd hatched their plan – Lindi's plan. By now Priscilla Motlantshe should have received a call from Harry Seaton. Kagiso knew it was a bigger gamble than he'd taken in all the years of his clandestine activities. Sabotage took careful planning, trustworthy accomplices, some cunning, plenty of courage but, most important, the option of bailing out if something wasn't right. He was always in charge of events, not the other way round. This was different. This whole scheme depended on Mrs Motlantshe, a woman he'd met only once, reacting in a way Kagiso hoped she would. It was based on a hunch, not a calculation, an assumption that mother and son had shared a bond that transcended her duties as a wife. What if he was wrong, and right now, instead of thinking of a way to get to Francis Xavier Church, she was on the phone again, alerting Josiah, or Willemse?

Lindi came out of the bathroom and saw Kagiso staring out of the window.

'Hey! What are you thinking?'

'I was just thinking there is nothing more I can do. It's down to you now, you and Ma Khethiwe.'

It had been Kagiso's idea for Lindi to have Ma Khethiwe with her when she went to the church. He chuckled.

'What?'

'I was just thinking of you and Khethiwe together. That's quite a scary combination.'

'You bet.'

Lindi took one last, lingering look at the room and shut the door.

21

Sharmi Meer woke up and looked around the room, like someone trying to familiarise themselves with the surroundings. From the sofa-bed, she gazed up at the elaborate pressed-tin ceiling, then across to one corner where an impossibly healthy rubber plant had had to adapt its upward trajectory. Sharmi got her bearings. She'd picked up the plant at an end-of-day sale at Rosebank market and handed it over as a not entirely convincing gift. Its size and vigour now, many years later, were a tribute to her friend's nurturing skills but also to the steadfastness of their relationship. Her friend was out; she was on her own. This was the third, maybe fourth, bed she'd slept in since deciding to abandon her own apartment after that last meeting. It was like a farewell tour.

Sharmi was on the verge of getting up to make some coffee but slumped back into the cushions. What was the rush? She still had time. Long enough to wonder how she had reached this point of no return. Would it be like the movies? She realised she didn't even know whether the police in South Africa read out your rights. Perhaps that was just an American thing. At what point did they take the photo, those black-and-white mug-shots in which the suspects always seemed to look guilty? Thank God she'd had a haircut.

She'd already decided to present herself at Johannesburg Central Police Station, the old John Vorster Square, where so many anti-apartheid activists had been beaten and bruised, some never to be seen again. They'd all been dragged in, kicking and screaming against the oppression they were fighting.

But Sharmi would just walk in, like she was volunteering for duty. And it was a kind of duty. That was how she saw it now. Handing herself in to protect the others. Of course they'd get pulled in, too, but she'd be able to prove that they knew nothing about what had happened to Lesedi. She owed it to them – she owed it to Kagiso. Yes, even Kagiso. Especially Kagiso. She knew that now. It wasn't an ending she was looking for but a new beginning.

She was going to call time on her duel with Kagiso. She'd let it define who she was. Now she would shape the rest of her life – whatever happened – on her own terms. It had never been about wooing him back, not for some years now. She'd given up on that a long time ago. One evening in Cape Town, one night in Muizenberg, and a journey across the vastness of the Karoo, that was all it had been. There hadn't been much of a relationship to start with. That was what she had told herself for years. Just an affair, a fling, a mistake. God knew she'd made enough of those when it came to men. She'd always been able to walk away unscathed. Not with Kagiso, though. She'd never stopped long enough to work out why. It was different now: she'd had plenty of time to think.

Just a few days ago she was still up for the fight. Ready to run, to hide, to lie, to do whatever it took to stay a step ahead of the authorities. That was why she'd got rid of the car, a link to her movements in Mpumalanga. She was ready to tough it out. Then came all those news bulletins about a radical priest (she knew him by reputation) who'd died in a mysterious car accident and the hunt for what the police had called the ring-leader of an underground cell of activists.

They, Willemse and his mob, were picking off their enemies one by one. Lesedi's death gave them a free hand. It was the ideal cover to silence their critics. She began to imagine a headline: 'Lesedi Murder Ring-leader Killed In Police Operation'.

She wouldn't put it past them. That was when she'd known she had to make a choice: come clean or wait to hear that Kagiso had paid the price for her silence. That was when she'd discovered she hadn't expunged the curse of intimacy. With the other men in her life she'd been looking for something. In Kagiso she had found something.

It was eight in the morning. They drove into Johannesburg earlier than they'd planned to, Lindi and Khethiwe, with the driver in the front cab and Kagiso lying low in the back of the windowless van. The road heading west was quiet, and most of the checkpoints were on the other side of the road, for traffic heading towards the Mozambique border. On the one occasion they'd been stopped, just outside Machadodorp, Ma Khethiwe had scolded the soldier. Vaguely pointing to the back of the van she'd said she had supplies for her *spaza* shop in Benoni: was he going to pay her for lost earnings when she did not turn up on time for customers?

The man, though he was barely old enough to warrant that description, had pointed at Lindi and asked what the white woman was doing. Khethiwe broke into Zulu, saying the stupid woman was standing on the roadside looking for a lift and if Khethiwe hadn't picked her up she would have got a lot more than a lift. They'd both laughed, the joke on white people and their stupidity.

Once they entered Johannesburg, there was a strong sense that all was returning to normal. A city that had been knocked off its stride earlier in the week was back doing what it did best, making money. The spasm of xenophobia that had seen tens of thousands of Mozambicans fleeing for their lives was conveniently being forgotten, the newsstand photos of the Ponte building on fire were fading and the taxi drivers were, once again, vying for pole position on the commuter run to Braamfontein, Rosebank, Sandton, Randburg and beyond.

Anonymity, that great gift of the city, was just what they were looking for.

They decided to lose themselves in the hustle and bustle of Joubert Park till it was time for Lindi and Khethiwe to head for old Sophiatown. Kagiso stepped out of the back of the van, squinting into the winter sun, and stretched. Lindi slipped her hand under the tail of his shirt, which was now hanging loose.

'And how were things back in economy class?' she asked, stroking his back. Kagiso saw Khethiwe's disapproval of this open display of affection. He stepped aside and tucked in his shirt.

If Priscilla Motlantshe turned up, the plan was for Lindi to head for the shopping mall at Rosebank where Two-Boy would be waiting at a café. They'd chosen it because it had Wi-Fi and was always full of customers staring at screens. Lindi was to hand over the laptop or whatever Priscilla gave her and head to her rented office. Two-Boy had been confident it would take him just minutes to find whatever Lesedi had on Willemse, assuming there was something to find. Kagiso would head for the flat in Hillbrow and wait for Two-Boy's call. If Lesedi's story stood up, Kagiso planned to phone Lindi with the details and she would alert SABC, the BBC and Anton. He'd join her later and they'd hold a press conference – the two of them side by side.

'So, let's get some breakfast,' Lindi said.

'I'm going to wait here,' Khethiwe said. 'Let the driver come with you. He can bring something for me. Put plenty of sugar in my tea,' she said, smiling at Lindi. They'd stopped for a snack the previous night and Lindi's dietary fastidiousness had been the source of some mirth.

A slight breeze was catching the thin and gentle spray from the fountain in the middle of the park, wafting it over towards some of the surrounding benches where it fell, like mist, on one of the many home-less men who started their wandering day in Joubert Park. Lindi walked into the cloud of spray and tilted her head so she could feel the contrast between the warming glow from a rising sun and the chill droplets of water.

It reminded her of the Seatons' old home in Observatory, how she and Ralph would shriek as they ran in and out of the watery arc of the lawn sprinkler. She remembered how Maude used to shout at Kagiso for joining in, telling him she didn't have an endless supply of clean clothes for him, though her job was to ensure that that was precisely what Ralph and Lindi had at their disposal. Ralph would always end up stark naked but Maude never let her do the same, especially if anyone outside the family was around, and that included Kagiso. 'Girls don't do that,' she used to say.

Lindi looked across at Kagiso, who was watching her. So much for modesty, she thought. There was a café just across the street from the park. Lindi and Kagiso walked towards one of the gates.

'You are lovebirds. You need something to remind you of this happy day!'

One of the many hawkers came towards them, a camera swinging from his neck. 'Madam, don't you want a picture with this handsome man of yours?'

'And who says he is so handsome?'

'Well, a pretty lady like you can only have a handsome man,' he shot back, beaming.

'Is that what you tell all the girls?'

'Only when it is true, madam.'

'Now that's what I call a sales pitch. Come on,' Lindi said, turning to Kagiso.

He hesitated.

'You see, your beautiful lady, she wants a little memento. And me, I need the business. People have been staying away these last few days.'

'Come on, you'd be doing him a favour,' she said, prodding Kagiso.

All those rules about not drawing attention to yourself, blending in with the crowd, Kagiso knew he was about to ignore every one of them. It was turning out to be that kind of day.

'All right. But we are in a hurry. How long will it take?'

'Just let me take the photo and you'll have your picture now-now.'

The man positioned them carefully, pulling and pushing their shoulders into place so that you could see enough of the fountain behind them. He shouted at one of the vagrants, telling him to get out of shot. Lindi felt Kagiso's hand on her waist. Kagiso turned to look at her just as they heard the electronic swipe of the shutter.

'Okay, follow me and I will organise your picture.'

He went over to where two or three other men were standing, cameras at the ready. Arranged on the retaining wall of a flowerbed, a Canon printer was attached to a car battery.

'So what's your name?' Kagiso asked.

'My name is Mlungezi Moyo,' the man said, connecting a cable from the camera to the printer.

'So you are from Zimbabwe.'

'Yes, sir,' the man said.

Kagiso noticed a certain reticence in his voice.

'Have you been affected by this trouble?' Lindi asked.

'No, madam. This time they were only looking for the Mozambicans.' He pressed the power button on the printer. 'Next time they will be after us. That's how it is with these South Africans.'

He looked anxiously at Kagiso, as if he were expecting a rebuke.

'Well, you are doing a good job,' Kagiso said, by way of reassurance. 'Our people could learn some lessons from guys like you.'

'Oh, what a beautiful picture!' The photographer let it drop into his open hand. He blew on it and handed it to Lindi. 'This one is a good man, madam. Not like the other South Africans, hot one day, cold the next.'

Lindi counted twenty rand and then, as an afterthought, added another ten. 'I can't wait to show Mum and Dad,' she said, as they walked out of the park.

By the time they got back the driver had already returned with a couple of buns and tea for Khethiwe.

'Sorry, we got distracted,' Lindi said, sensing Khethiwe's irritation.

'Well, it is time to move,' Khethiwe said. 'This driver is not from here so we must leave some extra time.'

Suddenly the *joi de vivre* dissipated. Lindi felt her stomach clench. But it wasn't the old fear of failure that flooded in, ready to ambush her. She realised, with a clarity that had been absent till now, just how much was at stake.

'What will you do?' she asked Kagiso.

'Exactly as we discussed,' he said.

'No, I mean if she's not there . . . if it goes wrong.' She hadn't dared to ask the question before.

'It's not going to go wrong.'

Khethiwe was getting into the car. Lindi reached up and embraced Kagiso.

'See you later,' she said.

They'd parked the van outside Francis Xavier Church, just Lindi and the driver. Ma Khethiwe had gone straight into the church and the plan was for her to make sure that Priscilla Motlantshe had arrived and that she was alone. If she was satisfied that it was safe, Ma Khethiwe would come out, look into her handbag briefly, then go back inside the church. An hour had passed and still nothing.

From where they were, under a lone jacaranda tree, its dry, brittle branches giving little inkling of the nascent purple bloom it was incubating, Lindi could see both sides of the church and the front entrance.

Nobody had walked in or out while they had been there. A gardener made some speculative jabs at one of the flowerbeds before abandoning the task and heading back into a shed on the edge of the compound.

Lindi looked out of the window and checked the wing mirrors. Nothing. It was now just a few minutes before midday. She began to give up hope and wondered how she would break the news to Kagiso. She shut her eyes, steeling herself for the task.

Lindi felt the driver touch her arm. She looked up to see Ma Khethiwe on the steps of the church. She looked into her bag and walked back in. Surely there was some mistake. She asked the driver. He, too, was sure no one had been in or out. Perhaps there was a back entrance. They'd driven round the compound when they'd arrived earlier that morning and noticed some outbuildings, what looked like the priest's accommodation, but there had been no sign of a gate on that side.

She had to trust Ma Khethiwe. Lindi got out of the van, walked across the compound and into the church.

Ma Khethiwe was standing near the altar, talking to a priest, a white man who looked to be in his seventies, perhaps older.

'Is she here?'

'Good day, young lady. I am Father Vincent de Kok. I used to be the parish priest here many, many years ago but now it's my retirement home.'

'I'm so sorry, it's just . . . I was expecting to see someone else.'

'It's okay, it's here,' Khethiwe said.

'What do you mean? Where's Mrs Motlantshe?'

'She's not here, but she gave me something for you,' Father Vincent said. 'I have known Priscilla for a long time.' The priest made the sign of the cross and began to walk, surprisingly briskly, to the side of the altar.

'Our church was one of the few that had a mixed congregation and the Motlantshes used to worship here. Well, I think Josiah just came along for the ride.' He turned to Lindi with a knowing twinkle in his eyes. 'She called me yesterday and asked me to visit her.'

'Is there a reason she hasn't come herself?' Lindi asked.

'Well, yes. There's a police car outside her house. Such a fine property. I've often wondered how young Josiah made all that money.'

Again the wry smile. 'Priscilla says they are keeping an eye on the place, for her own protection, of course. But nobody cares about an ageing priest.'

They walked into the sacristy. Father Vincent pulled out a chair and placed it in front of a huge painting, which dominated the room, a black Madonna, nursing an infant Jesus.

'It's rather crude, isn't it?' he said. 'Funny how that sort of thing used to shock people – a black baby Jesus, I mean.'

He climbed onto the chair.

'Father, please!' Ma Khethiwe said. 'Let the girl do this thing for you.'

'Oh, don't worry. I'm not as doddery as I look.' He reached up and found a key that was sitting on the picture frame. 'There it is.' He stepped off the chair in a move that was less convincing than his ascent and walked over to a massive cupboard. 'Made of leadwood,' he said, as he placed the key in the lock. 'Not very commonly used in furniture. Lots of it about in Johannesburg, though, because it was used in the mine shafts. Hard as rock. Good for a campfire too, I'm told. The embers smoulder for a couple of days apparently.'

He parted some of the vestments hanging inside the cupboard and fiddled with both hands till he found what he was looking for. 'Still there,' he said, as if he'd had his doubts. He pulled out a sleek black case with a prominent zip along one side and a cardboard container about the size of a shoebox. Lindi reached out for them.

'Just a minute, young lady.' Lindi felt just the way she used to when Maude told her not to be greedy and wait her turn. Father Vincent looked her straight in the eye.

'Now I'm not sure exactly what you're up to, but I have a fair idea. Priscilla told me enough. She is a good woman, one of the best, and she is taking a big risk in trusting you and your friends. If you have any doubts about what you are planning to do with whatever you find here, then you must desist. This is a deadly business. We don't need any more people to come to harm.'

He paused and looked at both of them. Then he handed over the laptop and the box, as if they were a sacred offering.

'I haven't looked inside,' he said. 'But Priscilla said it's his computer and some personal effects the police gave back. She said there were no papers.'

The two women turned to leave, but Khethiwe paused. 'Please, Father, will you give us a blessing?' she asked.

'Yes, of course.'

Father Vincent placed his hands on their heads. He shut his eyes. 'Dear Lord, bless these your children. Give them the courage and wisdom to see through their mission, to bring justice where there is none and hope to those who long for it. In your infinite capacity to forgive, have pity on those whose sins may be exposed this day. And stay close to your daughter, Priscilla, for she needs your divine comfort more than ever before. We ask this through the blessed intercession of our Holy Mother, the Virgin Mary. God bless you, Khethiwe, and God bless you, Lindi. In the name of the Father, the Son and the Holy Spirit.'

It was the first time since she'd met him that Father Vincent had used her name.

'Go in peace, to love and serve the Lord.' He opened his eyes, smiling. 'Let me show you out,' he said, and headed back towards the church. 'I hear you were with Father Petro.'

It was as if the priest had thrown a grenade at Lindi. She stopped in her tracks. 'You knew him?'

'Oh, we are one big family,' the priest said. 'The bishop in Nelspruit and I are old friends. He was a novice when I did a stint teaching at our seminary. He told me he'd asked Petro to help you.'

'But did you know Father Petro? Was he a friend?'

'Well, I think we were kindred spirits, though he was a lot younger than me, of course. He used to stay here on his visits to the city.' Father Vincent looked around the church, at the empty pews. 'He said he could still hear the sound of protest here. He had imagination, I'll give him that.'

'He was running an errand for me when he was killed.'

'Who says he was killed?'

'Well, isn't that what most people think? We were threatened by some thuggish types that evening.'

'He certainly had his enemies but, no, he was not killed. It seems it was a terrible accident. The bishop has checked. Word gets round in those places. If something bad happens, people know about it.'

'How can you be so sure?'

'I'm not sure, not in the way you mean it. It's enough for me to know that he was doing God's work and he is with the Almighty now. He's in a better place.'

God's work. That was exactly how Father Petro had put it. Schooled in the casual agnosticism of a politically conscious home, Lindi had never been told about faith. There was plenty of talk about religion and doctrine – mostly excoriating – but rarely any mention of belief or the spiritual. She was beginning to feel she had missed out.

They shook hands, then Lindi and Khethiwe marched towards the van. Once inside, they hugged each other, relieved that they had what they had come for.

'I suppose we shouldn't really be counting our chickens before they've hatched,' Lindi said.

'What?'

'Oh, it just means we still don't know what's in this laptop.'

Ma Khethiwe told the driver to head for Rosebank. She rummaged through her bag and pulled out a sealed envelope. 'It's a letter for Kagiso from Mrs Motlantshe,' she said. 'The father gave it to me. He said that Kagiso must read it before he does anything.'

'But that's not going to be possible. The plan is for Two-Boy and me to talk to Kagiso over the phone, not to meet him.'

'Then you must read it,' Khethiwe said. She handed the envelope to Lindi who opened it with exaggerated care, as if it were some ancient manuscript and its contents might unlock a great mystery.

Dear Mr Rapabane,

I am trusting you with Lesedi's belongings because I know that my beloved son also trusted you. He paid a heavy price for trying to stop this filthy business with the land. I am the one who should have stopped it. I knew what my husband was doing but every time I was thinking he is going to stop. But he lost his way. All the time he wanted more. My husband is a bad man, but he is not the one who has killed our child. My husband thinks he is a big man but those fellows he is doing deals with, they are more powerful. For them, killing a child is nothing. I pray to Almighty God that you find this thing that Lesedi was hiding. You have to finish what he started. I am tired. My marriage to Josiah is finished. But I have two more children and I want for them to grow up in a South Africa that we fought for. Nkosi sikelel' iAfrika.

Priscilla Motlantshe

Lindi wiped away her tears and handed the letter to Khethiwe.

Kagiso tried sitting down. He tried standing up. He paced up and down the room. He checked both of his phones. The one Ma Khethiwe had bought for him and the one Two-Boy would use. They were both charged. Both had a signal. He was beside himself with anxiety. For a man who liked to be in control, this was like torture. He looked at his watch. It was nearly two. Even allowing for traffic, Lindi must be with Two-Boy by now. The fact that he hadn't heard anything must be a good sign. Surely she would have called him if Priscilla had not been there or she hadn't brought anything of Lesedi's with her.

Kagiso flinched, his body tensed even before he was aware of what had caused it. He heard a key in the lock of the door to the apartment. He backed away towards the window overlooking the street.

On the other side Sharmi opened the door with exaggerated caution, one centimetre at a time, till she could see into the room. She saw a figure silhouetted against the daylight and failed to stifle her shock.

Kagiso rushed at her, putting his hand across her mouth.

'I'm sorry,' she breathed, when he removed it. 'I didn't expect anybody to be here.'

She remained where she was, the door still open.

Kagiso moved around her and looked down the corridor. He shut the door. 'What the hell are you doing here?' he said sharply.

'I could ask you the same question,' she snapped back, then paused. 'Wait, wait, Kagiso. Let's not shout at each other.'

'Okay, fine, but what *are* you doing here?'

'I needed somewhere to be alone.'

'But this is the last place you should use. It's a meeting point and that's all.'

'I'm done with meeting points, Kagiso. It's over for me.'

'What are you talking about?'

Sharmi Meer realised this was one part of her plan she had not rehearsed. She'd thought about what she was going to say to the police, but not this. 'I'm handing myself in today.'

Silence.

'Say something.'

'You can't just call it a day. It doesn't work like that. There's the rest of us.'

'It was me.'

'What do you mean, it was you?'

'The Lesedi business. It was me.'

'But . . .'

'Hold on, let me finish.' She was relieved, grateful, a sinner given the chance to expiate her misdemeanours.

'You remember when you first told us that you'd had an approach from Lesedi Motlantshe. You said you were ready to give him the benefit of the doubt. I disagreed. Afterwards I put my own people onto it. I drove to Mpumalanga the day before his visit and gave the go-ahead. What they did, it wasn't what I wanted, wasn't what I planned. My instructions were to mess him up, enough to send a message that the Motlantshes were not wanted in the area. Something must have gone wrong. We've started a bandwagon rolling and all sorts have hitched a ride on it. My man's gone to ground so I can't tell you what happened. So you see, all this,' Sharmi pointed in the direction of the Ponte building, 'it was my doing.'

Kagiso walked back into the room and sat down. He didn't speak for an age.

'Why, Sharmi? Why? Why didn't you talk to me?'

'Because we never talk *to* each other, we just talk *at* each other.'

'But I brought it up at the last meeting. You could have said something.'

'Oh, sure! You at your sanctimonious best. Hardly the kind of atmosphere in which I could have said anything about this.'

'But this was about an operation. You should have talked.'

'It was *my* operation,' she said emphatically.

'But it went wrong, it was a disaster, and we were caught in the middle of it. You had no right to—'

'Look, I'm tired. I'm not here for a row. I've had enough of those. You and I have always disagreed about how to go about this whole business, but that's not it, is it? The rows, the arguments, they were not just about operations, not just about tactics, Kagiso, they were about us. You know that, don't you? And that's why Lesedi's death is so tragic. Actually, I think people like him are asking for it, but that's not why he ended up being killed. He died because you and I never learned how to just talk to each other, to explain ourselves to each other, to tell each other what was going on in our heads.'

Kagiso let the words sink in. She'd drawn him in, made him as culpable as she was. He wanted to throw the accusation back. He stared at Sharmi, as if to make sure this wasn't just another front she'd opened. She looked spent. He knew her well enough to see there was no fight left in her. She wasn't pointing a finger at him or trying to blame him. Not now, not this time. There was no judgement. She was trying to describe what had happened but he didn't recognise the picture.

'But – but you can't hate me that much . . . not enough to go and do a thing like that?'

'I don't hate you. I don't think I ever have.'

'Then why this?'

'You tell me, Kagiso. Let's not play games. By morning I'll be all over the news. By this time tomorrow you'll either have to be out of the country or you'll be pulled in, too. So tell me. Why have we been trying to destroy each other?'

'I don't know what you want me to say.'

'Just tell me the truth.'

'About what?'

'About us. I know what I did, what I carried on doing. I'm not proud of it, any of it. I've worked it out now. I wanted us to talk about it a long time ago. But we never got the chance – you walked away.'

Sharmi and Kagiso had met some years earlier. She'd just finished working on a feature film that had been shot on location in South Africa, hired as one of the English director's local assistants. There was a cast party and Kagiso had turned up, invited by a woman he'd known at Stellenbosch, whose father had invested in the film. Apart from the uniformed staff serving an endless supply of food and drink, the two of them were the only people of colour. Sharmi had seen the woman on the set occasionally, all white linen and lovely. For Sharmi each day on the shoot had been like a trial: she'd felt the need to prove herself, to say something, to do something that might catch the director's eye. The other woman, fragrant and ethereal, would turn up whenever it suited her and make straight for the director's chair, flopping into it like she owned it. Her conversations with the director would always start with a reference to some encounter they'd had off location. Daddy this, Daddy that.

The contrast between the two women could not have been greater and – over the course of that evening – Sharmi had lost no time in reminding Kagiso of the fact. That was when the sparring had started, that very night. It had begun as joshing, energetic disagreements charged with a sort of sexual frisson. Neither understood at the time that something else was at play – though they would find out in time, but too late to do either of them any good.

The party, and the events that had followed it, had shaped their relationship. They didn't talk about it any more but it sat there like a mutant gene that disfigured their lives.

The woman was just another of those people Sharmi had wanted to get even with, and Kagiso had offered her the means to do it. Sharmi never forgot the exquisite pleasure of watching the reaction on the face of Kagiso's Stellenbosch blonde when she heard that he would be leaving the cast party in her VW Beetle and not Daddy's BMW. In the car back to her digs in Muizenberg, Sharmi had, with some relish, described the look. 'First time the spoiled brat had anything taken away from her,' she'd said. 'Probably thought she'd had you bedded, her first black man.'

It had led to another argument, their second or third of the evening.

'Why, why must you turn everything into a political battle?' he'd asked.

'Because in this country everything is political, Kagiso, even who you fuck,' she'd replied. They'd ended up in her room later, Kagiso tearing at her clothes and lunging at her from behind with a ferocity that had left her dissatisfied and only just on this side of humiliation. But she hadn't tried to stop him. Earlier that evening, at the party, in the car, she'd goaded him, needled him, and he had reacted like a wounded animal. They were even.

That evening, each of them had revealed something to the other. In being exposed in that way, they had reached a point in minutes that might take months, even years, for others. It was a bond of sorts.

She'd woken the following morning to find that Kagiso had gone, leaving what she thought was a ludicrously formal note to say he'd be grateful for the lift back to Jo'burg if the offer was still open. (They'd talked about it at the party.) She'd called him straight away.

'What do you mean, "if the offer is still open"?' she'd said. 'You weren't *that* bad!'

'I'm sorry,' he'd said.

'Christ, I'm joking, Kagiso. We were both a bit over the top.'

'It won't happen again.'

And it didn't. Not on that journey. Never. She might as well have had a complete stranger in the car. They talked about everything except what had happened. The first part of the journey was through the sparse and arid beauty of the Karoo. She'd imagined the two of them, in the bubble of the car, their intimacy a cocoon protecting them from the vast and unforgiving desert around them. At first she'd let it go, hoping he'd open up. Then, when they'd broken the journey in Nieu Bethesda, Sharmi had confronted him.

'You can't do this, Kagiso. You can't walk into my life and then just walk away as if nothing happened.'

'I didn't walk into your life. We just ended up in the same bed. Anyway, I think it was you who walked into my life.'

Sharmi had slapped him across the face. 'Oh, so that's it. I suppose you think I make a habit of picking up poor, unsuspecting boys and dragging them into my bed. What do you think I am? Is that why you fucked me like you wanted to hurt me? Or is that how you get your kicks? Your bit of white fluff wouldn't have put up with that, would she? She'd have been straight off to tell Daddy.'

They hadn't used the room at the B&B and had driven through the night, all the way to Johannesburg, with barely a word uttered. That was it. They hadn't planned to see each other again.

A couple of years later, when Sharmi and Two-Boy had already begun the first steps towards direct action, he'd said she should meet a friend of his who was, as Two-Boy had put it, 'ripe for the picking'. It turned out to be Kagiso, a rising star in the Ministry of Rural Development and Land Reform. There was shock on both sides as Two-Boy did the introductions at a bar in Greenside. They'd managed to greet each other like old mates who'd simply lost touch.

They became like prize-fighters, circling each other, trying to punish each other, and discovering, when the blow was struck, that there is nothing more tactile or intimate than harming someone.

They were as close to each other as you could get – but neither seemed able or willing to admit it. So they went on trying to hate each other. For Sharmi every act of sabotage, every fire they started, every farm that was wrecked, was part of a proxy war she was still fighting against Kagiso. She pushed each secret project to its limits, waiting for the moment when Kagiso, as he always did, tried to row them back. That was when she would strike, saying he just didn't have the stomach for the fight.

In fact, she'd had little reason to doubt his commitment, except for a prejudice born of what little she knew about his background. None of them in the cell really knew much about the others. They were co-conspirators, not friends. That was partly a question of temperament but also design: it seemed simpler that way.

Sharmi didn't understand him – he didn't fit into any box, or not one that she recognised. Take the whole Stellenbosch University thing. What kind of black youth would have chosen to go to an old Afrikaans university? In her mind Sharmi saw a place of arcane initiation ceremonies and pretty blonde girls on the hunt for someone with a nice slice of the Western Cape in their inheritance. And then there was his white 'family', which was just bizarre to her. Kagiso rarely, if ever, talked about his childhood but Sharmi had picked up enough from conversations with François to piece together a picture of a black mother and her son locked in a humiliating embrace of dependency with a white family who basked in a self-righteous glow of generosity.

'It wasn't like that,' François had said, when Sharmi had asked him about Kagiso's past. The four of them, Sharmi, François, Kagiso and Two-Boy, had yet to coalesce into the group of underground activists they were now.

'How do you know?'

'Because he's had plenty of opportunity to forget, to bury them, since they left and he hasn't. He's genuinely fond of them.'

'Well, if he's so fond of them, as you put it, why don't we hear more about them?'

'One good reason is that he knows people like you are waiting to pass judgement.'

'Oh, come on, man! I pass judgement on your parents, with all their charitable foundations and shit, but you still talk about them.'

Francois's father had made a fortune in a catering business that supplied the South African security forces with ready-to-eat meals. He'd retired to Cape Town where the family owned a sumptuous villa over-looking Camps Bay. He and his much-altered wife divided their time between their home there, a penthouse in Sandton and a game ranch in the Tuli Block bordering Botswana. Jointly, they had established several charities to which they devoted enormous amounts of time, not to mention money.

'That's because in this twisted country where we live it's easier for me to say I love my parents, despite their dubious past, than for Kagiso to say he respects and loves a white family who tried to do some good. You see, Sharmi, you don't really hold it against me that I was the beneficiary of a wealthy upbringing, however ill-gotten it was. You allow me to leave my baggage at the door, but you don't allow Kagiso to do the same.'

'Christ! Spare me the fucking sermon.'

'No, this is important,' he'd said, leaning closer to her. 'You don't expect me to hate my parents, but you want Kagiso to disown his.'

'His what? What are they, François?' Sharmi had interrupted. 'That's the whole point. They're just another white family who got the fuck out when the going got tough.'

'No, it isn't the point. Whether Kagiso wants to think of them as part of his family or not doesn't matter. It's up to him. The fact is, he should be allowed to be grateful to them for giving him the same opportunity as me – except he had to be a lot smarter and tougher to get through than I did. Why can't you just leave it at that?'

'Because it affects the way he thinks. He sounds and behaves like a white liberal.' She had spat out the last word like it was a curse. During the struggle for freedom, especially in the eighties when the state had given up any pretence of looking for legal cover, those whites who clung to the hope that there was still some middle ground from which to effect change were vilified from both sides. The white establishment saw them as duplicitous, enjoying the fruits of apartheid while pretending to despise it, and many in the black liberation movements, increasingly drawn to violent opposition, saw them as irrelevant.

'Ah! So now we have it. A black man can't be a liberal.'

'I didn't say that. I just can't see how any self-respecting black man would *want* to be a liberal.'

'Would you prefer Kagiso was like those so-called freedom-fighters, who *toyi-toyi* with their imaginary guns and make inflammatory speeches, while they stuff money into the pockets of their Italian suits?'

'Don't be ridiculous. I just wish he'd show some passion – some proper blood-and-guts passion,' Sharmi had said.

Kagiso slumped back in the sofa. He shut his eyes and kept them shut as he spoke. It was as if he were talking to himself. 'Every meeting, every argument, you remind me that the person I've become is not the person I want to be.'

He opened his eyes. Sharmi began to move towards him. 'No, don't,' he said. 'You see, I'm not really sure if any of this, this whole thing that we've been doing, I'm not sure if it is really me. It's what I thought I should do, not what I wanted to do. Every time we did something, blew something up or whatever, a part of me thought it was wrong. You see, I know I've been happiest when I've brought people together – not this, not what we've been doing, dividing people, making them hate each other. That never made me happy. And yet I carried on. But you, everything you do, you're so clear, so sure, so committed. I should have pulled out a long time ago. That's what you would have done. I didn't have the guts to act on my conscience. I wanted to be more like you, have your certainty, but I just didn't have it. So I guess it was easier to tell myself that I didn't like what you stood for, the way you went about things.'

'I don't buy that,' Sharmi said. 'This thing is older than the Land Collective. It goes all the way back to Cape Town.'

'You're right. It goes all the way back to that night. You remember?'

'How could I forget?'

'I mean the party, not what happened afterwards. You were there because you'd earned your place there. I was there because – I can't even remember her name now – because I was brought there. I was tagging along. I'm good at that.'

'That's *kak*, man, rubbish.'

'How would you know, Sharmi, you with your self-belief, your family's history in the struggle? You're the real thing. Me, what am I? You think you're the only one who's looked at me and thought, I know his type – black skin, white brain? Be honest, that's what you think, isn't it? You thought that from the first time you laid eyes on me.'

'Did François tell you that?'

'He did but he didn't have to. You made it pretty plain all on your own. Don't worry, you weren't the first. Oh, no. By the time I met you I'd got pretty used to it. It's what happens when people – our people, black people – find out the only reason I was at a decent school was because some white folk paid the fees. It explains everything for them. If you see both sides of an argument – oh, that's the white thing again. If you look for compromise – Jeez, he's been brainwashed. You just happened to be the person who made me want to hit back, Sharmi. That's all. It wasn't that I didn't want you, it wasn't that I didn't like you, it was just that I didn't stack up against you.'

They stared at each other. They were like old warriors who'd fought themselves to a truce, looked at the damage they'd caused, the bodies piled high on the battlefield, and wondered how it could have come to that.

Kagiso broke the silence. 'I'm not sure what you expect me to do now.'

'*I* don't expect *you* to do anything.'

'Am I supposed to persuade you not to hand yourself in, pretend I don't care that Lesedi is dead and that his killer is still free and that you played your part in his murder?'

'I'm not here to tell you what you should or shouldn't do, Kagiso. I've made up my mind. It's up to you to decide what your next move is. You've just been talking about acting on your conscience. Maybe now you've got your chance.'

The phone rang. It was Two-Boy. 'It's me. It's not good. There's nothing on the laptop.'

'Are you sure?'

'I've checked and I've rechecked.'

'What about his papers?'

'There weren't any.'

'A back-up drive, a phone, an iPad. Anything else?'

'Nothing. I'm as certain as I can be. Did Les – did he give you any idea what he had?'

'Not exactly. He just said . . .' He paused.

'You still there?'

'Yeah,' Kagiso said. 'Maybe I misunderstood him, or maybe it was just talk.'

'What the fuck you saying, Baba? All this was just a hunch or what?'

'I need time to think. I'll call you.' He put the phone back into his pocket.

'What was all that about?'

Kagiso realised Sharmi could not have known, and still didn't know, what Lesedi had been trying to do. 'He was on our side.'

'Who?'

'Lesedi Motlantshe.'

'Give me a break.'

'It must have been more or less the last thing he did before your – your people dealt with him. He was ready to stop his father's Mpumalanga deal and told me he had the money trail and he was ready to go public. That was Two-Boy just now. We thought the evidence would be on Lesedi's computer, which we managed to get from his mother. But Two-Boy says there's nothing.'

Sharmi had been standing more or less where she'd entered the room.

Now she shuffled towards the adjacent wall and leaned against it. 'But I don't understand, Kagiso. You could have said something.'

'First, I didn't know till he came to Soil of Africa. Second, even if I had said something you'd have accused me of being naive. It wouldn't have been the first time. Maybe I was. Maybe it was just big talk from Lesedi. Maybe you were right, after all. I don't know where else we could look. It was our only chance. It's over. It's time to call it a day.'

'You've still got time to get out. You could make Zim or Mozambique this evening, or at least be well on your way.'

Kagiso's phone rang again. 'I told you I'd call when I'd decided what to do.'

'No, no, you don't understand. Lesedi has come good. We've nailed them, man. It's all here, just like Lesedi told you.'

'I thought you said you couldn't find anything.'

'I was looking in the wrong place. Priscilla Motlantshe gave us a box of Lesedi's things. It was there all the time!'

'Where? What do you mean?'

'His key-ring. A real fancy thing. You know personalised and what-what. His car keys, keys to his apartment, they're all hanging off this silver . . . What you call it?'

'Fob, whatever. What about it?'

'It's got a memory stick inside it. It's all there, Kagiso. It's dynamite. There are bank numbers, everything. Willemse is in it up to his neck. But he is not the only one. All the names are here. There's even someone in the president's office. It goes right to the top.'

'That's good, Two-Boy, very good.'

'What do you mean good? This is everything we've been fighting for.'

'No, we didn't fight for this. Lesedi died for it. Okay, let me call Lindi.'

'She already knows.'

'I was meant to do that.'

'I'm sorry. She didn't go straight to her office. She was here when I found the stick.'

'Where is she now?'

'She's on her way – should be there any minute now. Waiting for your call. We going to *jol* tonight, *bru*.'

'Sure. Check you later.'

Kagiso got up and went over to the window. He stood there, oblivious to everything else.

'I said, who's this Lindi?'

'Sorry, I was miles away. Lindi? She's from London. She's been helping me.'

'She the one who called you that night, at the last meeting?'

'Yes. She's the daughter of the family my mom worked for.'

'So she obviously turned out okay. I'm sorry – I was so mean about them, her family.'

'Well, that's a new tune.'

'I've had time to think, I've been doing a lot of that the last few days.'

'Apology accepted. I guess that's what I'm supposed to say. Anyway, we've got bigger things to worry about.'

'I think I was jealous.'

'Jealous? Of Lindi, you mean? You don't even know her.'

'I don't mean her as a person. I mean the whole set-up, the way you were so close to them. Not the white-family-black-servant thing but . . . you really liked them and they really cared for you. I'm probably not making a whole lot of sense . . .'

Even as she searched for the words, Sharmi knew where she was heading: an admission she should have made a long time ago. She used to accuse Kagiso of being naive for taking his relationship with the Seatons at face value. Now she knew it was a strength, not a weakness. She was incapable of doing that. The baggage of history had weighed her down, got in the way and conditioned her reactions. It was the prism through which she saw everything. It looked like 'certainty' – that was how Kagiso had just described it – but it was nothing of the sort. It was a prop. If anything went wrong, blame history.

'What I'm trying to say . . . I'm not as strong as you think. I'm tough, that's for sure. I'm good at fighting, but I'm not so good at the other stuff.'

'Stuff?'

'At . . .' she hesitated '. . . at love.' Even using the word she felt as if she had laid herself bare.

A phone rang again. It was the one Ma Khethiwe had bought. Kagiso knew it would be Lindi. He moved back to the sofa.

'Is everything okay? I've been waiting for your call. You've heard, haven't you?'

'Yes, I have, and, yes, everything is fine, Lindi.'

'You don't sound like everything's fine, Kagiso. Come on. You've won. This is everything you've worked for. You've bust open this thing.'

'I don't feel like a winner. We haven't bust open anything, Lindi. We made a lot of noise. But one man did bust it open and he did it quietly – and now he's dead.'

'Jesus. What's brought this on? Look, I understand how tired you must be, how difficult these last few days have been. But we've got to finish this thing. When are you going to get here? We've got to prepare a statement, I've got to talk to Anton, and presumably you've got to talk to the rest of your people. There's a lot to organise.'

Kagiso paused.

'Kagiso! You still there?'

'I'm not coming, Lindi.'

'You're not coming to the press conference?'

'I have to think things through.'

'What's there to think through? I don't understand.'

'I can't tell you now. We'll talk later.'

'And I'll just twiddle my thumbs till then, shall I?'

'Do what you have to do. Take care, Lindi, *hamba kahle.*'

Kagiso ended the call. He looked up at Sharmi. Something clicked into place. It was as if he was seeing her for the first time. 'What now?'

'I have stuff to do,' she said. 'I'm going to call Two-Boy, you call François. You've got about five, maybe six hours before the shit hits the fan.'

Kagiso stood up and walked over to Sharmi. They embraced, perhaps the only real act of intimacy they had ever shared.

Anton's phone rang. It was Lindi's usual number.

'So did it work? Did Lesedi Motlantshe's mother show up?'

'Yes, it worked.'

'And?'

'Did you get my email? I've sent you a file attached to it.'

'I checked my inbox a few minutes ago. There was nothing from you.'

'I didn't give it a subject and you won't recognise the address. Check your junk mail – it will have ZA for South Africa.'

'Hold on, let's see, I'm looking, still looking . . . Yep, here it is.'

'Open it, make sure it's all there, and you can read it.'

'Christ! There's a lot of stuff – it's massive. Letters, looks like bank accounts. There must be dozens of pages.'

'Good, you've got it. Now let me explain. That's the evidence Lesedi had put together on the land deals. When you look at it you'll see how the deals were done, how the farmers got paid off, and how the foreign buyers were going to split the money with people here. Motlantshe, ministers, probably the president, they were all in it.'

'Girl, this is fantastic. You or whoever, the Land Collective people, you've handed this stuff to the police?'

'No, not yet.'

'What? Look, we're not a detective agency. This is evidence of corruption, possibly criminal. We've got no business sitting on it.'

The tables had turned: Lindi was skirting round the rules; Anton was urging caution.

'You don't have to tell me that,' she said. 'There's a strong possibility the authorities might try to suppress all this. I had to make sure you had it.'

'Okay, so we've taken care of that. What we've got to do now is get this off our hands and concentrate on what we're there for. You know, how we use all this to get a debate going on a proper land-reform policy. You could be there for some time, months probably. Lucky you.'

'Maybe not so lucky, Anton. I could be staying here for a while anyway.'

'How so?'

'I think the police here are going to want to interview me.'

'What the hell you talking about, girl?'

'Remember when we spoke on the phone after I had been to Lesedi's funeral? You said Kagiso had to know more about the Land Collective than he was letting on. You were right. He's one of them.'

'Bingo!' Anton crowed.

'Don't sound so smug. There's more to come.' She thought about how to say it. There was no way to sugar-coat this particular pill. 'The Land Collective was involved in Lesedi's murder.'

'Christ! How long have you known about this?'

'An hour or so.'

'Your man Kagiso, was it him?'

'No. He only found out himself a few hours ago. Apparently, it was organised by another member of the Collective. They just meant to teach Lesedi a lesson but it obviously got out of hand.'

'And then some! We've got to act fast. We've got to distance ourselves from this.'

'What if I don't want to?'

'What are you talking about? If you don't want to . . . what?'

'Distance myself.'

'Lindi, if it ever came out we sat on this for a minute longer than we had to we'd be fucked. You, me, the Trust, all of us. We can just pack up and say goodbye. We don't have a choice.'

'I do have a choice. I want a choice.'

'I'm not giving you a choice.'

'I can't believe I'm hearing this from you of all people. It was your idea to try to reach the Land Collective!'

'Don't give me that bullshit. I didn't know they were murderers.'

Anton the firebrand no more. It was as if they had changed places, swapped roles.

'All the time I've known you you've banged on about being with the little people, taking on the vested interests. I could give you the speech word for word. And now when we have a chance—'

Anton interrupted: 'Is this personal?'

'What do you mean?'

'Is this about your family's relationship with the guy? White guilt and all that *kak*.'

'How dare you? I'm not going to forget you just said that but, for the record, no, this is not personal. This is about following my instincts, doing what I think is right. The Land Collective are not murderers.'

'What's happened to being neutral? Gone, just like that.' Anton's frustration at being unable to get through to her was building.

'On this I'm not neutral.'

'The police will want to know what our links with the Land Collective are, how close we are to them. You've told me everything, right?'

'I've told you everything you need to know.'

'So what now?'

'You have to do what you have to do, Anton. That's the advice someone gave me just now. I guess it's the same for you.'

A few hours later, close to midnight in South Africa, Radio 702 broke the story. Within minutes every other radio station and TV channel was onto it. Police had arrested – that was what the press release said – and charged a suspect in the Lesedi Motlantshe murder case. The police released a mug-shot of Sharmi Meer. She was almost smiling. Defiant. The statement said the police were now looking for other members of what they called an 'underground terror cell known as the Land Collective'. One, an employee of SABC, had already handed himself in. The identities of two others were known and police were searching for them. All border posts and airports had been alerted. The photos of François Nel and Kagiso Rapabane were grainy blow-ups of snap-shots. Police were also keen to question a British national, thought to have had close links with the cell and in South Africa without a work permit.

There was a quote from Lieutenant General Jackson Sibande, police chief in Mpumalanga Province. 'This vile crime was an insult to the peace-loving people of Mpumalanga. We said we would find the culprits and that is just what we have done. Now justice will take its course, as it always does in our free and beautiful country.'

The press attaché at the British High Commission in Pretoria was woken up by a journalist. It was the first she'd heard of the story. A while later the High Commission released a statement: 'The High Commission is aware of the arrest of a British national in connection with the recent disturbances. Consular assistance is being given and

High Commission staff will, of course, be cooperating with the South African authorities.'

Overnight in London, South Trust's Twitter account announced a press conference at seven the next morning in connection with the recent disturbances associated with land sales in South Africa. There would be a statement from the Trust's director.

Anton Chetty didn't expect the small conference room at South Trust to be quite so crowded. Not so early in the morning. He recognised Robert Whitaker and one or two more Africa hands. There were a couple of other correspondents he'd bumped into before. The usual suspects. But who were all the others? There were several TV cameras on raised tripods at the back of the room – they looked like a firing squad. He hated this. Hated what he was about to do. What he *had* to do – that was what he told himself. Anton felt the perspiration on his back. He removed his jacket. He was accompanied by a member of staff. As they sat down behind a table at one end of the room, he asked her if she knew who all these people were.

'Over a hundred journalists follow us,' she whispered, 'so, no, quite a few of these faces are new to me. I think the business press are here in force, though – that's the woman from the *FT* by the aisle in the front row. There's bound to be questions about land reform so just stick to the bullet points we discussed earlier.'

She handed him a sheaf of papers.

'That's a reporter from the *Today* programme. You spoke to them a few days ago so he's bound to ask you how you could have known days ago that the murder was linked to agitation over land reform.'

Was that just six days earlier? It felt like a lifetime to Anton. He didn't know whether to stay sitting or stand up. There was a lectern next to the table. He decided to stay where he was.

'Another thing,' the woman said, wrapping her hand around the microphone. 'Just stick to the agreed wording on Lindi. It's been checked by the lawyer and the Chair has signed off on it. Bound to be questions about her.'

Anton cleared his throat. His colleague poured water into a glass and shoved it closer to him. He took a sip. He looked down at the notes. Where the hell were his glasses? He found them in the pocket of the jacket he'd slung over his chair.

'Good morning, ladies and gentlemen. Apologies for dragging you in here at this ungodly hour – indeed, no one could be sorrier about that than I am. At least it gives you plenty of time to write up your stories.'

Stop waffling. Just get on with it. He didn't have to turn around: he knew his colleague was staring at him, anxiety written all over her face.

'Now, late last night South Trust came into the possession of some documents relating to the sale of farmland in South Africa to foreign entities.'

What? 'Foreign entities'? Had he agreed to call them that?

'Our researchers have been looking at the documents through the night and they appear to show prima facie evidence that some – perhaps all – of these sales are irregular.'

Another of those weasel words. 'Irregular'. 'Corrupt' would be the right one.

'We, South Trust, are not an investigative agency. Our only interest, in accordance with our mandate, is to determine the causes of the recent unrest in South Africa and, if at all possible, to try to mediate between the competing parties. We have decided, therefore, not to publish the documents as yet. We have instead handed copies to the relevant authorities in South Africa and, indeed, here in London. Once we have had representations from our legal advisers we hope to publish the documents on our website, though, as I say, that will primarily be a legal decision and, of course, not ours alone. The authorities in both countries will have their own views on the matter.'

He could barely bring himself to continue.

'Now I want to turn to a related matter. You are, no doubt, aware of developments in South Africa overnight, which, according to the South African authorities, are linked to the murder of Lesedi Motlantshe last week. Two people are in custody . . .'

Anton's colleague leaned towards him and pointed to something on her phone. He couldn't tell what he was supposed to be looking at. She pulled the microphone towards her. 'Sorry to interrupt. It seems a third person is in custody. A former government employee turned campaigner. Thanks, Anton.'

He wished she would just carry on, finish the job.

'A British national is also being questioned, not under arrest, I must make that clear, but I can confirm this morning that she is . . . ' he reached for the water, swallowed hard '. . . she was working for South Trust.'

There was an audible crackle of activity: phone keyboards being tapped; notepads being written on; and the collective and unmistakable murmur of journalists who have found their top line. A British citizen, a Goody Two Shoes activist, caught at the heart of a murder investigation in a foreign land. The press officer took the microphone again.

'Mr Chetty will take a few questions but just a word of caution – I'm sure you'll all understand that, for legal reasons, he may have to be more circumspect than . . . than . . . well, than you would want him to be.' She pointed to the man from *Today*.

'Mr Chetty, when you say this British citizen was working for South Trust, do you mean she was an employee? Is she still an employee and what is her name?'

'Yes, she is a member of our staff and her name is Lindi Seaton.'

The press officer grabbed the microphone again. 'Just to be clear, I mean to expand a bit on what Mr Chetty was saying. Yes, she is still a member of staff but, for the moment and until her position becomes clearer, she is suspended with all the usual protections under employment law.' She pointed to another journalist. 'Just tell us who you represent.'

'Daisy Evans, the *Guardian*. In their initial statement and in other follow-up remarks, the South African authorities have made it clear that they believe the British national – Lindi Seaton, as you say – has what they're calling close links with this underground group, the Land Collective. How long have you been aware of those links?'

Anton took a moment. 'Look, let me put it like this. Our staff are given a great deal of independence when they're in the field. That's the way we work and it accounts for our success. They are not expected to be referring things to me all—'

'Could you just say whether it is true she had links with the Collective and how long you have known that?'

'Well, it depends on what you call links.' Exasperation ricocheted around the room. 'It is part of our job to make connections with all parties to a conflict. We don't make judgements.'

'I'm not asking you to make a judgement. Did your employee have links or not? It's quite simple, really.'

The press officer leaned over to the microphone. 'There is absolutely no way the Trust was aware of any connection or link between Lindi Seaton and this so-called Land Collective when she was assigned to this mission in South Africa. We were first made aware that she had met a member of the group just two days ago. The facts are hazy. For obvious reasons we have not had a proper chance to debrief Ms Seaton.'

Another reporter spoke up. He directed his remarks at the press officer, ignoring Anton. 'Surely any link would compromise your neutrality in the eyes of other parties.'

'Clearly that is an issue and one we take extremely seriously. It is one of the reasons Ms Seaton has been suspended. Mr Chetty will take a couple more questions. Yes, the *Financial Times*.'

'Mr Chetty, you said the Trust handed the documents to the British authorities and not just the South Africans. Why?'

'It is our view, our preliminary view, that some of those who stand to gain from these land acquisitions, which we, er, believe to be irregular – that some of these companies and individuals are UK-based.'

'Can you name any of them?'

'No, I can't. As I said, there may be legal implications. What I can say is that the beneficiaries range from individual investors to private equity—'

'I'm afraid we really can't say any more.' The press officer gathered her notes. 'That's all we have time for. Mr Chetty has – as you can imagine – some urgent meetings to attend but I will be around for a few minutes more. Thank you.'

Clive Missenden's phone bleeped. He was in the private dining room of a Dubai hotel, having a late breakfast. He looked at the message. It read: *Get out of there, dump the deal, whatever it takes.* Then he dialled a number.

'Josiah, hope I haven't woken you up. Not surprised you're still under the covers after last night's exertions. Wonderful evening. Thank you so much. Look, I'm just calling to say I'm heading out. The plane's being fuelled up as we speak.'

'But what about the meeting? This fellow, Kariakis, he's bringing the papers soon. They are all ready for you to sign.'

'Yes, yes. I'm sorry, it's going to be a wasted effort. The truth is, Josiah, dear boy, we were never really very keen on this Mpuma-what's-it business. Don't get me wrong, it did look quite promising at one stage but it does seem rather sticky now.'

'But – but what should I tell Jake and the others? I mean, they're expecting a call from me today.'

'Oh, I think you'll find Jake's got his hands full at the moment,' Missenden said briskly. 'Josiah, old thing, why don't you break the habit of a lifetime, get off your arse and just check your phone? Come to think of it, why not try the remote control for your TV? It's quite easy if you try. So long.'

And that was that. Time to move on. There were other continents, other deals to pursue. True, they'd had to put some money up front but, what the hell, it could all be written off. There was only one thing Clive Missenden couldn't stomach. That bitch Lindi Seaton. She'd got one over on him. He wasn't going to forget that in a hurry.

EPILOGUE

Later that day, when Kagiso had finally called Lindi – about the time Sharmi Meer walked into a Johannesburg police station – it was to tell her that the Collective was linked to Lesedi Motlantshe's murder and that he would be handing himself in: an act of solidarity with Sharmi. Shortly afterwards, Lindi was interviewed by the South African Police Service.

The next morning, having watched a live stream of Anton's less than convincing performance at the press conference, she leaked the contents of Lesedi's hidden file to the *Mail & Guardian* in South Africa.

She was subsequently expelled from South Africa. She was *persona non grata* and her passport was stamped to that effect. Banned from South Africa: like father, like daughter.

Lindi and Kagiso were unable to meet before she was thrown out.

In the wake of the online newspaper exposé, Jake Willemse, the minister for rural development and land reform, was placed under house arrest pending police enquiries. Parliament was due to launch its own investigation.

Josiah Motlantshe, whose name made numerous appearances in what was already being dubbed the 'Lesedi Papers', was thought to have flown straight from Dubai to one of his homes abroad, in Florida. A statement on his behalf said there was no question of his running, he was simply attending to business and would return to South Africa in due course. The statement came from a PR firm in London, one that had made its name looking after the interests of a British businessman accused of breaking arms embargoes to several countries, including the Democratic Republic of Congo.

In the absence of her husband, Priscilla Motlantshe became the focus of press attention. Finally, she agreed to face the journalists, reading a handwritten statement outside the front door of the family's Houghton home.

'My heart is sore. I have lost the two men in my life. My marriage to Josiah is over. He is not the man I met so many years ago in Soweto. He fought like a lion for our freedom, but now he has forgotten those days. I never thought of a future without him – that is what I face now. But as I prepare for this I know I am not alone. I carry inside me,' at this point she held her clenched fist against her chest, 'the memory of my beloved Lesedi. No mother wants her son to oppose his father but Lesedi did the right thing. You see, I believe that the true spirit of the father lived on in his son.'

Sharmi Meer, Dudu 'Two-Boy' Modise, Kagiso Rapabane and François Nel, who had been arrested on the Botswana border, were all charged under terrorism legislation, some of it dating back to the apartheid years. Sharmi Meer refused to name her accomplices in the Lesedi murder and it was assumed she could not escape a lengthy jail sentence. As for the other three, after the revelations of the Lesedi Papers, public opinion was on their side. There was even talk of a presidential pardon. It was a gesture urged on the president by supporters who believed such a move might help to ease the pressure for the role of the Office of the President to be included in the forthcoming parliamentary inquiry.

In London, Harry Seaton stood in the hallway of his house, staring at the wall of photographs. He had another to add to the collection. He'd decided that the picture of Lindi and Kagiso arm in arm, taken a few weeks earlier in Joubert Park, should go right next to the one of the family taken in the week before they'd all left South Africa. Harry tapped the hook into the wall. He slipped the newly framed print over it and stood back, looking at the two photographs side by side. In his mind there was a sort of symmetry to them: a relationship begun in the old country and cemented in the new one. A friendship that transcended time and place. There was enough truth in that. Another photo, another story.

ACKNOWLEDGEMENTS

Several people read this novel in its various stages. Milton Nkosi and Steve Lenahan in Johannesburg, friends from a time when South Africans were first working out what to do with their freedom, have helped to give this story its authenticity. One of them black, the other white, they grew up in different South Africas but come Freedom Day they shared a passionate hope in the new country. I first knew Kamil Naicker as a child when her parents were working clandestinely towards an end to apartheid. Kamil is one of freedom's children and now, as an academic and writer, her understanding of the challenges facing her generation made her comments on this book invaluable. Sophie Raworth, a newsroom colleague turned stalwart friend, put her talents as a journalist and bookworm at my disposal. Richard Allen, who has known me since our days in school, was my one-man focus group. I was happy and relieved to hear that he kept turning the pages.

I am indebted to Hannah Knowles, Senior Commissioning Editor at Canongate, for listening to the voices in this novel and deciding to let them be heard. She's been a supportive and inspiring editor whose interventions have improved this book.

I am grateful to my copy-editor, Hazel Orme, who combined an eye for detail with an enthusiasm for the narrative.

A huge thank you to my agent, Maggie Hanbury, who has guided my excursions into the world of publishing for twenty years and more. This is my first work of fiction and she has supported me every step of the way.

Frances Robathan has lived with these characters from the moment they started to form in my mind and has helped to shape them. She has done so with her usual grace and generosity.